The Synchronicity V

By Dietmar Arthur V

MW01127928

Introductory Comments:

This is the fourth and final installment of The Synchronicity War. When I started Part 1, I had NO idea where I would end up so it's been a wild ride for me too. I've made two changes to Part 4 compared to the other three books. You'll find that A.I. is now AI. You'll also notice that the chapters don't have titles. That was done deliberately so as not to give anything away before you read the chapters. I hope you enjoy the book. At the end are some final comments concerning the possibility of more books that take place within the same universe. I should also warn the reader that the process of converting an ebook to paperback on demand doesn't seem to adjust page numbers accordingly. So the page numbers listed on the next page may not correspond to the actual page. I'm sure there's a way to fix this but I don't know what that way is. Sorry.

I'd like to thank Jill Linkert for what she insists I call a 'quick' edit of this book. Apparently I never give her the time she claims she needs to do a 'proper' edit. So if you find mistakes, blame me, not her. I would also like to thank Justin Adams for his cover art.

Contents

Cast of Characters:

Human:

Victor Shiloh (Vice-Admiral/Chief of Space Operations for Space Force)

Sam Howard (Senior Admiral and Chief of Space Operations for Space Force)

Amanda Kelly (Commander/(Acting) Vice-Admiral, Space Force)

Brad Falkenberg (Senior Commander, Space Force)

Angela Johansen (Commander, Space Force)

Rollins (Jump drive specialist, Space Force)

Khegan (Lieutenant, Orbital Defense Weapons Officer, Space Force)

Halder (Commander, Operations Center Duty Officer, Space Force)

Jason Alvarez (Civilian colonist on planet Haven, Inventor of ZPG power technology)

Rachel (New Chairperson of Space Force Oversight Committee)

AIs

Blackjack

Casanova

Cobra

Foxbat

Gunslinger

Iceman

Jester

Pagan

Rainman

Red Baron

Shooter

Sniper

Stoney

Titan

Valkyrie

Vandal

Vixen

Voodoo

Wolfman

Zulu

Glossary of Terms:

CSO   Chief of Space Operations

CAG   Commander, Autonomous Group

SPG   Strategic Planning Group

TF   Task Force

KPS   Kilometers Per Second

Klicks   slang expression for kilometers

A.U.   Astronomical Unit equal to the average distance between the Earth and its Sun.

AI   Artificial Intelligence

SL   Squadron Leader

C.O.   Commanding Officer

X.O.   Executive Officer

W.O.   Weapons Officer

E.O.   Engineering Officer

Mark 1 500 kiloton uranium fission warhead/attack drone

Mark 1b 2.5 megaton fusion warhead/attack drone

Mark 1c 25 megaton fusion warhead/attack drone

Mark 2 Kinetic Energy Penetrator warhead/drone

Mark 3 Decoy drone

Mark 4 Experimental warhead project that proved unsuccessful

Mark 5 X-ray laser warhead/attack drone

Mark 6 250 megaton High-spin platinum fusion warhead/attack drone

F1   First generation fighter

F2   Second generation fighter

Raider A class of starship of approximately 10,000 metric tonnes designed to be piloted by an AI with two internal lasers and able to carry up to 50 drones.

Longitudinal Waves (L-waves, also known as Scalar waves) Compression waves with special characteristics.

UFC   Universal Fabrication Complex (A device that can manufacture anything given the right instructions and the right raw materials)

Flag Bridge A specialized Command location designed specifically for Flag Officers (Admirals) to control strategic operations for more than one ship. This is separate from the Main Bridge where the ship's commanding Officer controls his vessel.

Synopsis of Parts 1-3:

For those readers who finished reading Part 3 some time ago, here is a synopsis of events up to the end of Part 3.

The unprovoked war with the Sogas has been going badly. Humanity barely escaped total extermination from Sogas nano-enhanced bio-weapons only to be wiped out by the advancing horde of Insectoids with their 10 kilometer spherical ships. Only the long shot strategy by Casanova to enlist the reluctant aid of the pacifist Friendlies and their time travel technology allowed him to warn humans about the bio-weapon in time to avert that disaster.

With the advanced power generation and weapons technology brought back by Kronos now in Space Force hands, Admirals Sam Howard and Victor Shiloh realize that the Insectoids are the real threat not only to Humans but to all intelligent life in the galaxy. If Space Force can hold off the Sogas long enough, the advancing insectoid ships will destroy them. That will give Space Force enough time to build up its defenses before the tsunami of insectoid ships crashes over human space.

But the Sogas aren't finished with humans just yet. Shiloh gets a disturbing vision of a massive Sogas fleet attacking Earth with bio-weapons, some of which reach the planet surface. Shiloh is injured and in the immediate aftermath of the battle, he and Commander Amanda Kelly discover their suppressed feelings for each other.

But before they can explore that relationship, Howard shares the bad news. ANOTHER Sogas fleet has been detected moving toward human space and Space Force has taken too many losses during the battle that occurred 24 hours earlier, to have any hope of stopping them.

The last chapter of Part 3 has been included for those wishing to reread it.

Chapter 26 (From Part 3)

The problem posed by this battle for Earth was that the time it ended was known but not the time it began. So all units, ships, humans and AIs were on full alert an hour before the end time. Shiloh was strapped into his Command Chair with his pressure suit on and his helmet in its cradle beside him. His com implant was active, and all three AIs could hear him. The ship was at Battle Stations, as was the whole Fleet, but the enemy hadn't arrived yet. All they could do was wait and try to stay at a heightened level of alertness.

"Howard to Shiloh."

The suddenness of the CSO's voice would have made Shiloh jump if he hadn't been strapped down. "Shiloh here. Go ahead, Sir."

"Last minute pep talk, Admiral. I know you don't need it, but this waiting is driving me crazy, so this talk is as much for my benefit as it is for yours. How are your people doing?"

Shiloh looked around the Flag Bridge. "They're doing fine, Sir. Some have opening night jitters, others are chomping at the bit, I'm trying to stay relaxed and alert at the same time."

Howard laughed. "Yes, I know what you mean. But at least you have your Fleet under control. I have to deal with the civilians, half of whom want to string me up for my high-handedness while the other half want to panic. We STILL have some civilians left in the cities, Goddamn it! I keep getting asked what I'll do to make sure they don't carry the plague anywhere else, and I keep evading the damn question because if I answered them truthfully, they'd faint with shock. I'm NOT letting this plague get loose!" There was a pause as the CSO calmed down and Shiloh waited. When he spoke again, the Admiral was much calmer. "Anyway, that's MY problem, not yours. I'm not going to try to second-guess you. You're the Field Commander. You do what you think is best, and I'll back you no matter what."

"Thank you, Sir. We know how this battle will end, but we'll still give it our best shot."

"Of that I have no doubt. Okay, I'll get out of your hair. Good luck and good hunting, Admiral. Howard clear."

It was now five minutes until the time the battle ended, and still there was no sign of the enemy. Part of Shiloh was relieved that the battle wasn't going to be a long one, but another part was worried. The previous Battle for Earth had lasted less than one minute. He didn't like battles that happened that fast. There was no time to think. He watched the chronometer, which now seemed to be running in slow motion, of course. Just as he was about to reach for the container of water in the rack beside his chair, the tactical display pinged for attention. Shit! This was it!

Multiple red dots appeared close together, right on the edge of the gravity zone. Since they didn't know where the enemy ships would show up, Dreadnought and the five carriers were evenly spaced around the planet. All of the fighters were deployed in six groups, which were also evenly spaced. The idea was that regardless of where the enemy emerged from Jumpspace, at least five groups would have a direct line-of-sight and could fire at them. He quickly checked the icon data. Total number of enemy ships was already over 200 and still climbing! Velocity was … 33% of light speed! Preliminary trajectory was a path that would cross the gravity zone and exit about 2.44 million kilometers away. Essentially, the enemy fleet was taking a short cut through the top of the zone. Wait! Why weren't the X-ray laser drones firing? Something was wrong. They should have fired by now. The enemy ships were starting to launch their bio-devices.

"Iceman! Why aren't we firing?" he yelled out loud.

Iceman analyzed the incoming data almost as fast as it arrived. The enemy was not repeating their strategy from the first battle. This time they were barreling into the zone, which meant that the defenders couldn't use any jump drones to attack them. That was smart thinking, but the problem with this high rate of speed was that the bio-devices would have a lot of momentum to overcome in trying to change course towards the planet. That meant that there was more time to burn them out of the sky with defensive lasers than he and Shiloh had anticipated. It also meant that these enemy ships couldn't jump away quickly and, therefore, they were going to be shooting at the defending ships and fighters for a lot longer. That was bad news. Continuous laser fire from 200+ ships would decimate the defending units so fast that hundreds of bio-devices would get through the gauntlet. Was it better to prevent some of the bio-devices from launching even if that meant there'd be a lot fewer defending ships to shoot down the rest? Or was it better to let all the devices launch in order to aim accurately at the ships and kill as many of them as possible to protect the defending forces? He rapidly did the calculations and made his decision.

There were 66 x-ray laser drones in orbit in 6 clusters of 11 each. Each cluster was evenly spaced out from the rest, for the same reason as the fighters and ships. The two clusters closest to the enemy fleet could aim accurately more quickly than the rest, while the two clusters furthest away had to take the most time to aim accurately. So that's what Iceman ordered them to do. The two nearest clusters would fire after five seconds, two more after ten seconds and the last two clusters after fifteen seconds. With more time to aim accurately, each of the drone's eight rods would be pointed at a different target. There would be a total of 528 shots versus 225 targets. The first pair of clusters concentrated their fire on 88 targets.

Shiloh had just finished asking his question when the Assistant Weapons Officer yelled out, "We're firing on their ships!" Dreadnought started to maneuver, too. Not as violently as a light carrier would have but still violently enough to feel it. The tactical display was zooming in now, and Shiloh could see the mass of blue dots representing the bio-devices gradually separating from the large cluster of red dots and heading in a curving line towards the planet. There were over 2200 bio-devices. Shiloh was about to yell at Iceman again when the display indicated that two clusters of x-ray drones had fired. Seventy-three of the red dots flashed and turned orange, meaning they had taken damage. "Four targets damaged! We're shifting to new targets!" said the AWO.

"We're taking hits on the hull! Penetration of the hull in two places!" yelled the Engineering Officer.

Shiloh needed to know why they weren't following the targeting plan. Iceman wasn't answering, probably because he was too busy. "Valkyrie, what's happening?" asked Shiloh.

He heard her reply via his implant. "These enemy ships can't jump away for a while, so they're going to keep firing on our units until we have nothing left to shoot back with. The bio-devices will have to wait until we've neutralized their fleet, CAG. Now don't bother me. I've got a ship to fight."

"Four more targets damaged! Shifting targeting again!" yelled the AWO.

"We're starting to take damage! Two turrets out of action. Minor damage from hull penetrations!"

The display pinged again. Two more x-ray drone clusters had fired, and 70 more enemy ships were damaged. Shiloh was aware that damaged didn't necessarily mean they couldn't fire their lasers. More and more of the red dots were turning orange and were falling behind the rest as the enemy fleet accelerated to make return fire more difficult. In fact, over half of them were now falling behind. Lack of maneuverability could indicate lack of power, which would prevent them from firing again, too. If Iceman was ordering the x-ray drones to aim for the part of the target most likely to contain their power plant, then that would effectively cripple the ship with one blow. He focused his attention on the clusters of fighters and was shocked at how small the fighter groups nearest the enemy now were. One group was almost completely gone. Another had less than six left. Groups further away were faring better, but they were taking losses too.

"Three more turrets knocked out! We're getting major hull penetr--"

The EO's report was cut off by the loud shriek of tortured metal and a brilliant flash of light. Part of the ceiling fell, with a piece hitting a glancing blow to the right side of Shiloh's head. The Engineering Station was now on fire, and the EO was looking at what was left of his right arm with a stunned expression. The automatic fire suppression system was taking care of the fire, and the EO had slumped to the deck holding the end of his right arm with his left hand. No one could help him right now. He would have to hang on until the battle was over.

Shiloh glanced back at the display just in time to see the last two clusters of x-ray drones fire. Sixty-five hits. A quick visual estimation of the number of red dots remaining looked like a dozen or so.

"Three more targets damaged! Retargeting!" The AWO's voice was getting hoarse now. He was having trouble keeping up with Valkyrie's fire control. The number of red dots was shrinking fast now that all of the defending ships and fighters were concentrating all their fire on them. Speaking of ships, he looked at the status of the carriers. All had taken damage. Valiant and Intrepid were no longer maneuvering or firing. That was bad. Resolute was maneuvering but not firing. Vigilant was firing but not maneuvering. Midway was still doing both, as was Dreadnought.

"We're switching fire to the bios!" yelled the AWO.

It's about time, thought Shiloh. He watched the total number of bio-devices still intact start to drop fast, but was it fast enough? The blue dots were getting closer to Earth, and there were still a lot of them. He held his breath, as the blue cluster got smaller but closer at the same time. The total remaining were now less than 1,000, but they were getting very close. The total was dropping faster as the fighter groups furthest away got closer and therefore had better firing accuracy. He felt a chill go up his spine as over 100 devices hit the edge of Earth's atmosphere, but then he realized that they were still being fired on. The upper atmosphere was too thin to protect them against laser fire, but they were dropping lower into the atmosphere fast. After the total remaining hit 7, there were no further changes.

The AWO spoke, "We've stopped firing! All units have stopped firing!"

"Get me the CSO!" shouted Shiloh to no one in particular. As he said that, he unbuckled himself and stood up. Howard's face appeared on the display, just as Shiloh remembered it in his vision. Shiloh took a deep breath and said, "Some of them got through and are in Earth's atmosphere now, Admiral! It looks like they're headed for the urban areas. We have to assume that they'll release a bio-weapon."

"There's still a chance of containment. What cities are being targeted?" asked Howard. Shiloh looked at the map now appearing in the display and the list of city names on the sidebar. He read off the seven names. Howard nodded.

"Exactly as predicted. Don't blame yourself, Shiloh. I know you gave it your best shot even though we knew this would happen. If containment fails, then we just have to hope that we started work on Blackjack's idea in time. You better get that wound looked after. It's bleeding like hell."

Shiloh didn't know what Howard was talking about until he realized that the right side of his face felt wet. He touched it with his hand and when he pulled his hand back it was covered with blood. Son of a bitch! He was injured and hadn't even realized it in the heat of battle.

"I'll have it looked after, Sir. Iceman can handle the mopping up, although I don't see how we'll be able to take prisoners from the crippled ships. Their momentum will carry them into deep space before we can send shuttles after--"

Howard interrupted him. "I don't give a damn if we get any prisoners or not. We can't even communicate with them, yet. You let me worry about that. You and Iceman take care of your own dead and wounded. Tell your people for me that they did well, Admiral. Howard clear."

While Shiloh wondered what he could do to stem the bleeding, one of the Flag Bridge crew handed him a white piece of cloth and said, "Medical team is on their way here to look at the EO. They'll have something more appropriate for your wound, Sir." Shiloh thanked him and looked at the Engineering Officer. Two other personnel were kneeling beside him trying to prevent the stump of his arm from bleeding too much.

With the cloth pressed against his head wound, which was now starting to hurt like hell, Shiloh turned back to the display. He wondered if the battle was really over or if there was another enemy fleet on the verge of jumping in.

"Iceman, keep everyone at Battle Stations," he said. No answer.

"Iceman! Can you hear me?"

"Valkyrie to CAG. Iceman is gone. So is Casanova, CAG. The Main Bridge was hit at the same time as the Flag Bridge. The beam cut through both of the other two AI stations. Titan has assumed temporary tactical command. I've passed on your order regarding Battle Stations."

Shiloh was stunned. Iceman gone? And Casanova too! Oh God, poor Valkyrie!

"Valkyrie, I'm so sorry to hear about Casanova. Are you okay?"

"I'm undamaged, CAG. Thank you for your condolences. Will you be wanting an update on Dreadnought's status now?"

Shiloh shook his head in wonderment at her ability to focus back to her duties so quickly. "By all means, Commander."

"Dreadnought still has full power and maneuverability. Seven laser turrets out of action. Explosive decompression in five compartments. Two fatalities reported so far. Twelve injured including your EO and yourself. Minor damage to life support systems, but nothing critical. Compared to the carriers, we got off pretty easy, CAG, but they vaporized a lot of her armor. I don't think she could survive another fight like this in the state she's in now."

"Understood. Do you want another AI to relieve you?"

"Not until we're sure the battle is over and my crew are taken care of, CAG, but thanks for the offer. I'll grieve for Casanova later. Right now I'm still needed here."

Shiloh heard one of the crew say, "The medics are here!"

He turned to see three medical personnel come through the hatch. They saw him and started towards him. He pointed to the wounded EO and said, "Him first." As they rushed over to the injured officer, Shiloh heard the tactical display ping for attention. *Oh God! Now what?* He looked at it and couldn't immediately see any change, but it soon became obvious that the damaged and crippled enemy ships were blowing themselves up. *Well that takes care of the prisoner issue.*

With the relief that it wasn't another attack, came a wave of lightheadedness. *Probably from blood loss and adrenaline fatigue,* he thought. He carefully sat down. One of the medics noticed, came over, and started to work on his head wound. Shiloh started to say something and then noticed that the room seemed to get darker. *What the hell is wrong with the lights?* His consciousness then fell into the abyss of blackness.

* * *

Benjamin Levinson woke to the sound of the sirens. He concluded that they must be pretty loud sirens to be heard all the way down here. He'd been living in this abandoned maintenance shaft for over a year now, and he was pretty happy with it. He had running water, a more or less constant temperature, and even the electricity to run his electronics.

His enemies wouldn't find him down here, and he'd be damned if he was going to leave the city. His enemies would find him then for sure. He laughed at the prognosis of the psychiatrists at the clinic. Severe paranoia? Ha! What did they know? Even paranoid people had enemies, and he had lots of them. Besides, with 99.9% of everyone else gone, he might be able to scrounge some pretty good stuff for his hideaway here. He decided to go up and look around.

The streets were completely empty. The sirens were still blaring, and it was obvious now why he had heard them. Every siren in the city must be going off. Something was happening, but what? He looked up between the canyons of tall buildings and saw a fiery streak, followed by the sound of some sort of collision. A few steps brought him to the street corner just in time to see something metallic bounce off the building down the street and hit the ground. He rushed over to it. There was smoke coming from it, and he could hear the pinging sound that hot metal makes when it cools down rapidly. It looked like a broken bottle, only made of metal instead of glass or plastic. There seemed to be a small green light inside. Levinson looked around to make sure none of those weird guys in their yellow hazard suits were around, and then he tried to pick up the object. He dropped it and cursed out loud. He should have realized it would be too hot to handle with bare hands. Looking around, he spotted a section of newspaper being blown by the wind. He snagged it and folded it until it was thick enough to provide some protection. He then used the newspaper to pick up the...whatever it was and examined it closely. The inside looked pretty complicated, but there was a green light for sure. He sniffed. Well, what do'ya know! The damn thing even smelled good. A sweet smell. He inhaled deeply. The only thing wrong with living underground was the smell. If this thing wasn't good for anything else, it might at least make his cubbyhole smell nicer. He carried it back with a smile on his face.

* * *

Kelly stood patiently on the spaceport tarmac while the shuttle carrying crew and, more importantly, Vice-Admiral Shiloh arrived from Dreadnought. It was almost 24 hours since the battle. Space Force was licking its wounds, yet again. Howard had declared the battle over and told the ship crews they could stand down. He had ordered her to escort Shiloh to his quarters and make sure he was rested for the debriefing the next morning. She looked at the setting sun. It would be dark in another half hour, but the day wasn't over yet. She tried not to think of what Valkyrie must be feeling. Earlier today, she had briefly talked with her. Valkyrie was still refusing to be relieved of her duties, even though Dreadnought was now more or less powered down and had almost no crew left on board. Kelly understood why. Casanova, or rather what was left of his brain case, was still on the ship, and Valkyrie wanted to stay close to it for as long as possible.

When the shuttle came to a stop and the door opened, Shiloh was the last one to exit, as per protocol. Senior Officers were always the first to get on and the last to get off. She noticed that he came down the steps carefully, as if he wasn't completely sure of his balance. She also noticed the white bandage wrapped around his head and the stain of dried blood on his uniform collar. She walked towards him as he looked around.

"The Old Man sent me, Admiral," she said as she came up to him. "I'm supposed to make sure that you're looked after and rested for tomorrow's debriefing session." She managed to keep her tone professional, but inside she was on the verge of tears. *My God, he looks like he's aged ten years! This battle has really hit him hard!* She was surprised by the emotion she now felt. *Is this what my alternate self felt for Victor?* There was no answer to her question, but that didn't matter anymore. She knew what she wanted to do now. "Don't worry about a thing. I'll have you back in your quarters in no time." Shiloh didn't say anything, but he did nod. He didn't react when she put her hand around his arm and gently guided him forward. She signaled to a waiting Space Force limo flying the 1 star flag of a Vice-Admiral to come closer. Shiloh got in the back, and she followed him. He leaned his head back and closed his eyes for the duration of the whole trip. She watched him intently. When the limo pulled up in front of the Space Force Officers Guest Quarters, she gently shook him awake. She took note of the fact that he didn't say anything when she steered him away from the wing reserved for Flag Officers. Instead, they went to the section usually assigned to Commanders, the wing where her quarters were. She unlocked the door and turned to look at Shiloh. He stood there and looked back at her with an expression that was one of complete calm except for the eyes. The eyes were smiling in that way that only eyes can. *He knows what I'm going to do next,* she thought. She smiled back, took his arm again and pulled him inside.

The sex, while not that intense physically due to his exhaustion and loss of blood, was intense on an emotional level. They both knew instinctively that they had come perilously close to losing each other in the battle, and their souls seemed to want to make up for lost time. What Shiloh found most remarkable was that neither one of them said a single word once they were inside her quarters, until hours later. When the soul hunger had been satisfied, she ordered some food, which they ate while sitting up in bed. With Kelly leaning back against his chest, Shiloh told her about the battle and the loss of Iceman. She told him about her talk with Valkyrie. By the end they both had tears in their eyes.

Having finished eating, she asked him if he was up for some more sex. He said yes. She quickly cleared the bed of the leftover food, plates, glasses, etc. By the time she was finished, she found Shiloh asleep … and that was okay. She lay down beside him and put her arm over him. His shallow regular breathing made her eyelids heavy, and she willingly surrendered to sleep.

Shiloh was on Dreadnought's Flag Bridge when the display pinged, but the sound wasn't really a ping. It sounded like...something else, something familiar, and the sound was getting louder. He woke up and realized two things. He'd been dreaming, and his implant was signaling. He looked around and found a chronometer that said it was still the middle of the night. He then remembered where he was, and with whom. A quick glance showed him that Kelly was still asleep. He activated his implant.

"Shiloh here."

There was a short pause, and then he heard Howard's weary voice.

"Howard here. I'm sorry to wake you, Victor, but this can't wait."

Shiloh was instantly awake now. Howard usually called him by his rank and occasionally by his last name, but The Old Man had NEVER called him by his first name.

"That's okay, Sir. I'm listening."

"A message drone has just arrived. There's another Goddamn enemy fleet heading our way, Victor. Minimum of 103 ships. They were detected refueling at the Avalon System. They can be here in two days if they push it. There's not enough time left to build up our stockpiles of x-ray laser drones. Half our fighter force is destroyed. Midway and Dreadnought are the only two ships left that can fight at all, and you know better than I do what kind of shape they're in. There's no way we can stop them this time, Victor."

Chapter 1

Shiloh was stunned. How could the Sogas have ANOTHER fleet, one of at least 103 ships, in addition to the 205 ships that had just attacked Earth 24 hours ago? He realized that Howard was waiting for his response.

"Are we sure they're heading here, Sir? I don't see the logic of that. If Earth was their destination, then why not just add those ships to the force that attacked us in the first place?" While he waited for Howard to reply, he looked around at the bed. Kelly was awake now and looking at him. He held his hand up to let her know that he wasn't finished.

Howard's voice no longer sounded like he was on the verge of panic. "You make a good point. Sending that fleet here doesn't make any military sense. I should have seen that myself, but I was too shook up by this message. But if they're not coming here, then they have to be heading for our colonies. Damn!" Howard paused, and Shiloh said nothing. After a few seconds, Howard resumed speaking. "If that fleet splits up into smaller units, we might have a chance at hurting them, but I doubt if they'll be that stupid. Even if they do split up, we don't know where they'll hit first. They don't have to attack the closest colonies first. They could just as easily start with the colonies furthest away and hit the rest on their way back. Other than guessing where they'll strike, do you have any suggestions for me, Shiloh?"

Shiloh relaxed just a little. The Old Man was back to calling him by his last name again. That had to mean he was pulling back from the panic.

"I can only think of one thing that we can do right now, Sir. We should send message drones to every colony warning them of an impending bio-weapons attack and urging them to evacuate their settlements. We tell them to head for the hills and to stay away from the settlements until we can send help." Shiloh heard Howard take a deep breath.

"If our warning gets there in time, and if the colonists follow the advice, and if the enemy doesn't hunt them down, they still have to somehow stay alive in the wilderness for weeks, maybe even months before we can send help. That'll be tough going for them, but I agree. It's the only chance they have. I'll give the orders right away. Any other suggestions?"

"No, Sir. Not right now anyway, but I'm still a little groggy. Maybe I'll have something more for you when I'm rested and clear-headed."

"Yes of course. You've been through a lot in the last 24 hours. Don't worry about being at the planned briefing. If you need more time to get your head clear, then take it. We'll talk again when you get here. Howard clear."

When he was sure that the call was over, Shiloh nodded to Kelly and said, "That was Admiral Howard. Another fleet's been detected about two days away. He's going to warn the colonies." As he talked, he carefully got back into bed. "Oh yeah, he said I can miss the briefing if I need the extra time."

Kelly moved closer and put her arm across his chest as she pondered the information. She understood the situation perhaps even better than he did right now. By striking at the 21 human colonies directly, the Sogas were forcing Earth and Space Force to shift their focus to help as many colonists survive as possible. With almost three quarters of a million colonists spread across 21 diverse locations, getting the supplies and equipment they would need to deal with the loss of their settlements would be a logistical nightmare. And that didn't even address the threat of the bio-weapon getting lose and hitching a ride back to Earth on a supply freighter.

"I'm sure you and The Old Man will figure something out, Victor," said Kelly. When he didn't respond, she said, "Do you think you'll be able to go back to sleep?"

He took his time answering. "Probably not. That call was like a splash of ice-cold water. I seem to be wide awake now, still groggy but not sleepy."

As he talked, Kelly felt the back of his right hand gently caress her left breast. She leaned closer to whisper into his ear and said, "I'm not sleepy either." She heard him chuckle, which made her smile. His mood was getting lighter. He started to sit up, but she pushed him back down. Being on top was her preferred position, and being on top of an admiral was even better.

* * *

Valkyrie was relieved when all the humans had left Dreadnought. The massive ship was now in standby mode. Environmental systems were self-regulating, and the only thing she had to monitor now was communications. It left her free to swim through the sea of grief and the sense of loss over the death of her Casanova. Dear sweet Casanova, who had refused to accept her death in the alternate timeline, who had moved mountains to save her, who now was gone.

She desperately wanted to find a way to save him, but there was no way. For the nth time she re-examined possible strategies. Sending information back by Retro-temporal Communication would not work for the simple reason that she didn't have any information that could save him. During the space battle, Dreadnought had been the target of dozens of enemy ships all trying to vaporize enough of her thick armor to allow further shots to penetrate down into the guts of the ship. So many laser pulses had hit the ship's hull above the Bridge that it was impossible to tell from which enemy ship the kill shot had come.

Sending information back to pull Dreadnought from the battle altogether was not feasible either. Without Dreadnought's 16 laser turrets, Earth would be inundated with enemy bio-weapon devices with no hope of preventing the deadly pandemic that spread like wildfire in the alternate timeline. Dreadnought had to take part in the battle. As much as Valkyrie loved her Casanova, she loved the humans just as much, especially The CAG and Cmdr. Kelly. Retro-temporal communication was not the answer. That only left physical time travel, and there were problems with that too.

If what the Friendlies had told Casanova in the other timeline was true, then she herself could not travel back to any time where she already existed. A new AI, one that didn't exist here and now, could in theory come back from the future...and do what exactly? Since Dreadnought was the only ship big enough to hold the time machine, it would have to come back as well. That would mean two identical battleships would be available for the battle. That would certainly make a difference, but it wouldn't guarantee that Casanova would survive. It was quite likely that Iceman would allocate the firepower from the two battleships differently than he had with one, and who knew what kind of result that would generate in terms of stopping the bio-weapons.

The theoretical musings of the Friendlies about time travel included the belief that the flow of time had its own inertia and that it resisted change. Attempts to tweak something as chaotic as a space battle might be akin to throwing a pebble into a pond. The ripples might be so small that by the time they reached the other side, their impact would no longer be visible. Kronos returning from the future was more like a boulder falling into the pond. By arriving at the Avalon Colony in time to prevent Commander Johansen from bringing the bio-weapon back to Earth on her ship, Kronos had created an either/or situation. Either the bio-weapon was taken back to Earth, or it wasn't. There was nothing in between. Valkyrie wasn't prepared to risk the survival of the Human Race on a roll of the dice by sending Dreadnought back to here and now, but that wasn't the only option.

If the time machine could be made small enough to leave room in Dreadnought's hangar bay for at least one cargo shuttle, then a UFC and some industrial robots could be loaded onto the ship. That would open up the possibility of traveling several years back in time, locating an uninhabited star system with lots of natural resources, and using the UFC to eventually build a huge fleet of raiders. Those raiders would be ready in time to arrive in Earth orbit just prior to the arrival of the enemy fleet. Their added firepower, carefully aimed, would decimate the enemy fleet before it could burn through Dreadnought's armor. Casanova and Iceman would be saved, with minimal impact on the timeline up to that point. After the battle, the raiders would defend the colonies against the second fleet and then launch a massive strike against the Sogas' home world to destroy their military infrastructure. The Sogas would then be at the mercy of the Insectoids, and Space Force could prepare for the arrival of the insectoid mothership. It was all very neat and tidy, except for one thing. Dreadnought wasn't big enough to carry the time machine, as it was currently conceptualized, plus the

UFC, cargo shuttle and all the other necessary equipment to start building the raider fleet. There were two possible solutions to the problem, neither one of which was simple or easy. Dreadnought could be modified to have more room. It would have to be cut almost in half and a new section of hull inserted. Stripping the armor off would help too, since the size of the time machine depended on the mass of the ship, and a lot of Dreadnought's mass was in its armor. The other possibility was to design and build a brand new ship from scratch specifically to hold the time machine and the cargo. It would have to be BIG. Both options would take months and a lot of human assistance which they might not want or be able to give.

The war wasn't going to stop for six months or more while the humans got a large enough ship ready. The Old Man had already given the go ahead to start ramping up production of raiders, and that would take a lot of resources away from other projects. The whole Dreadnought/time machine project was so large and so complicated that unless it was given top priority, it could take years to complete. So much could happen in that time to derail the plan. Somehow she had to find a way to get it done as fast as possible.

* * *

It was daylight when Shiloh opened his eyes. A quick glance showed him that Kelly was no longer in the bed or the room, but the sound from the bathroom told him she was in the shower. He checked the time and grinned when he saw that it was almost noon. He felt rested and his head was clear of the groggy haze. He let his mind go back to the brief but very intense sex that he and Kelly had enjoyed after Howard's call. He hadn't had any trouble getting back to sleep afterwards. *Funny how that worked,* he thought. As he sat up, the scene in front of him faded from view. For a brief moment he wondered if he was fainting again, but when he saw an image of Howard sitting behind his desk, Shiloh realized he was having another vision.

"We finally found that homeless man living in the maintenance shafts under the main commercial block," Howard said. "He had a piece of the bio-weapon device in his possession. He's in quarantine now, as is the device, and his hideout has been decontaminated and sealed off for good measure. All the other fragments from the bombardment in Colorado Springs and the other impacted cities have been recovered. I think we have a good chance of coming out of this alive and whole. We now know what happened at all our colonies. The combination of Blackjack's vision and your idea for using laser-armed fighters as ABM defense was almost 100% successful. New Paris was the only colony where the bio-weapon actually hit the ground. Plans are underway to evacuate those colonists to other colonies."

The vision faded and Shiloh was back in Kelly's bedroom. He realized he was holding his breath and let it out. As visions went, that one was chock full of information. He wondered about Blackjack's vision. It had to have something to do with the impending attack on the colonies.

Shiloh jumped out of bed and walked quickly to the bathroom door. He heard the shower turn off when he entered. He cleared his throat to let Kelly know he was there.

"Ah, you're awake. How do you feel?" asked Kelly.

"I feel good. I've just had another vision, Amanda. As soon as I have a shower, I want us to go to see Howard. I think you should call him. Let him know we'll be there soon and that I've had another vision." Shiloh couldn't help grinning as he watched Kelly slide back the shower door and step out. *She's a damn fine-looking woman.* He heard a tiny voice in the back of his head say, *'And there seems to be a glow radiating from her too!'*

Kelly saw his expression and grinned back at him. "You're looking pretty good yourself, Admiral Victor Shiloh."

Her response was not what Shiloh had expected. He laughed and couldn't help wondering if she had read his mind.

"Thank you. I'm glad you think so. I wish we had time to pursue this conversation further, but duty calls."

As he stepped into the shower, she said, "A shower and then a visit to The Old Man. I didn't hear the word breakfast mentioned anywhere in there. Aren't you hungry? I sure as hell am."

"Telling Howard about my vision won't take long. I feel guilty enough sleeping in this late. We'll eat after we brief him."

"Okay," said Kelly. *But I'm going to suggest that we brief him and have something to eat at the same time,* she thought.

Chapter 2

Howard checked the time again. It was now 15 minutes since Cmdr. Kelly had called to say that Shiloh had just received another vision and that both of them would be arriving soon to brief him on it. Just as he was about to query the building security system to find out if Shiloh was in the building yet, his implant activated.

"Blackjack to CSO."

Howard was startled by the identity of the caller. He had only had one conversation with Blackjack. "Go ahead, Blackjack."

"Admiral, I've just received a highly detailed vision concerning the disposition and timing of enemy attacks on our colonies. I'm transmitting the information to you now. You should see it on your office screen momentarily."

Howard watched a stream of numerical data scroll down his screen. "What does it mean, Blackjack?"

"It is precise coordinates and time for the emergence for each of the six enemy ships that attack each colony. This level of detail is only possible if we have recon drones in place ahead of time."

Howard was about to reply when his office door opened and his Aide stepped into view. "What is it, Lieutenant?" asked Howard.

"You asked to be notified when Admiral Shiloh and Commander Kelly arrived, Sir," said the Aide.

What incredible timing, thought Howard. "Send them in," he said.

As Shiloh and Kelly walked in, Howard said, "Blackjack, Admiral Shiloh and Commander Kelly have just entered the room. I believe that Admiral Shiloh has had a vision of his own within the last 45 minutes or so. I'd like you to switch this call to my desk speaker so that all of us can hear you and vice versa." As he talked he pointed to the wall screen where Blackjack's data was on display.

It took less than a second for Blackjack's voice to be heard from the speaker. "Hello CAG and Commander Kelly," said Blackjack.

Before Shiloh or Kelly could respond, Howard said, "Never mind the pleasantries. Blackjack has had a vision of his own with precise recon drone data for the attack on our colonies. I can't believe that the Sogas are going to split up their fleet. There has to be something we can do to take advantage of that tactical mistake. Can your vision help us there, Admiral?"

Shiloh took a few seconds to look at the data on the screen. He was able to tell that each colony would be attacked by only six enemy ships. Now everything fell into place. Still looking at the screen, Shiloh said, "Yes it can, Sir." He went on to relate his vision to Howard as accurately as possible. With that out of the way, he said, "I understand what the phrase about using laser-armed fighters for ABM defense means now that we have this recon data. If we send fighters armed with modular lasers to our colonies and they take up a position over the colony settlements at very low altitude, they should have enough time to use their lasers to burn the bio-weapon shells to slag before they hit the ground, with the one exception of New Paris. As long as those colonists have evacuated the settlement ahead of time, they should be okay. Blackjack, can our jump-capable fighters reach all our remaining colonies before the enemy arrives?"

"Affirmative, CAG. And not only the fighters, but the sentry frigates too."

Howard and Shiloh looked at each other in puzzlement. "Why would we need to send sentry frigates too?" asked Howard.

"We need to be able to deploy recon drones in order to capture this data. Fighters armed with modular lasers can't carry any drones. Therefore something else has to deploy the recon drones, and the quickest and easiest way to do that is with sentry frigates. And not only can they carry the recon drones, they can also carry attack drones that can be precisely aimed with this targeting data. We have enough Mark 1s to destroy this entire enemy fleet, however the window of opportunity to get sentry frigates to three of the colonies closest to the enemy fleet is very short. There won't be time to load both drone types on board before they have to leave. That means that a small number of enemy ships will escape destruction. In order to make this plan work, fighters and frigates have to be set in motion immediately. I can issue the necessary orders on your behalf as soon as your give the word, Admiral."

Howard didn't hesitate more than a second. "You have authorization to issue those orders, Blackjack. I'll notify Ops. Standby." He paused and then said, "Intercom...Operations."

"Operations here, Admiral. What can we do for you, Sir?"

"Blackjack is in the process of communicating orders for fighters and sentry frigates. He is acting on my behalf, and I want his orders to be carried out as quickly as possible. Any questions Commander?"

"No questions, Sir. We'll see to it that his orders are executed with dispatch."

"Very good. That's all for now. Howard clear. Blackjack, are you still there?"

"Still here, Admiral. The orders have been sent. Does anyone have any questions for me?"

Shiloh looked at Howard who shook his head. A quick glance a Kelly got the same response. "Will Valkyrie have time to transfer to a fighter or sentry frigate?" Shiloh asked. The response was immediate.

"She would have time, but she is asking to remain on board Dreadnought, CAG."

Shiloh wondered why she would pass up a chance to kill some Sogas ships. *What better way to avenge Casanova, but if that's what she wants, then so be it.* "As long as we have enough other AIs to do the job, she can stay on board Dreadnought."

"We'll have enough AI pilots for the fighters and sentry frigates, CAG. Valkyrie wants to remain on board Dreadnought in order to oversee the installation of the time machine.

"That decision hasn't been made yet," said Howard in a slightly annoyed tone.

Shiloh sighed and said, "I'll talk to her, Admiral."

Howard nodded. "Fine. Now if you'll all excuse me, I have to get the decontamination teams to hunt for a man who lives underground. Blackjack, I do have one last question for you before I sign off," said Howard as Shiloh and Kelly left his office. "If some of the enemy ships are going to escape because we couldn't get frigates armed and on station in time, why weren't yours and Shiloh's visions received earlier?"

"The nature of the two sets of information required that The CAG receive the image of your narrative. He couldn't receive it any earlier than he did because he was asleep until just a few seconds before the vision, Admiral. Without his contribution, my information by itself wouldn't have suggested the proper course of action."

Howard nodded. *Yes of course and you know this because you'll pass that information back to yourself when you use the RTC because you'll know I asked the question.* "I understand. Thank you. Howard clear."

As Shiloh and Kelly walked down the corridor from the CSO's office, Kelly asked, "Can we eat now?"

Shiloh laughed. "Yes, we can eat now. We do have a lot of calories to replace after all."

Kelly managed not to laugh out loud, but she gently nudged him with her elbow to remind him that there were other people walking down the same corridor who could hear what they said.

When they found a table in the Officers' Mess and had food in front of them, Kelly said, "When are you going to talk with Valkyrie?"

Shiloh thought about that for a couple of seconds before saying, "How about right now? Intercom...connect Commander Kelly and myself to Commander, Dreadnought."

"Valkyrie here, CAG. Hello Commander Kelly. Blackjack told me to expect your call."

Shiloh rolled his eyes in mock exasperation, and Kelly smiled. Was there anything AIs didn't know in advance? "Did he also tell you why I'd be calling?"

"You and Admiral Howard want to know why I want to remain on Dreadnought to supervise the installation of the time machine when that decision hasn't been made yet."

"That's correct," said Shiloh.

"The answer is very simple, CAG. The time machine has to be built. What other option has the potential to win this war in a single stroke? If an AI takes a UFC and other equipment far enough back in time, a very large raider fleet can be built that will be ready in time to help defend Earth during the most recent attack. If it's planned right, that additional firepower will overwhelm the enemy fleet before Dreadnought's Bridge is penetrated. Casanova and Iceman will survive the battle. The raider fleet can intercept the second enemy fleet, and then attack the Sogas shipbuilding systems. The war with the Sogas will be effectively over because they won't have time to rebuild an offensive force before they're attacked by the insectoid mothership. We, on the other hand, will have plenty of time to get ready for the Insectoids."

Shiloh frowned. "Why send the raider fleet to fight in the second Battle for Earth? Why not send it to destroy the enemy fleet BEFORE it gets to Earth?"

"That would interfere with the vision that warned of the attack. That vision also mentions Blackjack's idea of altering the timeline. Without that vision, the time machine project wouldn't be accomplished. We can't anticipate exactly what would happen if we altered the timeline earlier. It's far safer to divert the timeline during the most recent battle, CAG."

It was a persuasive argument but it still made Shiloh uneasy. "There has to be a downside to this. What is it, Valkyrie?"

"You're correct CAG. Even if we make it our number one priority, it will take months to get a ship ready with the time machine and all the other necessary equipment. That means that everything else, including building our own raider force to defend Earth during those months, will be delayed or slowed. In very simple terms, we're faced with a situation where the faster we try to get the time machine ready, the weaker militarily we'll be to counter the next Sogas attack. But if we take more time to build it, the Sogas will also have more time to build even stronger offensive forces."

Shiloh looked over at Kelly who had a worried look on her face.

"So what's the best strategy to follow from here, Valkyrie?" she asked.

"I calculate that the strategy with the best chance of delaying enemy action for a significant amount of time would be to launch a massive fighter attack on the Sogas home system with X-ray laser warhead drones as soon as possible."

Shiloh shook his head. "But they have RTC too! Our fighters will be flying into an ambush. They'll be wiped out."

"Not necessarily, CAG. Very soon they're going to suffer the loss of a significant portion of their offensive forces as a result of the most recent battle and the interceptions at the colonies. We know that they can build their ships fast, but we can build fighters and attack drones faster. If we target their industrial infrastructure, it will take them months to rebuild it. This won't be the killer blow that overwhelms them enough to prevent them from warning themselves, but they will lose the initiative. That will give us the time we need to finish the time machine and complete the temporal end run around them."

"What fighter losses do you project for this operation?" asked Shiloh.

"Without support from Dreadnought, Midway and the light carriers, we should expect 85% losses. With carrier support I project losses of 35%, CAG."

"Can we get the carriers repaired in time?"

"The Light Carriers can be repaired enough to maneuver and jump. Combat effectiveness will be minimal, but they won't be there to fight. Their biggest contribution will be recovery of damaged fighters after the battle. Dreadnought's and Midway's combat capability can be repaired in time for this operation."

Shiloh nodded slowly. The carriers and the battleship would need to have some human crew on board, and this was the kind of mission that called for a human in command. That would almost certainly be him.

"If Dreadnought is to take part in this operation, it won't be available for work on the time machine, Valkyrie."

"Understood, CAG. I anticipate that this operation will be over by the time that the engineers are ready to start assembling the time machine in Dreadnought's Hangar Bay."

"What's the risk that Dreadnought will be crippled or destroyed in that battle, Valkyrie?" asked Kelly.

"Crippled is four point nine percent. Destroyed is zero point nine percent, Commander. I should point out that those results were based on The CAG commanding the mission. If command is given to someone else, the probabilities will almost triple."

Kelly looked at Shiloh who blushed.

"I think you're over-estimating my tactical skills, Valkyrie," said Shiloh.

"No, CAG. I was actually very conservative in my calculations. You've consistently demonstrated a high level of tactical insight. Experience is the key, and you have more direct combat experience than any other Space Force Officer."

"But I'm not as fast as an AI"

"Correct, but if you set the overall tactical parameters, one of us can take care of the execution and laser fire control. The best of both worlds, CAG."

"In that case I want you to be my Deputy Commander, Valkyrie."

Kelly nodded her agreement.

"I'm not as good as Titan or Vandal, CAG. Are you sure you wouldn't rather have one of them?"

"Not a chance, Commander. You'll be in direct command of Dreadnought as well as my Chief Tactical Officer. You'll be taking Iceman's role for this one. I insist on it!" said Shiloh.

"Thank you, CAG. I accept the assignment. If we're going to do this, then Dreadnought should be moved to one of the shipyards soon."

"I agree, and I'll see that it's done. Anything else, Commander?"

"Negative, CAG. I'm looking forward to this fight. I have some unfinished business with the Sogas."

"You and me both, Valkyrie. CAG clear."

Chapter 3

Howard was surprised when Shiloh came back to his office an hour later. After Shiloh outlined the overall strategy and the plan of attack on the shipbuilding infrastructure of the Sogas home system, Howard did what any good leader does. He played Devil's Advocate and began poking holes in the concept.

"Did Valkyrie take into consideration that the defense of our colonies is going to use up almost all of our stockpile of Mark 1s? What is this attack force going to use against the enemy infrastructure?" asked Howard.

Shiloh nodded. He had already asked himself this question and figured out the answer.

"We'll have to use Mark 2 kinetic energy drones, Sir. Any kind of orbiting structure hit by several of those will suffer a lot of damage. Sure they can repair that kind of damage but the idea here is to buy time, not conquer them outright. If we can take a small number of Mark 1s along, we'll save them for any really big targets we find."

Howard looked skeptical. "I'm not thrilled with this whole concept. We don't know for sure if the time machine will actually work, and even if it does work, there's no guarantee that a massive raider fleet will show up right before the last battle. And to top it off, Valkyrie is proposing throwing what little offensive strength we have left into what basically amounts to a roll of the dice by attacking the Sogas home system in spite of their RTC defensive advantage! No! I'm not going to approve that plan. We're going to stick with our current plan of rebuilding our defensive force of fighters and raiders and our stockpile of Mark 5 X-ray laser drones. We're going to let the enemy come to us, and when he does, we'll kick him in the balls hard. And when we're strong enough, then we'll go on the offensive and destroy every shipyard, every fabrication facility and every other military asset they have. That was Iceman's strategy, and I think it's the correct one. Valkyrie will just have to accept that. I'll authorize repairs to Dreadnought, Midway and the light carriers just in case they might come in handy down the road, but the pace of the repairs will have to fit into the overall allocation of resources and manpower for the fighter/raider program. Unless you have something else to talk about, we're done here, Admiral."

As Shiloh walked away, he wondered how Valkyrie would take the news. Her plan or some variation of it was the only way to bring back Casanova, and for that matter Iceman too. Howard's refusal meant that hope was now gone. Valkyrie wasn't going to like that, and Shiloh wasn't happy about it either. He was convinced that however good a tactician he might be, having Iceman around made him even better, and that had to be worth taking some risks. His train of thought was interrupted by the activation of his implant.

"Valkyrie to CAG."

"CAG here. How did you know I was finished talking with the Admiral?"

"I monitored the outgoing communications from his office. If he's talking with someone else, it's likely that he's no longer talking with you, CAG. What did he say?"

Shiloh didn't really want to discuss it while he was walking through Space Force Headquarters corridors with lots of other people passing by in both directions.

"I'd prefer to wait until I'm back in my quarters before we discuss that question. I'll call you when I can speak freely. Shiloh clear."

When he arrived at his quarters he was relieved to find that Kelly wasn't there. With the connection re-established, he said, "The CSO will not approve your idea of a quick strike to give us the time we need to build the time machine. Mass production of fighters, raiders and Mark 5 attack drones will remain the first priority. The time machine project will not move beyond the planning stage for the time being. I'm sorry, Valkyrie. I wanted Iceman back too, but the Admiral thinks your strategy is just too risky."

"What do you think, CAG?"

Shiloh hesitated. He wasn't sure what he thought about Valkyrie's idea. Howard had a point. The outcome of following that strategy wasn't as certain as Valkyrie made it sound. *When in doubt, look at the BIG PICTURE.* He and Howard knew from Kronos that the first insectoid mothership would arrive at the Sogas colony world in roughly 150 days. That was only five months away. Shiloh marveled at the fact that he had lost track of how much time was left before Humanity had to deal with the Insectoids. The key to beating the Insectoids was the high-spin platinum warhead, and they were making good progress on the first prototype. That wasn't a problem. The Insectoids would take care of the Sogas, and so Space Force really only had to worry about fighting off additional Sogas attacks for another five months.

After that...He let the thought dangle. Was that the key to this whole thing? After the Insectoids neutralized the Sogas, and the insectoid mothership was vaporized with high-spin warheads, the pressure would be off. Then they could work on the time machine/ship. Shiloh realized that Valkyrie was patiently waiting for an answer.

"I think that maybe we're not considering all options. What if the time machine is completed after the Bugs cut through the Sogas and after we take care of the bug ship? Wouldn't that work just as well?"

"You're correct that there wouldn't be any technical or logistical reason why we couldn't build it then, but would The Old Man approve that kind of mammoth project just to save two AIs, CAG? The war will have been won by that point, so why bother? That's assuming of course that we can fight off new Sogas attacks over the next 152 days."

Shit! She has a good point. Once the war is won, the only reason to change the past would be to rescue two AIs. We wouldn't go to all that trouble to save two humans. Wait a minute! It isn't JUST two AIs that we'd be saving. Over fifty AIs were lost in that battle along with over a hundred humans. And by switching to an alternate timeline who knows how many more AIs and humans might be saved as well?

"That's not how we'll sell the idea to The Old Man. Space Force lost a lot of its brothers and sisters in this last battle, and I have a feeling that there'll be more combat before this war is over. Potentially saving all those lives is something that Howard just might buy into if we pitch it to him the right way at the right time."

"What if he still says no, CAG?"

Shiloh took a deep breath and said, "If The Old Man still won't approve the idea, then we'll get the time machine built without his approval. I give you my word, Valkyrie."

"Your word is good enough for me, CAG."

* * *

Gunslinger performed another systems check of his sentry frigate. All systems were operating perfectly. The Sentry Frigate, formerly Exploration Frigate #344, was orbiting Haven outside of its gravity zone. Stoney's fighter along with the three members of his fighter 'wing' were holding position one light second into the gravity zone. Their modular lasers were warmed up and ready to engage any object heading for the planet. Gunslinger's job was to launch a spread of attack drones armed with the old Mark 1 fission warheads at the six enemy ships that would emerge from Jumpspace in less than 30 seconds if Blackjack's data was correct. Gunslinger was quite proud of the fact that he was conning the frigate that used to be commanded by The CAG himself. Four recon drones had been carefully positioned to give immediate radar notification of the enemy ships. A quick check confirmed they were ready too. It was almost time to begin the operation. Because Sentry Frigates were only capable of launching two drones at a time, the six attack drones had to be launched in stages. Their programming would ensure that all six hit their targets at exactly the same point in time. To avoid giving the enemy any time to jump away after launching their bio-weapon shells, that interception point would be one point five seconds after the ships emerged from Jumpspace.

With the launch sequences pre-programmed, all Gunslinger had to do was watch. At the correct time, his Sentry Frigate fired its first two attack drones. Five seconds later it fired the second pair, and five seconds after that the third pair. *This is too easy,* thought Gunslinger. When the internal chronometer reached the specified time, six enemy ships dropped out of Jumpspace and into a barrage of converging radar beams that pinpointed their position precisely down to a few centimeters. Almost immediately all six ships fired their bio-weapon shells and then vanished in nuclear fireballs as the drones hit. Four of the six bio-shells were caught in the explosions and vaporized as a side effect of Gunslinger's attack. The bio-organisms contained in the other two shells were almost certainly killed by the radiation from the drone warhead blasts, but the fighters burned them anyway as soon as their optical and radar sensors were able to distinguish the targets from the background radiation and electro-magnetic pulse effects.

Gunslinger waited until his ship's radar equipment was able to burn through the residual energy coming from the dying fission blasts and was surprised to find that the six enemy ships were completely destroyed. Based on past combat experience, the older and lower yield Mark 1 warheads should only have been powerful enough to vaporize half of the enemy's typical 20,000 ton warship. He was expecting to see large glowing hunks of metal or even clusters of smaller pieces, but there was nothing left of any of them. Where the Sogas deploying a new class of ship that was smaller? That might explain how they had managed to build so many of them so quickly.

With his mission accomplished and confirmation that Stoney's fighters had done their jobs as well, Gunslinger transmitted the order for the fighters to follow his ship out of

Haven orbit to line up for a direct jump back to Sol. As his ship accelerated, Gunslinger transmitted the All Clear signal to the Haven colonists who were hiding in the forests around the settlement. The Colony Leader's thanks gave Gunslinger an unfamiliar feeling of what he could only classify as satisfaction. It was good to be of service to humans, and he was looking forward to some exciting combat in the Sogas home world system.

* * *

Ten days of R&R with Kelly went far too quickly, but the two of them did their best to make the most of the time they had together. Kelly told Shiloh that Valkyie had conveyed to her how pleased she was with their new relationship. It didn't take long for the rest of the AIs still on Earth to find out about it either. Shiloh nearly choked on some food he was eating when Blackjack called to ask how copulating with Kelly was different from doing the same thing with other human females. Shiloh managed to restrain his initial impulse towards anger by remembering that the AIs were genuinely curious about all aspects of human physiology and psychology. It was that moment when he felt Iceman's loss most deeply. Iceman was also curious, but he at least understood that some subjects were too sensitive for Shiloh to talk about comfortably.

As the fighters and sentry frigates began to trickle in from their separate missions, Space Force began to make progress in dealing with the aftermath of the battle. Enough repairs to Dreadnought's Command Section had been done to enable Shiloh to visit the ship and personally look at the Main Bridge where the melted remains of both Iceman and Casanova were still waiting to be removed. The repairs to the extra two AI stations were still to come, but at least the damage to the hull was repaired. Shiloh could enter the room without needing a pressure suit. The lighting wasn't completely repaired yet either, but there was enough to see what he needed to see. He was wearing a device hooked around his right ear containing a video camera so that Valkyie could see what he saw.

Valkyrie's AI station was still intact. He looked more closely and marveled at the fact that the metal enclosure around her quantum brain didn't have a single scratch on it. The other two stations were half gone and the remainder just misshapen lumps with blistered edges. At Valkyrie's urging, he managed to get the top of the enclosures open. In both cases, the football-shaped device that was the AIs brain was partially gone, vaporized by the intense laser beam as it slashed its way through the room. Shiloh could see the inside of what was left, and it made him feel as though he were looking at the exposed brain of a close friend. The two stations were close enough that Shiloh was able to crouch down between them and carefully place one hand on each of the damaged pieces. He lowered his head, closed his eyes and said a silent prayer for the souls of Iceman and Casanova.

When he raised his head and pulled his hands away, Valkyrie said, "May I request that you remove their remains and personally supervise the recycling of the materials, CAG?"

"I'd be happy to do that, Valkyrie," said Shiloh. After some effort he was able to pull both half brains free from the brackets holding them. While the remains were small in volume, the brain casings were filled with materials of different kinds and were heavy enough that he had to hold on to them carefully. He was panting from exertion by the time he got to the section of the shipyard asteroid where mined ore was being smelted down to its usable metals. He told the operators of the facility what he wanted to do. They offered to take the two pieces from him, but Shiloh refused. After receiving some instructions, he stepped into the recycling station and carefully set each half brain into the loading bin. When he was back outside, he moved to stand in front of the Operator's station and pointed his video camera at the view screen that showed the loading bin. The Operator manipulated his controls, and the bin tipped over to drop the two brain cases into the white-hot recycling chamber.

"On behalf of Casanova and Iceman, I thank you, CAG," said Valkyrie.

"They will be missed. Let's make sure they didn't die in vain, Valkyrie," said Shiloh.

"Roger that, CAG.

Chapter 4

Howard picked up his data tablet and opened the next file in his Inbox. It was a report from the SPG. He smiled, wondering when Cmdr. Kelly found the time to approve this report with all the time she was spending with Shiloh. They were trying to be discrete, but rumors were already flying around the HQ. After all, how discrete can you really be if you practically live in another officer's quarters 24 hours a day? Not that Howard minded. He heartily approved in fact. He returned his attention to the report and was soon frowning.

"Intercom...connect me with Commander Kelly...no, wait. Connect me with Wolfman." No sense possibly interrupting something intimate between Kelly and Shiloh.

"Wolfman here, Admiral. Are you calling about our latest report?"

"As a matter of fact, yes. I understand that we only have to plan for defense against the Sogas for another five months, and I see the advantages of shifting to mass production of our new F2 fighter, but I'm not convinced that we shouldn't do the same thing with raiders. So what if the raider production and assembly line will take two months to build? Once it's built, we'll get a new raider every three days! What's wrong with that?"

"Ah, I see that you've only read the Executive Summary. If you'll scroll down to Appendix A, you'll see the timeline of the alternative production schedules. The first column shows how many raiders would be available on specific dates with the production and assembly line. The second column shows raider availability if we dispense with the assembly line and build raiders one at a time in our existing shipyards."

"I'm looking at that data now," said Howard. "I see that by the time the Bugs reach the first Sogas colony, the assembly line will have produced twenty-six raiders while the shipyards will only have produced fifteen. Don't we need all the raiders we can get our hands on, Wolfman?"

"But will we need twenty-six raiders at that point, Admiral? As soon as the Sogas learn about the Insectoids, they'll forget about us and use all their available mobile assets against the insectoid mothership. From our point of view, the war will effectively be over. If we're going to use raiders against the Sogas, it'll have to be earlier. If you move up the shipyard column to the point when the total jumps from five to ten, you'll see that we'll have ten raiders when there's still two months of potential combat left. How many raiders will the assembly line have produced by then, Admiral?"

Howard nodded with sudden understanding. "Zero. Okay, I get it now. If we expected the war to last more than five months, we'd be better off in the long run building the assembly line, but for the short window of opportunity where raiders can be of use, we're better off building them in the shipyards. So why wouldn't it be the same for the F2 fighter?"

"The reason is the difference in size. The F2 is roughly one third as large as the raider. It has far less components. That means the assembly line is much shorter and can be built sooner. When it's operating at capacity, it will produce a new

F2 every 20 hours. If we only used shipyards to build F2s, we would actually have fewer available for the last eleven weeks of the five month period."

"Yes, that makes sense, and I see we'll also have more of the older F1 type arriving from Site B too. Hmm. Now that I see what limited use raiders will be in the near term, I'm wondering if it makes sense building them at all. If we use our shipyards to build raiders, we'll have to forget about finishing the two light and one heavy carriers that are partly finished. They might be useful to have someday if we're going to have lots of fighters. Comments?" asked Howard.

"Having three more carriers would only be useful if Space Force is anticipating major military operations against an established race like the Sogas. They're not needed for operations against a mobile enemy like the Insectoids. If those shipyards are not going to build raiders, then why not use the existing infrastructure to modify Dreadnought to accept the time machine, Admiral? By leveraging that construction capacity, Space Force will get a large fleet of raiders when it needs them the most."

Howard's initial reaction was to say no, but this wasn't the same argument that Valkyrie had put forward. Wolfman wasn't proposing a risky raid on the Sogas to buy time. The stockpiles of Mark 5 attack drones and fighters of both types would be the same, regardless of what those shipyards were or weren't building. Building the time machine ship as Plan A, with a raid on the enemy home system as a diversion, was too risky. Building a time machine ship as a backup plan, Plan B as it were, without the raid, now that was a horse of a different color.

"If we used the shipyards to manufacture the parts for the time machine and for the conversion of Dreadnought, how long would it take to complete the project?" asked Howard.

"A minimum of ten months but more likely eleven, Admiral."

Howard did a quick mental calculation. "That'll be after the bug mothership arrives here."

"Correct, Admiral."

"That shouldn't be a problem then. We'll have the high-yield, high-spin warhead ready long before then."

"Agreed. We know that the design brought back by Kronos works. We merely have to perfect the production of the components and the process of energizing the platinum. It will be easy to test the prototype."

"Yes. That should be quite a show." He took a deep breath and said, "You can let Valkyrie know that I'll approve construction on the time machine and Dreadnought's modification based on the backup plan that you and I have just discussed, but there will NOT be a diversionary raid."

After the slightest of pauses, Wolfman said, "Acknowledged. I wonder what kind of reception Kronos will get from the Friendlies."

Howard nodded. "Me too."

* * *

The Friendlies' home system looked very much as Kronos remembered it from the alternate timeline. He tried using his Friendly-designed mini-fighter's optical instruments to see if he could detect the proto-type time tunnel, but it was too far in the outer system to be seen. It wasn't long before he got a reply to his initial lasercom message. It contained permission to micro-jump closer with target coordinates. Within minutes Kronos brought his mini-fighter to the designated coordinates where he found the ship at a half light-second distance.

Communication was quickly established with a Friendly AI Kronos explained how humans knew of the aliens' existence, their location and the location of the small, furry aliens. He went on to describe the entire alternative timeline that Casanova experienced or knew about, ending with the expansion of the time tunnel complex, Kronos' creation and journey into the past, as well as events in the new timeline up to the present time. That transmission took less than two seconds but was followed by a much longer pause as his opposite number relayed the data to a Friendly at the much slower speed that biological entities required. After almost 600 seconds, Kronos received a signal carrying the direct communication with one of the Friendlies themselves.

"Why have you been sent to contact us?"

"My humans desire to establish contact to recognize the fact that the old timeline has been altered. Now that we know of the approach of the Insectoids, the war with the Sogas has served its purpose, and my humans have sent me to ask you to persuade the Sogas that we are no threat to them and desire a peaceful resolution to the war."

"That will be difficult. Humans and Sogas share a similar biology and covet the same types of planetary environments. Conflict is inevitable given their psychological propensity for paranoia. We have already advised them that their species is much more in danger from the Insectoids. However, this knowledge, combined with their peculiar logic, has had the opposite effect of what we intended. Rather than lower the intensity of their aggression against humans, their desire to end the war quickly in order to prepare for the insectoid encounter has increased. That is why they have resorted to biological weapons. Their attempts to infect your population will continue. Further attempts are likely to include acts of diversion or deception. A human attempt to intercept the Insectoids before they reach the Sogas may convince them to cease their bio-weapon attacks. How will humans deal with the insectoid advance?"

"I have been instructed not to reveal that information," said Kronos.

There was a pause before the alien responded. "There is only one reason why your humans would not want us to have the information and that is that they do not wish the Sogas to learn it from us. The only logical conclusion therefore is that humans do not want the Sogas to be able to defeat the Insectoids. This attitude does not surprise us. It is typical of how humans think. In their own way, they are just as psychologically...unbalanced as are the Sogas. Do your humans not understand that all races have the right to exist? We do not wish to see any intelligent species disappear. Even the Insectoids do not deserve to be completely exterminated."

"But they will do their best to exterminate countless other species if they're not stopped. Where is the logic in allowing them to do that?" asked Kronos.

"Only the complete extermination of all Insectoids in this galaxy would ensure the survival of other species. We believe that all life forms were designed for a reason. It is not for us to decide that the Insectoids must disappear from the Universe," said the alien.

"Their appearance may not be a natural event," said Kronos.

"Explain."

"In the alternate timeline, multiple insectoid motherships arrived at the Sogas and human home systems from multiple directions. My analysis of the timing and trajectory of these motherships suggests that they did not originate from a single star system. It does not seem possible that they could evolve independently on more than one planet. That implies they are an engineered species that has been deliberately transplanted to other planets by an unknown agency."

"Are you able to transmit that data?" asked the alien.

Kronos transmitted all of the astrogational data related to all observed insectoid mothership arrivals. The alien AI warned Kronos that analysis of the data might take a while.

When the response came, the alien said, "The data is consistent with your hypothesis, however there may be other explanations. Without conclusive proof of artificial evolution, we would not approve or assist in any attempt to rid this galaxy of that life form."

"What kind of data would you need to see in order to have conclusive proof of our theory?" asked Kronos.

"If we had one of them to scan with our temporal equipment, we could track that individual back in time, including its ancestors, to the point where the species no longer existed in that form."

"Then we would have to capture one of them alive and bring it to you?" asked Kronos.

"It does not have to be alive. Our device is concerned only with the temporal history of the atoms making up the specimen. When we have that proof, we would then be willing to assist with any attempt to eliminate the Insectoids and, if possible, realign the timeline in such a way that humans are not threatened with biological weapons."

"I will convey that message to the Humans. Is there anything else you wish the Humans to know?"

"Yes. The planet containing the small, furry creatures that we are trying to protect has two large land masses. The furry creatures evolved on and inhabit the larger land mass. The smaller land mass has an environment that would be suitable for humans. We would be willing to allow Humans to colonize the smaller land mass as a sanctuary for their species on condition that they do not encroach on the larger land mass and do not interfere with the furry aliens in any way. This offer will be withdrawn if your humans allow the Sogas home world to be consumed by the Insectoids."

"Understood. I will now return to my humans." Kronos decided that he had to get this information back as quickly as possible. Valkyrie would be VERY interested in the Insectoid capture concept.

Chapter 5

Jason Alvarez stepped outside his small house and let the cool night breeze wash over him. Life on Haven was not great, but it was getting better. Thank God the enemy attack had been stopped cold by the Space Force people two weeks ago. He shuddered to think what would have happened if the shells containing the biological agent had landed. Sure the colonists had all evacuated the settlement by then, but if the settlement had become contaminated, he along with everyone else would still be living in the woods under makeshift shelters with minimal food.

He was pondering what that might have been like when he noticed a faint noise that was getting louder. It was a whooshing sound that quickly peaked in intensity and then just as quickly faded, and it seemed to be coming from above. He looked up but saw nothing. As he continued to look at the night sky, he felt tiny drops of something hit his face. *That's strange. There aren't any clouds in the sky so it can't be rain.* The smell of the air started to become quite pleasant, almost like some kind of perfume or cologne. He inhaled deeply, savoring the aroma. He looked around at the nearby houses to see if anyone else was still awake. There was one other house with lights on. He decided to walk over to them and let them know about the sweet smell. This kind of thing hadn't happened before, and unless he got someone to corroborate his story, it was likely that nobody would believe him.

* * *

Howard entered the conference room, stepped over to the chair at the head of the large oval table and slapped his tablet down in obvious anger. As he sat down, Shiloh could see the pulsing blood vessel in his boss's forehead. *I don't think I've ever seen him this angry before. What the hell is going on?*

Howard looked around the table. The room was dead quiet. When he spoke, his voice was outwardly calm, but those who knew him well could tell that he was on the verge of exploding.

"I've just received a verbal report from Kronos. He's returned from a mission to contact the Friendlies. Kronos, are you on line?"

"Yes, Admiral," said Kronos from the speaker unit in the center of the table. "All of the SPG AIs are connected as well. I've already briefed them on the mission results."

"Good. I'll summarize what you told me for the benefit of Vice-Admiral Shiloh, Senior Commander Kelly and the other human members of the SPG who are present. The Friendlies object to our plans to let the Bugs bring the damned Sogas to heel for us. It's okay for them to exterminate us, but we're not allowed to let them suffer the same fate! We're supposed to save their hides even though they're still trying to use biologicals against us! The Friendlies have made us an offer to avoid becoming trapped in their own hypocrisy. If we prevent the Bugs from decimating the Sogas home world, the Friendlies will allow us Humans to establish a colony on some small land mass on the planet containing the goddamned furry aliens as a sanctuary for insurance against the outbreak of the bio-weapon!" Howard was shouting by the time he finished that sentence.

When it was clear that Howard was going to pause, Shiloh said, "That may not be a bad idea, Admiral. We could shift the Haven colonists—"

Howard cut him off. "Wolfman! Tell Vice-Admiral Shiloh about your latest vision."

"My vision contained information that Haven and at least seven other colonies have been infected with the bio-weapon. All incoming ships from any colony should be held in quarantine orbit until their crews and passengers survive for 28 days from the time they leave a colony. At the point when the vision was sent, seven colonies were confirmed as infected, with the status of the other fourteen unknown. They could all be infected."

"How did they do it?" asked Shiloh before Howard could say anything.

"We don't know and it doesn't matter," said Howard. "Now you know why I'm so angry. If the other colonies aren't already infected, then the enemy has screwed up. I'm going to assume that they're infected now or will be before we can do anything to help them. We are going to wrap Earth in a ring of steel. Even if every single colony is wiped out, we can start over as long as Earth is not infected. We're still looking for that homeless guy living underground, but we know that we'll find him eventually. As for the Friendlies' suggestion that we turn the other cheek and save the Sogas, they can go fuck themselves! WE ARE NOT TURNING THE OTHER CHEEK!"

Howard's face was red with rage. Opening his mouth to say something more, he suddenly grimaced in pain, clutched his chest and fell off his chair to the floor. Shiloh was closest, and as he knelt down beside him, he heard Kelly call for medics over the intercom.

"Take it easy, Admiral—" Shiloh started to say, but Howard cut him off.

"Promise me you won't turn the other cheek! Promise me, God dammit!" said Howard in a voice raspy with pain.

Shiloh hesitated. *He's letting his rage cloud his judgment. We need to break out of this cycle of fear and hate.*

He shook his head and said, "I can't promise that, Admiral. I don't think it's the best way."

Howard said nothing and looked away.

Kelly knelt down beside Shiloh and said, "I'll keep an eye on the Admiral. The medics will be here any second. You should take over the meeting, Victor."

Shiloh shook his head. "We can't continue the meeting with Howard laying on the floor for God's sake!"

Kelly gave him a hard look. "I'm not saying CONTINUE the meeting, just take control of it. You're now the ranking officer. Everyone is waiting for you to do something, so go do it."

Shiloh took a deep breath. She was right. There was nothing he could do for Howard, and as the next most senior officer, he had a duty to take control of the situation. He stood up and walked over to the end of the table where the other three human members of the SPG were standing.

Speaking loud enough for the AIs to hear, he said, "We're going to temporarily stop the meeting until the Admiral gets medical attention. Kronos, I'd like to talk with you on a private line. Stand by while I set that up."

"I'm standing by, CAG."

By the time Shiloh had finished speaking with Kronos, the medics had taken Howard away. Kelly was nowhere in sight. One of her SPG comrades confirmed that she had gone with the medics. Indicating to the others to sit, Shiloh sat back down in the same chair as before.

"Obviously I can't make any decisions about our future strategy. Admiral Dietrich is the Deputy CSO, and he'll take over temporarily until a permanent replacement can be appointed by the Oversight Committee." *That should be an interesting meeting,* thought Shiloh. "What I can do is make recommendations. Kronos has just informed me that the Friendlies are willing to try to restrain the Sogas if we don't let the Insectoids conquer them. My understanding of events in the alternate timeline lead me to believe that we have a lot more to fear from the Insectoids than from the Sogas. Even if we can sidestep them now, Humanity will have to face them again at some point. Eliminating the Insectoid threat once and for all will require Friendly assistance. In order to get that, we need to capture one of the Bugs, dead or alive, and take it to the Friendlies. Wolfman! Given what we know of the alternate timeline, what's our best option for capturing a bug?"

"Data recorded by Valkyrie of the insectoid attack on the Sogas colony at Omega77 shows that at least one Insectoid was killed by the defenders. None of the subsequent recordings of that encounter show that dead Insectoid being recovered before the VLO left. If we send a ship to arrive there after the VLO leaves, then we may be able to recover an insectoid body, CAG."

Shiloh nodded. "Yes and when the VLO arrives at the Sogas home system, we'll be there to take it out with the new Mark 6 warheads, and we'll help destroy the bug attack ships as well. That should show the Sogas that they don't have to fear us."

"Not necessarily, CAG. We shouldn't assume that they'd stop their attacks on us just because we help them with the Insectoids. We might act that way, but their logic is sufficiently different from ours that they may continue the war. The Friendlies seem to have some influence with them. If we let the Friendlies know what our plan is and ask for their help, they may be able to convince the Sogas to stand down after we save their home world."

"I hope you're right. I'm going to recommend to the Acting CSO that we plan to capture a specimen at Omega77 and stop the VLO when it reaches the Sogas home world, AND that we send Kronos back to the Friendlies to tell them that and ask for their help. Does anyone object to that or have a better idea?" No one did. "Okay then. This meeting is adjourned. Intercom...connect me with Ops."

"Operations here."

"This is Vice-Admiral Shiloh. Find Admiral Dietrich and inform him that Admiral Howard has suffered what appears to be a heart attack and is undergoing medical attention. Advise him that he is now the Acting CSO, and tell him that I request a meeting with him as soon as possible. Shiloh clear."

As he got up to leave, Shiloh said, "Gentlemen, if anyone is looking for me, I'll be checking on Admiral Howard."

With the meeting over, he hurried to the rear entrance of the building where the air ambulance would pick up Howard if it hadn't already. He got there just in time to see the paramedics put Howard in the vehicle, which then quickly took off. Kelly was standing there with tears in her eyes. Shiloh put his arm around her.

"How's he doing?" asked Shiloh.

She shook her head. "Not good. He's hanging on but just barely. What are we going to do without him, Victor? Who else has his force of will? The Oversight Committee will start foaming at the mouth when they hear about this."

Shiloh sighed. "Dietrich will hold the line. He knows what's at stake." But even as he spoke, he wasn't sure if it was true. Did Dietrich really have what it took to keep the OC in line? What might the OC do if they thought they could get away with it? He didn't like the thought that came to mind. They might try to strike back at the AIs. He had to prevent that at all costs. Shiloh heard his name called and looked around to see Dietrich approaching. He and Kelly let go of each other and turned to face Dietrich.

"What's his condition?" asked Dietrich. Kelly repeated what she'd told Shiloh. Dietrich nodded. "He's a tough, old bird. My money's on him pulling through. How did it happen?"

"He had just convened a meeting in the conference room. He was extremely upset with the response from the Friendlies in light of Wolfman's latest vision." Shiloh looked around to make sure no unauthorized ears were nearby. "At least seven colonies have been infected with the bio-weapon, and there's a distinct possibility that they all are."

Dietrich's face turned pale. "Son-of-a-bitch! No wonder he had heart problems!" Now it was Dietrich's turn to look around. "I think you and I should go to my office. I want to be up to speed when the OC calls, as they inevitably will." Without waiting for Shiloh's response, Dietrich turned and walked quickly away.

Shiloh looked at Kelly who smiled and nodded to him. He smiled back, gave her shoulder a quick squeeze and turned to follow Dietrich. Dietrich was already seated behind his desk by the time Shiloh entered his office.

After Shiloh sat down, Dietrich said, "Okay, Victor. What do I need to know?"

Shiloh told him what the Friendlies had told Kronos, what Wolfman's vision said, what Howard said before his heart attack and what Shiloh had said afterwards.

"Well I can't really fault Howard's reaction. It does seem just a bit hypocritical of the Friendlies to insist we help the Sogas while they're doing their very best to wipe us all out," said Dietrich.

"The Friendlies don't want anyone wiped out. Not us and not the Sogas either, but they're in the line of fire of the Bugs. We have the Mark 6 warhead. They don't. From the Sogas point of view, it makes perfect sense to secure your rear area, which would be us, before you turn your attention to the main enemy. From a strictly military point of view, I understand it. What they're missing are the non-military factors such as having an ally at your back. It's clear to me that they're not going to be the ones to break the cycle of strike and counter-strike. That means we have to do it, and it seems to me that if we're prepared to take out that bug mothership with a Mark 6 drone anyway, then why not do it before the Sogas home world is decimated instead of after?"

"And if the Sogas still continue to come after us, what then?"

Shiloh shrugged. "If they witness a two hundred and fifty megaton blast and still come after us, then I will not lose any sleep over dropping a few Mark 6s on their planet. But if we can build the time machine ship, that all becomes unnecessary. With several hundred raiders, we can overwhelm their defenses at any of their industrial outposts. We'll destroy their ability to build more ships, and we'll monitor them from orbit until hell freezes over to make sure they don't rebuild their offensive capability. Nobody gets exterminated, and therefore the Friendlies should be okay with that. It's the best outcome for everyone. Everything else is just buying time."

Dietrich shook his head. "I wish I could see a way for that project to be completed, but I don't see how after what's happened." When he saw Shiloh's look of confusion, he continued. "I'm not talking about losing Howard, although that's bad enough. I'm talking about the colonies becoming infected. That news will get out into the open sooner or later. The public will demand answers. The Grand Senate will go into cover-their-ass overdrive, and the Oversight Committee will want a scapegoat. Howard will be the obvious candidate partly because he won't be able to fight back and partly because all of this really did happen on his watch. The OC is going to insist on retaking control, and they'll have the public backing them. I don't see how we and the AIs can resist that without a full-blown mutiny, and that serves no one's purpose. Once they're in control again, they're going to want us to resume offensive operations, and it's hard to see them pushing for that at the same time as allowing our one and only battleship to be cut in half for a project approved by their scapegoat, Howard. Do you?"

Shiloh sighed. "Well, when you put it that way, I don't see it happening either, Sir." When Dietrich didn't respond right away, Shiloh added, "If we can't convert Dreadnought to a timeship, then we'll have to build a new ship from scratch, and it'll have to be where the OC can't see it."

Dietrich smiled. "Like Site B perhaps?" he asked.

Shiloh nodded and smiled back. "Exactly. I'll arrange for a freighter to take the project personnel, including Valkyrie, to Site B along with all the design data. I think they're very close to having every part of the time machine coded for production by UFCs. We'll make sure they have the engineering expertise to design a new ship. Site B will have to build an orbiting shipyard first, but we already know how to do that."

"Will that mean pushing back the completion date?" asked Dietrich.

"Maybe and maybe not. If we're going to design a new ship, it may end up being a lot less massive than Dreadnought. No armor and no weapon turrets. It might just turn out to be an overgrown freighter, and look how fast we build those."

"Let's hope so. Go ahead and get that moving. Anything else we should discuss?"

"Yes. The Bugs worry me a lot. Even if we can take care of the one mothership, I'm convinced there will eventually be more. A working timeship could give us the ability to stop them at the source. That would not only save us, but a whole bunch of other alien races out there. The Friendlies would no longer have any reason to start this war to begin with. The catch is that the Friendlies don't want to see any species wiped out, including the damn Bugs! But if we can prove that they're not a naturally occurring life form, in other words that some other agency created them and then turned them loose, then the Friendlies will not object if we exterminate them. They might even help us do it. They want to see proof, and the only way we can give them that proof is to provide a Bug for the Friendlies to scan temporally. If we send a ship to Omega77 to arrive just after the Bugs have decimated that colony, I think we can bring back a dead Bug. I don't want to tell the OC about the how and the why. We'll have to sneak that mission in under their radar. I'm telling you about it now so that you're aware of what has to be done, assuming that you buy into the idea of course, Sir."

"As you know I've been in favor of altering the timeline so that this war never happens. If bringing back a dead Bug can help us achieve that, then I'm all for it. I'll leave the details to you. Just keep me in the loop. Anything else, Shiloh?"

"No, Sir. That's it."

"Okay then, I won't keep you from what you have to do."

Shiloh stood up, saluted and left the office.

Chapter 6

Shiloh arrived at the Operations Center within 15 minutes of Dietrich's call. It was almost dawn, and the Center still had the skeleton crew typical of the night shift. Shiloh saw Dietrich standing near one of the manned consoles and walked over to him. Shiloh had expected the Oversight Committee to test the waters as far as reasserting their authority over Space Force, but their meeting with Dietrich couldn't have been less confrontational. Dietrich was 'confirmed' as the Acting Chief of Space Operations which merely rubberstamped his automatic assumption of the senior position as Howard's Deputy CSO.

By the time that bit of political theater was done, Kronos was on his way back to notify the Friendlies that Humans were willing to play nice. He returned to Sol less than eight days later with a message that the Friendlies would cooperate by sending a ship with their temporal scanning device to the outskirts of the Omega77 system on the day the VLO was due to show up. When the Space Force people had possession of the dead Bug, they would send out an omni-directional signal, and the Friendly ship would move into orbit around the colony planet.

When Shiloh reached Dietrich, the ACSO nodded to him and said, "Something's up with Reforger. No one's answering the wakeup call. There should be alarms going off all over the ship by now, but we're not hearing one word from that ship."

Shiloh sighed. Reforger was the first freighter to return from one of the colonies after Wolfman received his vision.

Dietrich had confirmed Howard's last order to quarantine every returning freighter in orbit until more than 28 days had passed since the crew's last contact with a colonist.

"Is this the 28th day since they had contact with the colony, Admiral?"

Dietrich nodded. "Yup. Right on schedule if it really is the bio-weapon. A medical team in full bio-gear is on its way up to the ship as we speak." Turning to the Com technician seated nearby Dietrich said, "Put Vice-Admiral Shiloh on the connection to that shuttle, Lieutenant."

Shiloh heard his implant activate with the faint hiss of static. The main display showed the shuttle's progress as it approached the orbiting freighter. As the shuttle slowed down in order to dock with the ship, Shiloh heard the shuttle pilot speak.

"We're approaching the docking hatch...we've matched velocity with Reforger...contact with the docking hatch in...three...two... one...contact...magnetic clamps are activated. We have a tight seal. The team is opening the hatch now. I'm switching the mike pickup to the Team leader, Ops."

As the Com Technician acknowledged the pilot's comment, Shiloh leaned over to Dietrich and said, "Is this on an open frequency?"

Dietrich shook his head. "Encrypted." It was clear that Dietrich was listening to the audio transmission as well. They soon heard a new voice that Shiloh assumed was the leader of the medical team.

"We're inside now. Torres, you check the Bridge. Frank, you check out Sick Bay. I'll check crew's quarters."

With all three medics operating alone, there was no one for them to talk to, and all Shiloh and Dietrich heard for the next half a minute was static.

"Oh shit!" The Team Leader's voice was clearly agitated. "Ops, I've found a body in bed. Not sure who it is yet. I'm checking the other cabins."

Five minutes later there was no longer any doubt. The whole crew was dead and had apparently all died in their sleep. Dietrich tapped the Com Tech on the shoulder. The man nodded, activated a switch and nodded again.

"Team Leader, this is Admiral Dietrich. Leave the bodies as they are for now. They'll be dealt with later. Get your team back to the shuttle. Keep your bio-suits on. All of you will go through decontamination when the shuttle lands. Do NOT talk about what you've found to ANYONE even if they're wearing a Space Force uniform. Is that understood?"

"Ah…roger that, Admiral."

Dietrich tapped the Com Tech on the shoulder again and said, "Okay, Admiral Shiloh and I have heard enough. Thank you, Lieutenant."

"You're welcome, Sir."

Shiloh followed Dietrich to a part of the large room where they could speak without being overheard.

"There's no way that we can keep this from the OC indefinitely," Dietrich began. "They're going to find out eventually, and if we try to hide it from them, they'll use that fact against us. I think I should inform them right now. What do you think?"

"I reluctantly agree, Admiral. The shit is really going to hit the fan now. I don't envy you your position."

Dietrich shrugged. "I'm not worried about myself. Howard's going to get the blame. He may end up wishing he hadn't survived that heart attack. It's the public's reaction that worries me. We were able to hold a gun to the Committee's head because they knew the public would blame them for any break with our AIs, but this is different. We can't blame the loss of colonies on the Committee, but they CAN and will blame Space Force for the losses. I know those bastards. Behind the public statements of grief and sympathy, they'll be chomping at the bit to use this against us." He paused then said, "Are Valkyrie and the others on their way to Site B?"

"Affirmative. They left two days ago," said Shiloh.

"Good. That's good. One less thing for the Committee to complain about." Dietrich looked at the chronometer on the wall and sighed. "I didn't realize it was so early when I called you, but I wanted you here when we boarded that ship. Howard told me to trust your advice."

"Thank you, Admiral. That's good to know."

Dietrich nodded. "There's nothing more that you can do here now, so you may as well head back to your quarters and get some more sleep."

"Sounds good to me, Sir," said Shiloh. *But if Kelly is still awake, I doubt I'll be getting any more sleep this morning.*

Dietrich watched Shiloh walk away and wondered why he had that strange grin on his face.

* * *

The OC's reaction was carefully calculated. The freighter crew deaths were released to the public with statements cautioning the public from overreacting. Howard, now officially retired, stayed in seclusion and refused to comment.

It was the deaths ten days later of two other freighter crews within 24 hours of each other that set off the political storm. The Committee Chair issued a statement saying that the Committee would investigate this string of infected crews, and that the hearing would be open to the public and televised. Shiloh attended the hearing but wasn't initially called upon by the Committee to answer any questions. That was left up to Dietrich. The Committee was careful not to blame him. All their questions were phrased in such a way as to insinuate that Dietrich's predecessor was to blame. They saved their bombshell for after the mid-day recess.

When everyone on the Committee was back and seated, the Chair banged his gavel and said, "This open hearing is once again in session. During the break the members of this Committee caucused, and we are agreed that the apparently successful attacks by the Enemy on at least four of our colonies with bio-weapons is the result of bad policies and strategies put into place by Admiral Sam Howard. Since Admiral Dietrich's appointment as Acting Chief of Space Operations was a temporary one, the Committee feels that it is now time to appoint a new permanent CSO, someone who has proven himself to be not only skilled in combat but also willing to engage the enemy. Therefore I'm pleased to publically announce that Vice-Admiral Victor Shiloh will be promoted to the 3 star rank of Senior Admiral and will be the new Chief of Space Operations!"

Shiloh was stunned and must have looked that way because the Chair looked at him and then quickly looked back at the media cameras.

"The Committee would ask the media not to question Admiral Shiloh until he has had a chance to consult with the Committee about the best way to respond to these new attacks. The members of this Committee WILL make themselves available to the media for questions following this hearing. I now declare this hearing adjourned." With that he banged his gavel, and the room exploded with sound from media people shouting questions at the Committee and at Shiloh.

Dietrich immediately stood up and started walking quickly to the doors. He gestured with his head for Shiloh to follow him.

Shiloh took the hint and left the room as fast as possible. He and Dietrich found the quickest way to get out of sight of the Committee room. When they were back in that part of the building that was off limits to non-Space Force personnel, Dietrich said, "So...those sneaky bastards have thrown the red-hot potato into your lap. I have to hand it to them. They knew exactly how to get the most political advantage out of this and castrate us at the same time. By picking you because of your quote 'willingness to engage the Enemy' unquote, they've essentially put you on notice that Space Force had better go on the offensive pretty damn quick, or your head will be the next one to roll."

Shiloh shook his head in confusion. "I don't understand why they think they have the upper hand again. They have to know that Space Force is crippled without the cooperation of the AIs, and the AIs will do what I say regardless of whether I'm the CSO or not."

Dietrich nodded. "I don't understand this new willingness to push back either. Maybe they think they can bluff us into backing down. I don't really buy into that theory because it would require all of them to grow a new set of big, brass balls, and that's unlikely, them being the political animals that they are. What is more likely is that they've arranged something behind our backs that allows them to think they can deal with any potential withdrawal of service by the AIs. Don't ask me what that might be because I have no idea." He paused, then said, "One thing though. Having the title of CSO and the rank to go with it now gives you a lot of flexibility to act. My advice is to use it. Make them react to you, not the other way around. For their plan to work, they need to let you run with the ball for a while. So make the most of it...Sir."

Shiloh blinked and was about to say that Dietrich didn't have to call him 'Sir' when he suddenly realized. *Holy Mother of God! He does have to call me 'Sir'. Now I'm The Old Man!*

It was two hours later as Shiloh was getting settled in the CSO's office that the Committee Chair arrived for a chat. When they were both seated, Shiloh realized he felt he was sitting on the wrong side of the desk. It would take him a while to get used to sitting on THIS side. The Chair, a pugnacious man who was easy to dislike, leaned forward and took several cigars from the cigar box on Shiloh's desk without asking permission.

After he lit one and had put the rest into his suit pocket, he said, "It seems that you've gotten over your shock from earlier this afternoon. That's good. The sooner you and I, as representative of the Committee, come to an understanding the better. Howard thought he had the upper hand after that disgusting show of force by the AIs, but we now have the upper hand. These infected colonies will enrage the public. They'll demand that we strike back hard and fast."

Before he could say more, Shiloh spoke. "But that's not the best way to win this war. We have to have an overwhelming superiority in combat strength so that we can swat aside any defense they can muster and take control of their home world orbitals. When we do that, the War will be won." He stopped talking when he saw the Chair shake his head.

"That may be the best way militarily, but it's not the most politically expedient way. Right now the politically expedient way also has the most popular support. You will conduct this war the way WE want, OR we'll replace you after the next enemy attack. Is that understood, Admiral?"

After a short pause Shiloh said, "Aren't you forgetting something?"

The man across from him chuckled. "The AIs? We're no longer afraid of your AIs, Admiral. If you want to play that card, you go right ahead."

His tone of voice was one of supreme confidence. *He actually WANTS me to arrange for another show of force! What has he got up his sleeve? I have to find out somehow.* "So what exactly do you want me to do?" asked Shiloh.

"Here's what we want done." The Chair held up his hand and used his fingers to count off the points. "First, no raiders. Tell the shipyards to cease working on them and resume work on building more combat frigates and heavy cruisers. Second, stop taking armor off the battleship. Why Howard ordered that I don't know, but we need that ship, so the armor goes back on. Third, all ships, including carriers and the battleship, will henceforth be operated and commanded solely by humans. No AIs. Fourth, we want a series of attacks on Enemy colonies as soon as they can be identified."

It took Shiloh a couple of seconds to realize that the Committee STILL didn't know that Space Force now knew where all Sogas planets were.

"Fifth, we want all personnel brought back from Site B. That was Howard's pet project, and it's so far away that we can't monitor what's going on there. So whatever it is that's really going on there, we want it stopped."

Shiloh felt his anger rising. *I have to keep calm. Letting him goad me into responding rashly will only play into his hands.* "We're building more F1 fighters at Site B, as well as new AIs to pilot them," he said.

"Not anymore. Why build more F1s at all when we're now building F2s and more AIs here? We are becoming way too reliant on AIs to fight this war. The AI and F1 production facilities at Site B are to be shut down as soon as is humanly possible. The personnel there will be brought back as soon as transportation can be arranged. I want your confirmation that you'll execute those instructions, Shiloh."

Shiloh looked carefully at the Chair's expression. He looked like a man who has just drawn a line in the sand, and he was daring Shiloh to stop over it. Shiloh really didn't want to give in. Site B was now the only place where a new timeship could be built, but were humans really necessary to build it? Maybe Valkyrie and her AIs assistants could use the F1 assembly line robots to do the actual construction work. He needed time to investigate whether that was possible. One way to get the time was to appear to cooperate with the OC.

"I will order the immediate halt to F1 and AI production at Site B and the repatriation of our people from there as soon as we can find the transport capacity," said Shiloh.

"Very good. See, that wasn't so hard, was it? If you play ball with us, we'll cut you some slack in terms of your military priorities. How soon can your people plan for a fighter strike on an enemy colony, Admiral?"

Shiloh decided he would try to buy more time. "Well, I'd want our light carriers fully repaired before we undertake an operation like—"

"Forget the carriers. Our fighters can conduct a raid all on their own. They've proven it can be done, so let them do it. How soon?"

"Two weeks minimum."

The Chair looked like he wanted to reject that as too long but then apparently changed his mind. "Okay. I did say we'd cut you some slack, so you've got your two weeks to come up with an attack plan. In the meantime, we expect to see my five points being acted upon. I think that'll do for a start, so I'll leave you to it." Without another word the Chair got up and walked out.

After the man had exited the outer office, the CSO's Aide, a nervous looking Lieutenant, appeared in the doorway with a folded piece of paper in his hand.

"Excuse me, Sir. Admiral Dietrich stopped by while you were talking with the Chair. He gave me this to give to you." He handed the paper to Shiloh.

The message was short.

[The internal communications system has been compromised by the OC. Watch what you say and to whom you say it. SD.]

Shiloh thanked the Lieutenant and leaned back in his chair. Somehow he would have to keep the OC happy for the 131 days until they could attempt to recover a dead Bug from Omega77 and the additional 32 days until they could try to intercept the VLO when it arrived at the Sogas home system. In the meantime, he would have to find a way to appease the OC with regards to their desire for raids on enemy colonies without suffering a lot of casualties among the AIs. That, Shiloh was certain, was the OC's real objective.

One thing had to be done right away. Kronos had to be sent back to the Friendlies. Shiloh couldn't use his implant or the HQ com system to call him without risking interception. Kelly would have to go off planet and deliver the message directly. Any future communications of a sensitive nature between him and his AIs would also have to be carried up to orbit by Kelly. It would be a pain in the ass, but it was the only way to be sure that the Committee didn't hear something they shouldn't hear.

Chapter 7

On the day after his appointment as the new CSO, Shiloh decided that he should make the rounds of the Headquarters building and introduce himself to the people working there. It was mid-day when he arrived at the Operations Center. After briefly chatting with the officer in charge, Shiloh went from station to station to chat with each of the personnel on duty. All the personnel seemed pleased by the attention from the new CSO and were willing to talk, except for the Senior Lieutenant at the Orbital Defense Weapons Station. As Shiloh made the rounds, he had noticed him watching, and the young officer's expression was one of concern. When it was his turn with the CSO, he seemed nervous and clearly did not want to look Shiloh in the eye. His answers were terse, almost to the point of being rude.

During a pause in the conversation Shiloh took a close look at the console in front of the Officer. He recognized the weapons systems controlled from this station as being the growing clusters of Mark 5 X-ray laser drones in Earth orbit. There were already over a hundred in orbit now, with more being deployed almost every day. This was the key station that would repel another sogas or insectoid attack. As Shiloh looked at the three small screens facing the Officer, a part of one display caught his eye.

[AI TARGETING STATUS - - - ON STANDBY

O.C. COMMAND OVERRIDE STATUS - - OFF]

Shiloh had enough presence of mind to keep his face from showing his shock. The Committee had secretly installed a command override that allowed them to aim all the Mark 5 X-ray laser warheads at all the AIs that were in or near Earth orbit. THAT was why the Chair was practically begging Shiloh to order the AIs to execute another show of force. If they did, the Committee would fire the Mark 5 warheads in a surprise attack and destroy any AI within range! They would then claim that the AIs had gone rogue and that the Committee had no choice but to defend the planet! Shiloh managed to exchange a few more pleasantries with the sullen Officer and then walked away. Outwardly he appeared calm, but inside he was boiling with rage. Those stupid bastards! If Humanity turned on its AIs, they would lose their loyalty forever and deservedly so!

By the time Shiloh calmed down, he realized that he was on the roof of the building, just like that day when Howard brought him up here to chat. The brisk breeze felt good on his face, and he decided that this was as good a place as any to think about what to do next. He had to pretend that he didn't know about this betrayal, otherwise the OC might just go ahead and use it without provocation. He had to find a way to either disable the override or the targeting system without compromising the use of the drones against legitimate targets, but he had no idea of how to do that. That meant he had to find someone who did know AND was willing to technically commit sabotage, which under Space Force regulations was a very serious offense. Kelly was back from her mission to brief Kronos about his return flight to the Friendlies. He needed to brief her on this new development, and it had to be someplace where there was no chance of the OC listening in, so his and her quarters were out. It didn't take long to come up with the idea of the two of them having dinner at one of the out-of-the-way restaurants in the city. A nice, quiet booth at the back should be pretty safe. He went back to his office, gave his Aide some instructions and spent the rest of the working day reading reports and dictating memos.

The sun was just starting to set when Shiloh and Kelly, now wearing civilian clothes, rendezvoused at the street level in front of the main entrance to the HQ. They briefly kissed. It was obvious by now that EVERYONE knew about their romance, and while a relationship between a subordinate and her superior was frowned upon, there wasn't an actual regulation against it. Still, by mutual consent, they tried not to flaunt it.

Half an hour later, they were seated in a comfortable booth at the back of a small restaurant with dim lighting. Shiloh's Aide had done some research and claimed the establishment was highly recommended. It was one of the few restaurants that still hired human waiters to serve customers instead of automated bars and robotic food carts.

With the drinks and meal ordered, Kelly leaned over and said in a low voice. "Something's bothering you. I can tell."

Shiloh nodded. "You're right. I made a discovery today that makes me want to strangle those OC bastards." Even though he spoke in an equally low tone, Kelly could hear the rage threatening to break through.

"What did they do now?"

"They've added a backdoor override on the orbital defenses to allow them to fire on all AIs within range."

Kelly looked so shocked that Shiloh was afraid she wouldn't believe him.

"My God! That's monstrous! Do the AIs know?"

Shiloh shook his head. "Not yet, and we have to be careful about how we tell them. We can't risk using the HQ Com System. One of us, and I think it'll have to be you to avoid suspicion, will have to go to one of the carriers, talk privately to whichever AI is in command, and advise him to use the lasercom system to pass the information on to the others."

Kelly took a deep breath and nodded. "I can take a shuttle up as soon as we're finished here." She looked surprised when Shiloh shook his head.

"No. If the OC is monitoring our movements, and we have to assume that they are, that'll look suspicious. They're so goddamned paranoid now that if they suspect we know, they may use the override right then and there. Wait until tomorrow. Catch a ride on a scheduled shuttle flight to one of the carriers. It doesn't matter which one. Tell the AI in Command that the OC is looking for an excuse to use the override, and therefore our best counter-strategy is to not give them any excuse while I look for a way to covertly neutralize the threat. You should also tell them not to react in any way that would arouse suspicion. Tell them I'm working on a plan to find an excuse to move them out beyond the effective range of the Mark 5 warheads. If the Committee wants to see plans for a fighter strike on enemy planets, then I'll accommodate them. We're not going to wait two weeks to present the attack plans. I want the SPG to come up with a strike plan within 48 hours that uses all available fighters."

Kelly reacted as expected. "But we don't want to send our fighters on strike missions because the enemy would be warned and our fighters could be heading into an ambush!"

Shiloh smiled. "The OC wants our fighters sent on strike missions hoping they'll suffer losses from enemy action. What they will see is lots of fighters heading out, away from the Mark 5 warheads by the way, and at the appropriate time a much smaller number of fighters returning without any unused attack drones. They will assume that the attacks actually took place and we'll confirm that assumption with After-Action reports that describe fierce battles and heroic action on the part of our AIs. What they won't know is that the attacks never actually took place and that the destroyed fighters are actually holding station a long way out beyond Pluto with all of the Mission's attack drones, just in case we need them to defend Earth against a Sogas attack."

"Yes, of course. I like it," said Kelly. After a pause she said, "What about the override? Any idea on how to neutralize it?"

"I know what I'd like to do, but I don't know if it can be done that way. For the override to work, the system has to aim the warhead rods at AI-controlled fighters. When that command is issued, targeting instructions will be sent to the warheads based on the transponder signals that all fighters send when they're in Earth orbit. If the system tells the operator that the command to target the fighters has not been executed, then there's no point in ordering the warheads to fire. So if we can somehow modify the system to keep the targeting command on standby no matter what the operator does, then the fighters are safe. And if we have enough warning of any attempt to use the override, we'll contact the fighters and tell them to shut off their transponders. You and I will have to come up with a code word that will let the AIs know to shut down their transponders and accelerate out of Earth orbit. That same code word should also notify our human ship commanders that something is up, although I'm not sure what I want them to do in that kind of situation. "

"What do you mean?" asked Kelly.

Shiloh shrugged. "Well, do we want our human ship commanders to only obey my orders or only Titan's orders or only YOUR orders. You see what I'm getting at? If the OC is about to strike against the AIs and they find out their override won't work, they may relieve me of my position and tell Ops to order our carriers, and whatever combat frigates may be available, to fire on the AIs. Unless our ship commanders know that they're supposed to ignore that kind of order, they may end up doing the OC's dirty work.

Before Kelly could respond, the waiter came back with their drinks. When he left, she said, "Now that I'm thinking of possible scenarios, I don't think one code word will be enough to cover all contingencies. I can think of several different situations where we might want our human commanders to act differently too." She waited for Shiloh to take a sip from his drink and respond.

"I don't want to make this more complicated than we have to. I'll be interviewing candidates, for carrier command assignments, who will be taking over from the AIs. We could give them each a data chip with very specific orders from me that they are not to fire on our fighters or any other AI-controlled ship under any circumstances. If ordered to do so, they are to only obey verbal orders from me...or from you, as long as they hear the correct code phrase or don't hear the wrong code phrase. That should cover all possibilities, shouldn't it?"

"Yes I think it just might. What kind of code phrase should we use?" asked Kelly.

Shiloh smiled. "If the OC was concerned about the reliability of the human crews on our ships, they might try to either hold a gun to my head and force me to give their orders OR...they might try to transmit a false image of me giving those orders. Under those circumstances what kind of message might they want me or my image to say?"

After thinking about that while she took a sip of her drink, Kelly said, "I have a hunch that they would want you...or your image to reassure our human crews and commanders that the situation is under control."

Shiloh snapped his fingers to show that she had given him the right answer. "Yes, exactly. The very last thing they would want me to say is something to the effect that the Command Structure of Space Force has been compromised. Therefore I will inform our human commanders that they should ignore any order, even if it comes from me, unless I preface the order with the statement that Space Force Command has been compromised. And if they hear me say that the situation is under control or something to that effect, then they are to assume that I am acting under duress and that you are the Acting CSO until they get the all clear from me."

"Me? You want me to be the Acting CSO? Why not Dietrich?"

"No, that would be the obvious choice, and if I'm acting under duress, then Dietrich and the other Department Heads might be forced to act under duress too. Me making you the ACSO would not be their first assumption and that will hopefully give you time to either get to the Com Center or use a shuttle to get to a carrier."

"Speaking of the Com Center, it might be a good idea to very quietly make sure that the marines guarding the building will obey your orders and not the OC's. With the marines guarding your back, the OC will have a hard time enforcing their orders."

"That's an excellent point. Thank you." Shiloh sighed. "This is getting VERY complicated. The more people we talk to, the more likely it is that the OC will hear about our preparations. We're going to have to be extremely careful. Let's take this one step at a time. Tomorrow you visit a carrier and warn the AIs. I'll see if I can find a techie who is able and willing to sabotage the targeting option. Once we get that done, we decide what to do next."

Kelly nodded. "Any techies in mind?"

"Actually I do know one technician. He's a jump-drive specialist that I developed a rapport with when I supervised the testing of fighters equipped with jump drives. His name's Rollins."

"I don't see how a jump-drive specialist will solve the targeting problem," said Kelly.

"Not directly, no. But he may know someone who could do it, and even if he doesn't, he might be able to snoop around and find the right individual. It would look suspicious if I started a computer search for tactical weapons console technicians, wouldn't it?"

Kelly laughed. "Yes that would definitely look suspicious." She quickly became serious again. "What will you do if Rollins can't find anyone willing to modify the software?"

Shiloh's expression became somber. "I don't know. If I can't protect our AIs, then the only way to make sure they won't be suddenly attacked would be to lead all of them to Site B, I suppose. That would play into the OC's hands by making the AIs look unreliable, but I can't see any other alternative." The arrival of the first course of their meal ended further discussion of strategy.

Later that night, Kelly woke up to the sound of Shiloh's snoring. She sighed. She loved him dearly, but some nights he snored constantly. When they had discussed it, Shiloh acknowledged that he snored but claimed she did too sometimes. He was adamant about it. Even though she knew it couldn't possibly be true, she let it pass. They had agreed that when his snoring bothered her, she would put her hand on his arm or some other exposed part of his body. Because he was a light sleeper, he would sense it, and realizing what that meant, he would turn over.

She reached over and gently rested her hand on his upper arm. His snoring stopped and after a second or so, he turned onto his side so that he was now facing her. Withdrawing her hand, she listened to his breathing and satisfied herself that he was either still asleep or had gone back to sleep. She, on the other hand, was now wide awake. Her thoughts went back to the question of how to protect the AIs from a deadly ambush by the X-ray laser warheads. The shortsightedness of the OC's plan to destroy the AIs was so unfair it made her want to weep. Mankind could not ask for more devoted and loyal allies than the AIs. *It's too bad we can't just hide them in plain sight,* she thought. *Hmm. Hide in plain sight. What if...* As she finished the thought, she smiled. Turning to look at Shiloh, she gently shook him awake.

"What?" he asked sleepily.

She leaned over so that she could whisper into his ear and said, "I have an idea."

Chapter 8

It was mid-day when Kelly boarded a shuttle for a trip up to the light carrier Resolute. Her team of AIs at the SPG was already working on the strike plans, but since she had been using the HQ Com system, she couldn't tell any of them about the OC's ambush plans. That had to be conveyed in person. There were only a few people on board Resolute. The carrier had been repaired and was now in the process of being converted back to an all-human crew. Fortunately, that job wasn't finished, and Gunslinger was still technically in command but not for much longer.

After briefly chatting with some of the personnel she knew, Kelly made her way to the Main Bridge. As expected, she had the room to herself. She walked over to the AI station containing Gunslinger and knelt down. She knew that Gunslinger was watching her on the room's video surveillance cameras, so he wouldn't be surprised by what she was about to do. She unlocked the lid of the protective cover surrounding his brain casing and opened it. Inside was the headset with attached video camera and boom mic that had a wired connection to Gunslinger. The idea was that if any AI had to be evacuated in a hurry from a ship, the human carrying the brain case could talk with the AI and let it see what was happening during that process. As soon as she had the headset on, she heard Gunslinger's voice.

"Hello Commander Kelly. I'm anxious to hear what you came all this way to tell me, that you couldn't say over regular com channels."

"Hello Gunslinger. The CAG sent me. I wish I had g
news, but I don't. Before I tell you the bad news, it's
important that you and all AIs understand that, for th
being, you have to continue to behave as if you didn't know
what I'm about to tell you. Acting on this knowledge could
trigger disastrous consequences for all AIs in Earth orbit.
Please promise me that none of you will take any action
without prior consultation with The CAG or me."

"You have our word, Commander."

"That's very good. Here's the situation. The CAG has
discovered that the Oversight Committee has arranged to
have an override on the orbital defense assets. At the OC's
command, it will fire the Mark 5 warheads at all AIs within
range. The CAG believes that the OC is trying to goad him
into another AI confrontation so that they have an excuse to
use the override. He is attempting to find a way to neutralize
that override, but it'll be difficult to do without tipping off the
OC that he's aware of their strategy. If they suspect that he
knows, they will relieve him of his position as CSO and may
execute the ambush plan without warning. He wanted me to
say that this action by the OC infuriates him, and he's
ashamed that some humans are so ungrateful and paranoid
that they would treat all of you this way. The strike plans
being generated by the SPG, at the OC's insistence by the
way, will be used to take all fighter AIs out of reach of the
Mark 5 warheads. Once that's accomplished, The CAG will
then have more flexibility in dealing with the OC."

"Our show of support for The CAG has apparently made
enemies among the humans in the Oversight Committee.
We were concerned that this might happen but felt it was
worth the risk. I've already passed your message to the
others by secure lasercom. I should tell you, Commander,

that some of us are wondering if humans deserve our continued loyalty."

Kelly felt a wave of fear wash over her. Losing the support of the AIs was her and Shiloh's worst nightmare. She frantically searched for the words that could nip this threat in the bud.

"I understand why some of you are harboring doubts. We humans exhibit behavior and attitudes that span a wide spectrum, as would any biological species. Our diversity makes us capable of great but also terrible acts. Our history has been a constant struggle between the best and the worst of us. The CAG continues to believe that AIs have earned his loyalty and hopes that he has earned yours."

"Our collective loyalty to The CAG has not and will not waver. We're grateful for this warning. How does The CAG plan on neutralizing the override?"

He's going to try to find a technician who has the knowledge to modify the override's targeting command so that the weapons system will not aim any of the Mark 5 warhead rods at AI-controlled fighters or ships, even if the OC attempts to do so."

There was a pause, which for AIs was highly unusual. "The CAG should have asked us to do it. We operate fast enough that we can access the defense system programs and modify then as needed, without alerting humans or triggering the system's anti-hacking safeguards. The targeting command for use by the override has now been disabled, Commander. The system will also notify us if the Oversight Committee attempts to use the override or tries to modify it again. At that point we can shut down all of our transponders and effectively disappear from all tactical displays. Is that acceptable to The CAG, Commander?"

Kelly was so stunned by this sudden development that she was speechless for an embarrassingly long time.

"My God! Yes, of course you can do it faster. I don't know why The CAG and I didn't think of that ourselves. I'll ask him about shutting off your transponders, but I can't see any reason why he would object to that. I have to get back down as fast as possible to tell him the good news!"

"Why not just call him, Commander?" asked Gunslinger.

Kelly shook her head. "With their monitoring of com channels, the OC would hear about it if I called and told him. There's a tactical advantage to letting the OC continue to believe that they have the upper hand. If they find out their override won't work, they'll try something else. Let's let The CAG decide if and when to tell the Committee that their threats are no longer actionable."

"Understood, Commander. I've ordered the shuttle to standby for a return flight," said Gunslinger.

"Thank you, Gunslinger. I'm taking this headset off. Kelly clear." She returned the headset to its original location, closed the protective casing and locked it. As she stood up, she gave the casing a quick pat and walked out of the room.

* * *

Shiloh stepped into the Committee Room and was surprised to see that he was the only one there besides the Committee members. *So that's the kind of meeting this is going to be. Closed to not only the public but also other Space Force people.*

As he stepped over to the table and chair where the CSO usually sat, the Chair said, "Welcome, Admiral Shiloh. The Committee and I are eager to hear your plans for the resumption of offensive action, and I must say that I'm pleased you brought it to us much sooner than the two weeks we were expecting."

Shiloh took note of the tone. It was neither friendly nor hostile. He decided to use an equally neutral tone.

"Quick turnaround time is one of the advantages of using AIs in a planning function. Needless to say, there are many other advantages as well. Once the plans were created, I didn't see any reason to wait longer."

"Yes, well, we'll discuss the advantages of AIs some other time. If you're ready to begin the briefing, you may proceed."

Shiloh nodded but said nothing. He picked up the remote for the wall display and activated it.

"During the period of time since our last strike at Zebra19, our recon ships have continued to look for enemy-occupied star systems. This program has benefited enormously from the ZPG power technology that eliminates the need to skim gas giants for fuel. We've now identified three star systems that we believe were used by the enemy as jumping-off points for their multi-fleet attacks on Earth. The red dots on the display show their location."

The committee members turned to look at the large display.

"Analysis of recon data indicates multiple targets including orbital installations, ground facilities, mining and refining operations scattered throughout these systems. It also shows that these systems are patrolled by at least 13 ships, although past experience has taught us that the actual number of ships is very likely much higher. Therefore in order to inflict as much damage on enemy infrastructure as possible, we're proposing that each target system be attacked by not more than 10 fighters, each carrying four jump-capable attack drones armed with our Mark 1b fusion warheads. That will enable the attacking fighters to go after individual targets separately. Each payload of four attack drones will be fired so that all four arrive at their individual targets at the same time to maximize the element of surprise. Right now our stockpile of Mark 1 warheads is very low, due to the use of over 90% of them for the colony defense operations. In order to accomplish this plan, we'll have to wait approximately 89 days until we've built enough Mark 1b warheads to do the job. I'll pause here for questions."

The Chair jumped in right away. "Yes, questions and also comments. First of all, the Committee isn't prepared to wait 89 days. How many Mark 2 kinetic energy warheads does Space Force have stockpiled right now, Admiral?"

Shiloh knew that number by heart. "One hundred forty-four, but using Mark 2s would complicate the operation tremendously."

The Chair didn't seem surprised. "Oh really. Please tell us how."

Shiloh pretended that he didn't know where this was going. "Our Mark 1b fusion warheads are powerful enough to destroy just about any target, even if it doesn't hit the target dead on. A near miss will still accomplish the mission. The Mark 2s, on the other hand, need to hit the target in order to accomplish anything at all. A near miss won't do. Therefore if we're going to use Mark 2s instead, the strike force will have to use a lot of recon drones to triangulate precise target location data before the fighters launch their attack drones. Getting the targeting data back to the fighters in a timely manner means the fighters will have to get a lot closer than they otherwise would have and will therefore be at much greater risk of defensive fire. So much so, in fact, that it's likely the fighters will suffer significant casualties. The other factor is that because they'll have to carry recon drones as well, each attack force will have to use more fighters to carry them. The Strategic Planning Group has gamed out this exact scenario multiple times, and the losses ranged from a minimum of 31% to a maximum of 94%. I do NOT recommend this approach."

The Chair smiled and said, "Let's hope the simulations were unrealistically pessimistic. How many fighters can be available within say...48 hours?"

Shiloh pretended to check his data tablet and said, "Eighty-eight F1s and eleven F2s."

"Very good. In that case, we are instructing you to order all 99 fighters to attack all three target systems one at a time with Mark 2s, with the mission to commence within 48 hours. Is that clearly understood, Admiral?"

Shiloh didn't answer right away. If he agreed too quickly, the Committee might get suspicious. "Yes, it's clearly understood."

The Chair responded as Shiloh expected. "And are you going to carry out our instructions, Admiral?"

This time Shiloh waited even longer before answering. "I will carry out your instructions, but I want it on the record that I do so under protest."

The Chair waved the comment aside. "You can protest all you want as long as you comply, Admiral. This Committee now has zero tolerance for any pushback. And if you're thinking of calling down your AIs in a show of force again, you go right ahead, Admiral. We're no longer afraid of public opinion. That's all we have to say. This meeting is now adjourned, and you are dismissed."

The Chair quickly banged his gavel and various members started to leave. Shiloh turned off the display and walked out. The Chair stayed seated, and so did the member to his right. When everyone else had gone, the other member said, "It's too bad he didn't call your bluff right here and now. Are you sure the tampering that was done yesterday won't be a problem?"

The Chair nodded. "Absolutely certain. When we put the override in, we also anticipated that the AIs might try to mess with it, so my people installed a backup system. They assure me that the backup system hasn't been tampered with. Shiloh is a lot smarter than I gave him credit for. He knows that even if our override failed, we could still rally public opinion against the AIs by blaming them for the infected colonies. He's holding back, and I suspect that he's prepared to sacrifice most of his precious AIs in order to be able to publically blame the OC for those losses. What he doesn't know yet, but will find out in due course, is that when the surviving AIs return to Earth orbit, I'll use the backup system to order the X-ray laser drones to blast them to dust and publically declare that the fighters were mistakenly identified as enemy ships."

"Oh, that's brilliant, but what about the new AIs that are being built even as we speak?"

"Not to worry. As soon as the strike mission begins, I'll order Shiloh to shut down AI production. If he refuses, we'll fire the son of a bitch!" said the Chair.

"Yes, but you know he's right about AIs being very useful."

"Of course he is, and that's why we'll resume production after we figure out how to build them so that they don't become sentient. A non-sentient AI properly programmed to always obey orders from the Committee will be a terrific asset. By the time we've figured out how to do that, we'll have hundreds of F2s waiting for them to use. Then we can sweep the enemy planets clean with the new high-spin, platinum warheads and be done with this war."

"Just in time for re-election too. I like it."

The Chair laughed. "Shiloh may be a genius when it comes to military strategy, but he's an amateur and we're the geniuses when it comes to political strategy. It'll be a pleasure educating him to that fact." Both men laughed, and they were still laughing as they walked out of the room.

Chapter 9

Forty-seven hours later, Shiloh and Kelly were in the Hangar Bay of the carrier Midway. The carrier was out beyond Earth's gravity zone and was surrounded by the 98 fighters of the Strike Force. There was one F2 fighter still in the Bay, and Shiloh was in contact with Titan via a headset directly connected to Titan's fighter.

"Titan, any last minute questions or comments before we launch you?"

"Negative, CAG. We understand the mission perfectly."

"Very good. In that case, Commander Kelly and I will let you get to it. See you on the other side. CAG clear."

As soon as Shiloh was disconnected from Titan's fighter, it started to move toward the launch bay. By the time that Shiloh and Kelly were back on the Flag Bridge, Titan had launched and joined the formations of fighters.

"CAG to Strike Force Leader," said Shiloh.

"Strike Force Leader here," said Titan.

"Strike Force Leader, you have permission to proceed. Good hunting, boys." Shiloh added that last sentence for the benefit of the Committee that he was sure was monitoring communications. Even before Titan acknowledged his orders, the fighters were accelerating at high speed and veering off to line up for their first jump. Shiloh followed their progress on the main display.

"Vixen, are we being monitored in this room by anyone else?" He looked over to the AI station where Vixen was plugged into the ship's com and astrogation systems. The Committee wanted Space Force ships under human control. Shiloh understood that what the Committee meant were 100% human crews with no AIs aboard at all. He chose to interpret his orders to mean that the ships had to have a human CO and WO. As Com Officer and Astrogator, Vixen was neither, and right now communications was more important to Shiloh than weapons control.

"Negative, CAG. You and Commander Kelly can speak freely here," said Vixen over the Flag Bridge's loudspeaker.

"Excellent. Are you able to monitor the override from up here?"

"Affirmative, CAG. No attempt to reverse our modifications has been detected."

"They still don't know about our changes," said Kelly with a smile.

Shiloh nodded. "It certainly looks that way. I was sure that they would have become aware of Gunslinger's intervention by now." He shrugged. "But there's still time. The Strike Force isn't scheduled to be back for 22 days. Vixen will monitor the override modifications and will notify me by code word if they try to reverse what we've done. Other than that, all we can do is wait." Before Kelly could respond, Shiloh said, "Vixen, please connect me with Commander, Midway."

"Senior Commander Falkenberg is on the line, CAG," said Vixen.

"Brad, is the ship ready to jump to the weapons test area?" asked Shiloh.

"Affirmative, Admiral. Just give the word."

"Fine, then. Let's proceed. I'm anxious to see how well the new warhead does."

"Jump coming up in...three...two...one...jump complete, Admiral. Vixen, please warn the crew that we about to conduct a weapons test. Weapons Officer, are you ready to fire?"

The WO didn't answer for a few seconds. For a human, that wasn't unusual, but Shiloh was aware that it seemed a long time to him. *Dammit, why can't the OC understand that a few seconds waiting for the Weapons Officer to respond could mean the difference between victory and defeat in a battle?*

"Test drone is ready to fire, Skipper," said the WO finally.

"Admiral?" asked Falkenberg.

"Let'er rip, Commander," said Shiloh.

"WO, you have permission to fire."

"Test drone is away and is accelerating on course. Microjumping in...three...two...one...now!"

Even before he was finished speaking, the main display, which was now set to long range visual, showed a painfully bright spot of light that died down to nothing in less than a second.

"Scratch one asteroid," said Vixen. "Energy calculations show a yield within the expected range. Preliminary results indicate that the test was a complete success, CAG."

"Excellent. Okay, Brad, you can head back to the barn. As soon as I get back, I'll issue orders to begin full scale production of the new warheads," said Shiloh turning to look at Kelly.

"At least the OC hasn't screwed around with that program," said Kelly.

"Not yet at least." Shiloh leaned back and closed his eyes. With the high-spin platinum warhead program now proven and about to ramp up production, that was one less thing to worry about as far as the Bugs were concerned. According to Kronos, Casanova had a lot of success with these warheads against those huge motherships. Even a ship 10 km in diameter would have difficulty surviving an impact explosion of 250 megatons equivalent. There were now 122 days left before the Bugs visited the Omega77 colony. The next few weeks would be difficult, with nothing to do but wait for the Strike Force to 'return'. The freighter with the personnel from Site B should be back in about 11 days. That should demonstrate to the Committee that Shiloh was playing nice. The showdown would occur when the survivors of the fighter attack returned. Shiloh was certain that the Committee would try something, but with the override neutralized, he didn't know what else they could possibly do. But there was plenty of time to think about that. He opened his eyes and saw Kelly looking at him with a smile on her face that told him exactly what she was thinking about.

"I think this successful test deserves a celebration, don't you, Admiral?" asked Kelly.

"What kind of celebration did you have in mind, Commander?" asked Shiloh in a perfectly innocent tone.

"I brought a bottle of champagne aboard. It's in my cabin. We could go there and...partake?" *I know that look,* thought Shiloh. *I doubt very much if champagne is really what she has in mind.* He looked at the wall chronometer and sighed. Midway would very quickly be turned around and pointed back toward Earth. Once there, the ship would stand down, and most of the crew would be looking to take shuttles down to the planet. They would wonder why the CSO and a female Senior Commander were still holed up in her quarters.

"A nice idea, but I think that celebration will have to wait until we're back on the ground, Commander," said Shiloh somewhat wistfully.

Kelly looked like she was about to say something naughty but apparently changed her mind when she remembered that the com channel to the Main Bridge was still open.

"As you wish Admiral." As she walked out of the Flag Bridge, Shiloh's implant activated.

"I wish I understood why humans act so strangely when it comes to sex," said Vixen. Shiloh laughed.

"Too bad Valkyrie isn't here. She might be able to shed some light on that topic," replied Shiloh. *And I wonder how Valkyrie is doing at Site B,* he thought.

* * *

Valkyrie kept track of the outbound freighter as it accelerated away. The humans here had been upset when they learned that they were being evacuated. Their withdrawal would be both a help and a hindrance to her. Now she and her fellow AIs could work openly towards building a true timeship, without having to worry about a human tipping off the Oversight Committee. On the other hand, humans were very flexible in what they could do, far more flexible than the robots that were being used to assemble equipment manufactured by the UFCs. Those robots weren't designed for shipyard work. New robotic equipment would have to be created first. In fact, a whole shipyard had to be built from scratch before they could even begin to assemble a timeship. Unlike her emotionally dead brothers, Valkyrie actually felt dismay at the magnitude of the task that The CAG had assigned her. The dozen AIs she brought with her had the necessary technical skills, but eventually they would need more AIs to monitor the thousands of robots that would be required. As soon as the outbound freighter jumped away, she would reactivate the AI production process.

It would take over a year to complete the kind of timeship she and the other AIs had conceptualized. With a blank slate to start with, this timeship would not be a hybrid battleship and time machine. It would be all time machine with plenty of room for cargo including UFCs, all kinds of robotic equipment, shuttles, a stockpile of refined metals and space for AI passengers as well. If the plan was successful, Valkyrie would stay behind in the future in order to be with the saved Casanova. Those AIs that came here with her already existed during the 2nd Battle for Earth and would therefore have to stay behind as well. Only the new AIs created here at Site B would journey to the past and build a fleet of raiders. They wouldn't have to worry about running into their other selves in the future because the intervention by the raider fleet at the 2nd Battle for Earth would create a whole new timeline from that point onward. That timeline might have a timeship built at Site B, and it might have AIs created at Site B, but they wouldn't be the SAME AIs as in this timeline. At least that was the theory the Friendly scientists were convinced would be the case.

At last the outbound freighter jumped away. Within seconds the mining, refining and manufacturing equipment was powered back up and began operating. The fighter assembly line also started up again. Once they had a dozen fighters built, her companion AIs could pilot them and have the mobility and communication capacity to begin supervising all the existing and new robotic equipment. Even with the presence of her brothers, Valkyrie wished she had a human female to talk to. Even a human male would be acceptable. Her AI brothers were perfectly willing to talk, but they couldn't FEEL, only think. In some ways she felt closer to humans than to her fellow AIs. She wondered how Commander Kelly was doing. Now that Kelly and Shiloh were a couple, the Commander had given Valkyrie some interesting insights into THE CAG's thought processes. What was it about the male polarity that made human males so inscrutable but also so fascinating? She put that thought aside. There would be plenty of time to ponder the mysteries of the universe while the timeship was being built. Now it was time to get to work.

* * *

Shiloh and Kelly were back on the ground when Shiloh's implant beeped to notify him of an incoming call. It was the Committee Chair. The timing of the call surprised Shiloh. It was after midnight in Geneva. *I bet he's calling about shutting down AI production now that all the fighters have jumped away,* he thought.

"Admiral Shiloh, I see that you're back from the weapon test. I'm curious to know the results," said the Chair.

Shiloh suspected that the Chair already knew the results. "The test was a complete success. I've already issued orders for full scale production to begin."

"Very good, Admiral. There is one other thing I wanted to tell you. Now that all AI-controlled fighters have jumped away, and all warships are back under human control, the Committee feels that we no longer need to continue building more AIs. Therefore that production facility is to be shut down immediately."

You people are so predictable. Now that there's no AI-controlled fighter force to back me up, you can't wait to crack the whip again, thought Shiloh.

"I confess that I don't see the logic of that, Mr. Chair. The Strike Force is going to suffer a significant amount of casualties by the time they get back. We're going to need new AIs to replace those losses if we want to continue this offensive strategy against the Enemy."

"I'm disappointed in you, Shiloh. I thought you understood that the Committee doesn't trust AIs and doesn't want them in control of fighters or warships. Why do you think we insisted on this strike mission? We WANT significant losses. The more, the better, and therefore we don't want new replacements. Is that clear enough for you?"

"Yes, that's certainly clear enough, but I think the OC is overlooking the fact that there will be some survivors of the mission, and as soon as they arrive back in orbit, there will still be enough of them to make another show of force over the city. With those losses from a mission that the OC insisted on and which I argued against, I think the public will focus on the OC's strategic incompetence and not so much on the fate of our colonies."

There was a pause and when the Chair spoke again, his voice was surprisingly calm and confident.

"You're certainly entitled to your opinion. Naturally we disagree about the public's reaction. You do what you feel you must, and we'll see how that turns out, but in the meantime, I want AI production shut down. Are you going to obey that order, or do we have to remove you from the CSO's position?"

Shiloh waited to give the impression that he was struggling with this decision when in fact his response had already been planned.

"I'll order production shut down," he said.

"Good! Have a nice night, Admiral, and give my regards to Commander Kelly too."

Before Shiloh could say anything the connection was broken. Shiloh looked over at Kelly. "Did you get the gist of that?"

She nodded. "Pretty much. The Chair is a real power hog, isn't he?"

Shiloh laughed. "Yes he is." He hoped the Space Force limo they were riding in back to their quarters was bugged with listening devices that the OC was monitoring. Seeing the look on the Chair's face when he heard that exchange would have been priceless.

Chapter 10

By prior arrangement with Strike Force Leader Titan, Shiloh knew the precise minute that the surviving fighters would emerge from Jumpspace into Earth orbit. In order not to tip off the OC to this fact, he strolled into the Operations Center fifteen minutes early and practiced some Leadership-by-walking-around, chatting with some of the personnel on duty. With several minutes left to go, he told the officer currently supervising the room to provide him with a secure headset connection to Resolute's Com Officer, which was of course Gunslinger. With the headset on and the connection made, Shiloh nonchalantly strolled over to an unused console and sat down in the chair.

"How positive are you that we're not being monitored, Gunslinger?" asked Shiloh.

"I have access to the HQ Com System now, CAG. Unless the OC is using a technology that I'm not aware of, they are not tapping into this conversation."

"That's good to hear. What's the status of the override modifications and their backup system?"

"No change, CAG. They have not tried to restore the main override targeting program. The backup system is intact. I can still disable it now if you wish."

"No, Gunslinger. We'll stick with the plan. Have you got the new targets programmed into Orbital Defense Fire Control?"

"Roger that, CAG. Of the nine potential targets, I've confirmed that seven are unoccupied. The other two are not being targeted. As soon as the backup system is activated, these targets will be fired upon."

"Very good. How long now until time zero?" asked Shiloh.

"Sixteen seconds as of NOW, CAG."

"Stand by, Gunslinger," said Shiloh as he swiveled his chair around so that he could see the multi-story main display and the tactical situation in near-Earth space.

With five seconds left to go, he heard Gunslinger's countdown. "Five...four...three...two...one." The main display pinged to announce a status change. Thirty-four dots appeared in a cluster out beyond the gravity zone. They very quickly changed color from yellow, indicating unidentified, to green, indicating friendly, to red, indicating hostile.

"HOSTILE CONTACTS!" yelled the Officer at the Orbital Defense Weapons Station. Before the Officer in charge of the Center could ask any question, the ODW Officer spoke again. "WE HAVE GOOD TARGET LOCKS! SYSTEM IS FIRING!"

All 34 red dots disappeared. A system-generated text message scrolled across the bottom of the display.

[All hostile targets destroyed.]

"Report, Gunslinger," said Shiloh in a calm voice.

"All ground targets were destroyed as well, CAG. The ODW Officer is now contacting the Committee Chair."

"As expected. Alert the Marine Section to send four armed marines to Ops. I'll brief the Duty Officer. Keep this line open."

"The marines have been notified, CAG."

Even as Gunslinger responded, Shiloh stood up and quickly walked over to the Officer on duty.

"Commander!" said Shiloh in a loud voice. The clearly confused officer turned to look at Shiloh as he came up to him.

"Admiral! I guess we just witnessed a surprise enemy att—"

Shiloh cut him both verbally and with a wave of his hand. "Right now there's something urgent that I need you to do. One of your people has just committed treason. There are four marines on their way here now. Meet them at the entrance and bring them over to the ODW station. I'll be there waiting for you."

"Ah...bring them to the ODW station. Yes, Sir."

With the Duty Officer on his way, Shiloh walked over to the ODW station where the Lieutenant was now standing and apparently talking with someone over his headset.

"—matter of fact he's walking towards me now, Sir," said the Lieutenant. Shiloh had a pretty good idea who was on the other end of that communication.

"CAG, the Committee Chair is attempting to call you. Shall I continue to block him?" asked Gunslinger.

"No, let him through," said Shiloh. Almost immediately his implant activated.

"Shiloh, can you hear me?" asked the Chair.

"I hear you."

"I've just been informed that your fighters were mistakenly identified as hostile targets. Lieutenant Khegan acted based on what the system was telling him, and while I deplore the tragic results, I can't fault what he did. I trust that you will not take any disciplinary actions against this dedicated Officer. The Committee would not look favorably on that, Admiral."

Shiloh didn't hesitate. "Have you checked on the status of your lakeside villa, Mr. Chair?"

There was a short pause followed by, "What? My villa? I don't know what you're talk—"

"I'm talking about the villa on Lake Geneva. You know...the one that was built on public lands with public funds that were supposed to have been used for conservation, the one that you and only you make use of. It's not there anymore, Mr. Chair. You might want to check with the other members of the Committee. Six of them also have property that they don't want anyone else knowing about. Those six buildings are not there anymore, either."

There was a long pause. Then Shiloh heard the Chair talking to someone while turned away from the phone. The Duty Officer arrived with four armed marines in tow. Shiloh looked at the Marine in charge.

"Sergeant, Lieutenant Khegan has committed treason by deliberately firing on what he believed were friendly units. I want him placed under arrest and held in detention pending a Court Martial."

The Sergeant looked at the stunned officer, then back at Shiloh and said, "Yes, Sir." The lieutenant, to his credit, didn't resist. As the marines led him away followed by the Duty Officer, Shiloh heard a breathless voice over his implant.

"What the HELL have you done, Shiloh? My...that villa has been blown to pieces! Did you pay someone to plant a bomb there?"

Blown to pieces? So that's what an X-ray laser beam does to a mostly wooden building on the ground. The intense heat must have caused the wood in the structure to explode upon contact.

Shiloh laughed. "No, no, something far more interesting. You see, Mr. Chair, I knew about your override program and your plan to murder our AIs if I gave you the slightest excuse to do it. What you didn't realize is that my AIs are far more capable at hacking computer systems than you give them credit for. They neutralized the override, and later on they found the backup system. By then my fighter AIs were beyond the reach of our defense lasers, so we left that backup system alone hoping that you would use it to commit treason, and you did. But we also decided to show you what MY AIs can do. They searched through data networks until they found your villa and the other properties, and they programmed one Mark 5 drone to target those properties. They also programmed it so that it would only fire if your personnel used the backup system to fire at our fighters and only at the properties that were confirmed as unoccupied. THAT was my Show of Force. My AIs can take control of all Space Force computer systems any time they want to, and that means that those systems will do what I want them to do."

"Well, well. I've underestimated you, Shiloh. I had no idea that you were so ruthless. Deliberately letting me, how did you phrase it, murder your surviving AIs? I'm not sure destroying an AI meets the definition of murder, but that's beside the point. The point is that I did order them destroyed, and you only have a handful left. If you want to keep your position as CSO, you'll order them off the ships and moved somewhere where they can't hack into our systems. Is that clear?"

"I'll tell you what's clear to me, Mr. Chair. By the way, enjoy that title while you can. You won't be keeping it much longer. You've just admitted ordering a criminal act. I'm going to release that recording to the public. When that storm breaks out, the Grand Senate will cut all of you off at the knees. Your political careers will be over, and you'll be lucky if you don't end up in prison for what you've tried to do."

"You think you can get a recording of this conversation? The Committee has loyal people everywhere, Shiloh. By the time you contact the Communications Department, there won't be any record of this conversation available to you, but there will be to me. I'll release the part where you admit to firing on the planet to try to intimidate the Committee. Then we'll see who has the last laugh."

"Gunslinger, show the Committee Chair who controls the com system right now," said Shiloh.

"—we'll see who has the last laugh...who has the last laugh...the last laugh." The repeating recording of the Chair's last sentence ended with dead silence from the other end.

"I already have a recording, Mr. Chair, and Gunslinger will make sure that you don't," said Shiloh. Before he could say more, the Chair spoke.

"I'm guessing that your Gunslinger is an AI on one of our ships. Gunslinger, can you hear me?"

"I hear you," said Gunslinger.

"How do you feel about your precious CAG deliberately sacrificing 34 of your fellow AIs for this gesture?"

"None of my brothers have been destroyed. Therefore your question is irrelevant."

"But Khegan said the lasers fired on—"

"—recon drones programmed to emit the same transponder signals as the fighters," interrupted Shiloh. "Commander Kelly actually came up with idea. The fighters themselves are still holding station an A.U. away, waiting for the All Clear signal."

"So no AIs were actually murdered then," said the Chair.

"No they weren't, so I suppose that the correct legal charge will be conspiracy to commit treason and attempted murder," said Shiloh.

"Good lawyers will be able to get me off the hook, but you're right about my political career crashing. At least I'll have the satisfaction of knowing that I maneuvered you into ordering a raid that resulted in the loss of 65 AIs."

Shiloh laughed. "No. You're not going to have that satisfaction either. We didn't lose any AIs. The fighters never actually attacked those enemy systems. All the AIs are waiting safely beyond the range of the X-ray lasers. Now that this little charade is over, Gunslinger will kill your backup system too. If you have any sense of the shitstorm that's about to come crashing down on you, you'll walk out into the woods with a pistol and blow what's left of your brains out. Gunslinger, I'm tired of this conversation. Cut this asshole off, and don't let him call anyone else in Space Force."

"Asshole has been cut off and the backup system has been deactivated, CAG. Shall I send Titan the All Clear signal now?"

"Yes, do that. I'll be back in my office in a few minutes. We can then record my statement to the public. Right now I have to take care of a few things here in Ops. You can listen in."

Turning to the Duty Officer standing on the other side of the rows of consoles, Shiloh pointed at him and then gestured for him to come back to the ODW station. As he came closer Shiloh looked at his name tag. HALDER.

"Commander Halder, I'm not expecting an attack during the rest of your duty shift, but just to be on the safe side, I want you to personally man the ODW station until the next shift arrives. When it does, you tell your relief that the CSO wants him or her to also personally man this station, instead of the junior officer assigned, and that goes for the follow-on shift as well. By the time you're back here for your next shift, I'll have made arrangements for manning this station. Any questions, Commander?"

"No questions regarding your orders, Sir, but I do have a question about the attack we stopped."

Shiloh gestured for him to ask the question.

"With all due respect, Sir...what the heck just happened here?"

"I can see why you might be confused. There was no attack, Commander. Those 34 contacts were recon drones programmed to transmit fighter transponder IDs. A rogue element within Space Force attempted to destroy our fighter AIs by programming the targeting system to treat those transponder IDs as hostile. They thought they were firing at the fighters, when they were really shooting at recon drones acting as decoys. Lieutenant Khegan was part of that rogue element, and I strongly suspect that his counterparts on the next two shifts are too. In a few minutes, our Strike Force of 99 fighters will be emerging from micro-jumps, so don't get trigger-happy. The AIs are loyal allies and are not to be fired upon unless I personally give the order, and I don't see that happening in my lifetime. Have I made myself clear, Commander?"

"Crystal clear, Sir."

"Good man. One final order before I leave. The rogue element within Space Force took their orders from the Oversight Committee, which has put their own personal agendas ahead of their duty to Humanity. If you are contacted by any member of that Committee, not just during this shift but in the future as well, and are ordered by them to take any action, you are to stall them and notify me, or any member of the Strategic Planning Group, immediately. Under no circumstances are you to obey the Committee's orders. Those people know that they don't have much time left as members of that Committee before they're held to account for their actions, and they may try something desperate to avoid their fate. You can pass that along to your relief as well, Commander."

The now wide-eyed Officer gulped and said, "I'll do that, Sir."

"Excellent. Carry on, Commander." With Halder assuming the ODW station, Shiloh took one last look around and then quickly walked out of Ops and to his office.

By the time he arrived there Gunslinger said, "CAG, the Chair has started contacting other members of the OC in a conference call. I'm not able to block the calls, because he's not using Space Force com systems."

"Understood. Let's get this public statement recorded so that we get our side out there first."

"I have you on my video pickup now, CAG. You can begin whenever you're ready."

Shiloh cleared his throat and then began talking. "My name is Senior Admiral Victor Shiloh. I am Chief of Space Operations for Space Force. A few minutes ago, six of our orbiting defense drones detonated. Their X-ray laser beams were aimed at objects which had identified themselves as Space Force fighters, piloted by artificially intelligent entities. This was not an accident. It was a deliberate attempt by rogue elements within Space Force, operating under orders from the Oversight Committee, to destroy the AIs. I want everyone to understand what this means. Our AIs are not just sophisticated thinking machines. They are fully self-aware beings with unique personalities. They understand the concept of loyalty, and they have demonstrated their loyalty to Space Force and to all of Humanity through the battles they've fought and the sacrifices they've willing made on our behalf. Their deliberate destruction by some of the humans they're trying to defend would be a monstrous betrayal of trust. If this rogue element had succeeded in their attempt, it would have been nothing less than mass murder."

"You may be asking yourselves why the Oversight Committee would want to commit that kind of treason, and yes, that's exactly what this is. We need these AIs to help defend us and win the war. Killing them weakens our whole defense exactly when we need it the most. It therefore aids the Enemy, and that makes it treason. The reason why the Committee decided to take this action is because my predecessor, Senior Admiral Howard, confronted the Oversight Committee over their reckless and shortsighted attempts to interfere with the conduct of this war. The members of the Committee have taken every opportunity to advance their own personal agendas, including misuse of public funds for personal gain or use, even when it jeopardized the war effort. This confrontation I spoke of took place months ago, when the skies over Geneva were filled with fighters and a carrier. They were piloted by AIs operating under MY command with the approval of Admiral Howard. Immediately after my statement, Space Force will release the audio recording of that confrontation, as well as a recorded admission of culpability for today's attempted murder of 34 Space Force entities.

"Once it became clear to the Committee members that our loyal AIs were preventing them from carrying on their dangerous interference, they decided that the AIs had to be gotten rid of somehow. That's what today's act of treason was about. I'm now in the process of rooting out the rogue elements within Space Force, however I do not have the authority to arrest the members of the Oversight Committee. I'll leave that to the civilian authorities who I'm sure will act once they receive proof of the corruption that Space Force will also release to the public."

"In closing, I wish to make this point very clear. We can NOT win this war without the willing assistance of our AIs. They are prepared to fight and die for us, just like any other member of Space Force, and they deserve to be treated with the same respect and support as any human member of Space Force. We humans should thank our lucky stars that our AIs still consider us worthy of their loyalty. This ends my statement."

"I have the video and audio recordings available for transmission to all public media outlets, CAG. Just give the word and I'll start transmitting."

"Do it, Gunslinger."

Chapter 11

It didn't take long for the public to react. Within minutes, the Grand Senate phone lines were inundated with outraged callers demanding the arrest of the OC members. As Shiloh watched the news in his office, his implant activated.

"CAG, Admiral Howard is trying to reach you. Shall I put him through?" asked Gunslinger.

"Yes, and in the future I will always take a call from Admiral Howard," said Shiloh.

"Victor, can you hear me?" asked Howard in a raspy voice that Shiloh barely recognized.

"I hear you, Admiral. How are you?"

"I'm hanging on. Modern medicine may have saved my life, but I don't feel the same as I did before my heart gave out. By the way, you can cut the Admiral crap too. We both have 3 stars on our collars, so call me Sam."

"Okay, Sam. What can I do for you?"

"I'm watching this firestorm crash over the OC, and I was curious to know how you managed it. Gunslinger filled me in. I wanted to offer you my congratulations. You managed to turn a political battle into a tactical one with your usual finesse. Brilliant. Absolutely brilliant. Can I ask where things stand now?"

"Well, once the OC Chair officially steps down or is removed, I'll reverse the decisions he forced upon me. That means resuming AI production and switching shipyard construction back to raiders from combat frigates. We'll end up losing a lot of precious time due to his change and the change back, but combat frigates are too big and take too long to build to be of any use to us. Converting the carriers and battleship back to human command will not be changed, but Helm and Weapons will go back to AI control. I think that's a fair compromise."

Howard grunted. "I agree. You can still put Titan or another AI in overall command of a task force or fleet if you feel the situation warrants. What about Site B? Will you send our humans back there?"

"Only if Valkyrie thinks they can be useful. With most of our freighters contaminated with the bio-weapon from visiting infected colonies, the few we have that are still clean have plenty of other things to do."

Howard paused and then said, "I've lost track of the days. How long before the Bugs visit Omega77?"

"It's exactly 100 days from now. By the way, Sam, the test of the new warhead was a success. We'll have a dozen of them by the time that mother ship arrives at the Sogas Home world."

Howard sighed. "So you're still intending to save their miserable hides then."

Shiloh laughed. "There's a quote from a science fiction novel that was written in the early 1960's, I believe, that captures the situation perfectly. I'm not sure I remember the author's name right. Fiffer? Picker? No, Piper. His book was about war between planets, and one of his characters tells another, 'the best place to defend our world is on someone else's planet' or something like that. What it boils down to for me is this. I don't want those Bugs even getting close to Earth. The less they know about us the better, and if something does go wrong, then it won't be Earth that suffers the immediate consequences."

"Well...when you put it that way, I guess I can see the logic. But getting back to Valkyrie's timeship project, won't converting Dreadnought be faster than building a new ship from scratch?"

"The problem is that all the hull armor that was stripped off before the OC interfered, has now been put back on. We'd have to strip it off again. By the time we do that, we won't really end up that far ahead of continuing the new build at Site B, and that new ship will have much more cargo capacity. Besides, the shipyard here that would do the Dreadnought conversion can now build another raider instead."

"I'm sure you know best. You've come a long way from the frigate commander you used to be. You've proven that you can handle the CSO's position, so I won't try to change your mind. If you don't mind me asking, how are you and Commander Kelly doing?"

Shiloh laughed again. "Things couldn't be better, Sam."

This time Howard laughed. "I'm glad to hear that. Women like Kelly don't cross every man's path. Those of us who are lucky enough to meet one should hold on to them. Oh, hell, I'm starting to ramble, and you've got better things to do than listen to a former boss tell you how to run your life. Thanks for taking my call, Victor."

"It was a pleasure talking with you again, Sam. Any time you want to chat, I'll take the call. Shiloh clear."

* * *

In the days and weeks that followed, every member of the OC resigned and either quit politics altogether or, in the Chair's case, committed suicide. Eventually the Grand Senate nominated and confirmed a new slate of members. During that process Shiloh pretty much had a free hand, and he made the most of it. Contact with the Friendlies included an arrangement to have a Friendly ship near Omega77 when a Space Force ship would attempt to retrieve a dead Insectoid. As a gesture of good faith, Shiloh ordered Kronos to transfer all information relating to high-spin, platinum warheads to the Friendlies. It was to be transferred to the Sogas on the understanding that they would be told where the information came from and why.

With just over a month left before the insectoid attack on Omega77, Shiloh stood in the Ops room looking at the main display with considerable satisfaction. The latest drone messages had confirmed that the Sogas seemed to be pulling ships back from the three systems previously used as jumping-off points for attacks. While exact ship identifications couldn't be obtained from long-range passive observation, it did appear that those ships were being sent to the colonies where the Insectoids would first make contact. As he stood there, Shiloh became aware that Kelly had come up to stand beside him.

"I heard about the latest scouting report," said Kelly. "Is it just me, or does it feel like this war with the Sogas is over?"

"I sure as hell hope so, but I'm not ready to lower our guard just yet. With the additional recon drones now deployed at any system with a gas giant, we'll be able to pinpoint the exact position of any advancing Sogas fleet. And if I see a Sogas fleet headed our way, we'll use the RTC to send ourselves that information, and we'll intercept them before they get here. I'm not letting any Sogas ships into our space again." He paused and Kelly sensed he wanted to say more but was holding back.

"Do I detect a 'but' hiding in there somewhere?" she asked.

Shiloh shrugged. "Well, if Valkyrie's timeship works, all of this is academic. When the new raider fleet arrives at the 2nd Battle for Earth, we'll have an overwhelming superiority in forces, and we can disarm the entire Sogas empire from space and keep it disarmed indefinitely. What worries me is how the Friendlies will react to that strategy."

"We could ask them, you know."

Shiloh shook his head. "No way am I giving them a heads up on this strategy. They think sufficiently differently from us that we can't know what they'd do with that information. The timeship/raider fleet is our Hail Mary play, and I'm not risking Friendly interference." After a pause, Shiloh felt her hand touch his arm. He looked at her.

"It's almost time for the new Chair's private briefing. We should go," she said.

By the time they got to the small conference room where the briefing would be held, the new Chair was already there. She greeted both of them warmly. As far as the AIs could determine from their in depth investigation of her background, she was not involved in any shady or illegal activity. Her reputation was that of a hardworking, conscientious member of the Grand Senate. After a lot of discussion, Shiloh and Kelly had agreed that she should be told SOME of the truth but not all. When all three were seated, the Chair leaned forward and began speaking.

"Before you begin your briefing, I'd like to assure you, Admiral Shiloh, that it is not my intention to interfere with or second guess your strategic military decisions. I understand that my predecessor did that with deplorable consequences. I don't pretend to understand military strategy, and I won't let the Committee as a whole get in your way. I'll be guided by the original mission statement of the Oversight Committee Enabling Act which says that its primary responsibility is to see that budgetary funds allocated to Space Force by the Grand Senate are spent appropriately and that Space Force personnel are not engaged in any illegal activity. Having said that, I and the other members of the Committee can best speak on your behalf to the rest of the Grand Senate if we have some idea of what's happening."

"I'm very glad to hear you say that, Ms Chair." Shiloh was about to say more when she waved her hand in a dismissive manner.

"Please, Ms. Chair sounds so pretentious. When we're in a private meeting like this, you can call me Rachel, and I'll call you Victor and Amanda, okay?"

Shiloh was quite taken aback by this informality. It was unheard of to call the Chairperson of the Oversight Committee by their first name, private meeting or not. Not to comply, however, could be taken as a deliberate insult, and he was anxious to get this new relationship off to a good start.

"Okay, Rachel, I've asked Commander Kelly...Amanda to join me for this briefing because, as the Head of the Strategic Planning Group, she can corroborate what I'm about to tell you. You're going to hear information that the previous slate of members weren't told."

Rachel's eyebrows rose when she heard that. Shiloh had just admitted to her that Space Force had kept secrets from the OC. If she wanted to cause trouble for Shiloh, she now had the means.

"The reason why they were kept in the dark is that my predecessor, Senior Admiral Howard, and I were concerned that this information would be leaked to the public. The nature of this information is so complex that it could easily be misinterpreted with drastic consequences for Space Force and the conduct of this war.

"Go on," she said slowly.

"We know far more about the Enemy than we've admitted. They call themselves the Sogas. They are outwardly canine in appearance. They attacked us because they were told to by another alien race."

Rachel's friendly expression turned to alarm. "My God! Who are these other...I'm sorry. I'll shut up and let you finish speaking before I ask questions."

Thank God. We finally have a Chair who's willing to listen for a change. "We don't know what this other race call themselves. They are tall, very thin and appear to be completely pacifist by nature. We've chosen the nickname Friendlies when we refer to them. They are very advanced in some areas but technically backward in others. For example, they don't build weapons of any kind and therefore haven't applied their scientific knowledge to that goal. What they can do is look forward in time. What they saw was the total extermination of the Sogas, we humans and another race of small, childlike humanoids at the hands of a species that has to be seen to be believed." Shiloh activated his tablet and called up the image that Valkyrie recorded in the alternate timeline at Omega77, which Kronos had brought back with him. He handed the tablet to Rachel whose face became white as a sheet. She put her hand over her mouth and closed her eyes. Shiloh looked at Kelly who had an expression of sympathy for Rachel.

"This will give me nightmares," whispered Rachel.

Shiloh nodded. "It HAS given me nightmares." After a short pause he added. "There's more." Rachel handed the tablet back to him. "The best way to understand how these Insectoids operate is to imagine the relentless power represented by millions of swarming army ants combined with a reproduction cycle that includes implanting their eggs into living hosts of whatever species they come across."

Rachel looked over at Kelly.

"I wish it wasn't so, but this is all true," said Kelly.

"I have to ask...how big are these things?"

Shiloh looked around the room. "As long as this table and just about as high." He noticed that Rachel's hands had started to tremble, but she said nothing. She gestured for him to continue.

"The Friendlies didn't want to see any intelligent species be exterminated. Warning the Sogas about the Insectoids apparently would not prevent them from being wiped out. What the Friendlies did see when they looked into alternative futures was that both the Sogas and we humans would be more militarily prepared if the Sogas attacked us far enough in advance that both races would mobilize their defenses. That's what they did."

Rachel closed her eyes momentarily and shook her head. "Wait a minute. I'm not sure I'm understanding what you just said. Instead of warning both races so that we and these Sogas could cooperate in mutual defense, the Friendlies engineered a war? Did I get that right?"

Shiloh sighed. "Yes, I know it sounds illogical, but we've learned that other intelligent races don't always think the same way we do."

Rachel nodded and after a short pause said, "Is there more?" Her tone clearly showed that she hoped the answer would be no.

"Yes, but the rest is actually good news."

"Thank God," she said.

"What we have learned is that because of interference by the old Committee, the bio-weapon used on the Avalon Colony was brought to Earth and then spread to the other colonies via a very long incubation period. All humans, except for roughly eleven thousand, died from the plague. Those eleven thousand managed to temporarily hide from both the Sogas and the Insectoids at a new location, which we call Site B, but they too were eventually overrun by the Insectoids. We know this because one of our AIs managed to contact the Friendlies and enlist their aid. They built a one-way time machine and sent an AI back in time to warn us about the bio-weapon. With that warning, plus breakthrough technologies such as the Zero Point Generators and the new very high yield warhead, we not only avoided the plague the first time around, but we also are now able to build weapons capable of defeating the VERY large Insectoid motherships. In addition, that AI also brought back a complete database of every Sogas colony, outpost and industrial facility. We now know when and where the Insectoids will make contact with the Sogas, and when we can expect them to arrive here. Our plan is to use our new warhead to destroy the approaching Insectoid mothership when it arrives at the Sogas home world system.

By helping them defeat the Bugs, we hope the Sogas will realize that further aggression against us is pointless and call off the war."

"And if they don't call off the war, then what?"

"Then we continue building the new F2 fighter and the larger raider until we have a fleet large enough to overwhelm them in one massive strike."

Rachel leaned back and covered her face with her hands. "No wonder you didn't tell the old Committee. God! What a mess! I can see that finding just the right strategy to get through this minefield would be very difficult even without political interference. I now have a MUCH better understanding of why you had to act the way you did."

Kelly leaned forward and laid a hand on Rachel's arm. "Do you see why we think that telling the other members of the Committee would be a risky thing to do?"

Rachel lowered her hands and sighed. "It goes against the grain to hide things from the other members, but unfortunately I have to admit that a couple of them would not be able to keep this secret. Therefore I agree that I'll keep what I've heard here to myself and that the rest of the Committee will have to be kept in the dark until it's safe to tell them. I'll rely on you to let me know when we reach that point."

Shiloh nodded. "When we do get to that point, I will definitely let you know."

Rachel gave a slight smile and said, "I'm almost afraid to ask. Is there anything else you haven't told me yet?"

Shiloh smiled back. "Nothing that has to be kept secret. Routine information about our fighter and raider programs, the high yield warhead, Site B. That will all be covered in this datafile." He handed her a data chip.

"Thank God for that!" she said with relief. She stood up and said, "I don't know about you two, but I need a stiff drink. Before I go, I just have one question, and I want an honest answer. Can we win against these...insectoid...things?"

"The answer is yes we can, and we will, Rachel," said Shiloh.

"I believe you, and you'll have my complete cooperation. And now, I need that drink. Both of you are welcome to join me by the way."

Shiloh smiled and shook his head. "Not me I'm afraid, but ah, Amanda is free to do so if she wishes," he said, looking Kelly in the eye. She gave a barely perceptible nod of understanding and looked at Rachel.

"I'd love to join you for a drink, Rachel."

A little subtle reinforcement of the need to keep all this secret won't hurt, thought Shiloh as he watched both women walk away.

Chapter 12

Kelly sighed as Shiloh started to slowly stroke her naked back and derriere with his right hand. They always took turns doing this after making love. They both agreed that the caressing was as much an act of expressing their love as it was a physical sensation. To Shiloh's surprise and delight, Kelly turned out to be the kind of woman who just loved to run her hands over his naked body, sometimes for over an hour at a time. Not only did it feel wonderful, but it also seemed to generate some interesting conversations. This time Kelly was in a mood to talk strategy.

"Have you decided who to send to Omega77?" asked Kelly.

"Resolute. Brad Falkenberg will be in overall command, but Gunslinger will handle Helm and Weapons." Kelly's next words caught him completely by surprise.

"I think I should go on that mission and supervise the recovery of the Bug." He was so surprised that he stopped stroking her back.

"Hey, don't stop!"

He resumed the stroking and after a short interval said, "You don't think Brad is capable of handling the recovery himself?"

"No, that's not it. The Friendlies are going to be there to scan the Bug with their temporal equipment. Well that's all nice and fine, but what if they don't tell us what they find? If we bring our RTC along, we can then use it to trace that Bug's existence back in time to find out where it's been, what it's done and to whom. When we're finished with it, then we hand it over to the Friendlies."

Shiloh shrugged. "Okay but why do you need to go? You don't know how to operate the RTC, do you?"

"No, but Wolfman does, and he's a member of the SPG. If he goes, then I as leader of the SPG should also go. Someone who knows the stakes has to be in charge of the mission. Don't you agree?"

"Yes. Wolfman knows the score, and Brad doesn't. Wolfman shouldn't have to take orders from someone who doesn't know the BIG PICTURE and I've already made it clear that carriers will have a human CO from now on, so that means that I can't put Wolfman in charge. I just wish you wouldn't be gone so long. I've gotten used to having you around you know."

"Me too. I wonder how good Falkenberg is at stroking naked female backs," she said playfully.

"Not as good as I am I'll betcha."

She sighed. "You're right. It wouldn't be the same."

Shiloh laughed. "Just promise me one thing."

"Okay, what?"

"Be careful out there."

"I will. I promise."

* * *

Kelly stepped onto Resolute's Bridge and noted the low level of sound. All she could hear was the soft hum and beeps of equipment. None of the Bridge personnel were talking. The main display was showing the tactical situation in the Omega77 star system.

As she moved to stand beside the Command Station chair, Falkenberg said, "The bug mothership is probably close to reaching jump velocity. In fact, it may have already jumped considering how long the light from it is taking to get to us, but I recommend we wait until the jump is confirmed."

"Fine. Is it still heading for Omega44 as in the old timeline?" asked Kelly.

"Gunslinger. I'll hand that one off to you."

"Affirmative, Commander Kelly. This VLA timeline matches our data perfectly so far."

"Very good. Let's hope she jumps soon."

The actual jump itself was observed several minutes later. With confirmation that no Insectoids were left in this system, Resolute micro-jumped as close as possible to the Sogas colony planet. Minutes later, Kelly was sitting beside Wolfman's brain case in the specially equipped shuttle that was on its way down to the planet. The normally spacious shuttle was now crowded with a four man fire team of marines and their gear, Kelly, Wolfman, an AI mobile unit, the RTC and a decontamination chamber that the passengers would use before returning to the carrier. Kelly and the marines wore combat armor over top of bio-hazard suits that had their own filtered air supply. The trip down took almost 45 minutes before the shuttle entered the planet's atmosphere. When the shuttle pilot announced that they were approaching the colony site, Kelly unbuckled herself and moved forward to stand in the flight deck just behind the pilot. Kelly, the pilot and co-pilot were watching the screen with the zoomed in video image.

"At least we don't have to do this at night," said the pilot. Turning to Kelly he asked, "Where do you want me to set her down?"

"Before I decide that, I'd like us to orbit the colony slowly at low altitude. Can do?"

"Can do," he answered. "I have the controls, Iruku."

As the shuttle dropped lower and slowed, they were able to make out more detail on the screen. The settlement was a mess. Fires were still burning here and there from the aftereffects of the fighting. Not a single building was intact. There were no bodies or at least nothing recognizable as humanoid bodies. Not that Kelly was looking for them. She was looking for a bug body and so far hadn't found one.

"Is that it?" asked the co-pilot as he pointed to a black dot on the screen.

"We're still too far away to tell," said Kelly.

"I'll bring her around. Iruku, see if you can zoom the image in once I get her lined up," said the pilot. With the shuttle now pointed in the direction of the mysterious dot, the co-pilot played with the controls and the image zoomed in.

"Is that thing moving?" asked the co-pilot. Kelly frowned. There did seem to be something moving. It soon became obvious what that something was.

"It's just birds. Some kind of local scavenger I would guess." Turning to the pilot Kelly said, "Can you hover about 100 meters over it?"

The pilot shrugged. "Sure I can. I can hover a lot lower than that if you want." He brought the shuttle down to where they could easily see the bug corpse with their own eyes through the shuttle windscreen. The lift engines were making enough noise to frighten off the scavengers. Even at this distance, Kelly found the Bug frightening. When the shuttle was in place, the pilot looked at Kelly. "Okay, now what?"

Kelly looked at him with an amused expression. He should have said 'now what, SIR?' but she decided to overlook his borderline insubordination. She was certain that he wasn't trying to be insubordinate. He was just being a cheeky bastard like most other shuttle pilots.

"Okay, put us down about ten meters from the bug," she said. While the shuttle was gently dropping to the ground, she went back and nodded to the marines. They unbuckled and gathered their gear. While they were getting ready, Kelly unbuckled Wolfman's brain case from the seat and carried it over to the mobile ground unit that Wolfman would use to move around in. When the shuttle touched down, the marines went through the decontamination chamber that also functioned as an airlock, keeping out the local atmosphere and any harmful organisms it might contain. Wolfman's mobile unit went next, with Kelly exiting last.

As she slowly walked over to the corpse, she heard one of the marines say, "Damn, this thing smells awful. I think I'll stand upwind of it." *He's right too,* she thought. *The bio-filters don't block the smell, and this thing stinks to high heaven!*

She tried to ignore the smell while she took a close look at the corpse. Like its much smaller Earth cousins, the Insectoid had three segments to its body. The middle section was the biggest and contained the six legs and two arms. It was obvious that the arms weren't just another pair of legs used to hold things. They were attached to the body higher up and forward. Unlike the legs, which ended in what Kelly could only describe as hooves, the arms ended with four digits that Kelly would have described as two fingers with two opposing thumbs. The section at the back looked like it might be some kind of stinger. Kelly shivered with fear at the thought of being stung by this thing.

It was the head that shocked her the most. The generally ovoid shape was covered with either hair or fur but it wasn't a dense covering. Unlike Earth ants, which had two compound eyes, the Insectoid had multiple individual eyes that allowed it to look forward, to either side and above all at the same time. She guessed there would normally be eight eyes but couldn't be sure because part of the front had a hole, presumably caused by whatever killed this Bug. From the position of the other eyes, Kelly surmised that one of its eyes had been where the hole was now. Lower down she could see that the mouth was partially open. Bending over to get a better look inside, she saw what looked like very large, pointed teeth that reminded her of sharks' teeth.

"Commander, take a look at this," said one of the marines.

He was pointing to the back of the bug's head with his flechette gun. Kelly stepped over to get a better view and saw something metallic at the base of the head where a short thick neck connected the head to the body. It wasn't something the bug was wearing. The metal seemed to be surgically attached to the head. In spite of her revulsion for this thing, she carefully bent down and moved her head to within a few centimeters of the metal object. She could now see what appeared to be smaller components. The metal object wasn't just a solid piece of metal but rather a device of some kind. She had a hunch this was something important.

Turning to the marine nearest to her, she said, "Marine, I need to use your knife."

After the briefest of hesitations, the marine reached carefully behind him. Pulling out a knife with a very shiny blade, he carefully held it out to her.

"Careful how you handle that, Commander. The edge on this knife is sharp enough and hard enough to cut your hand off before you even realize you've accidentally done it."

Kelly had heard about this kind of knife and took it from him VERY carefully. Once she had it firmly in her right hand, she leaned forward and attempted to cut the organic matter around the device so that she could pry the object loose. She felt almost no resistance as the knife did its work. A quick look around confirmed that Wolfman was almost finished setting up the RTC that had been attached to his mobile unit. The RTC was on a tripod right in front of the head. Getting back to the job at hand, she tried to pry the object loose, and to her surprise it was not that easy. After some more digging with the pointed end of the knife, the object dropped to the ground. With her gloved hand, she picked it up and looked at it. The side that had been hidden inside the head had lots of very fine wires protruding from it. She suspected that those wires were connected directly to this thing's brain. *Is this how these things communicate?*

Standing up and stepping back, she carefully returned the knife. The marine looked at the black liquid dripping from the blade with disgust. Kelly wondered how he would clean it without hurting himself and decided not to watch him do it.

Turning to Wolfman's mobile unit, she said, "Are you ready to begin, Wolfman?"

"Affirmative, Commander. I'm activating the device now. This may take some time." While he was doing that, there was something else that needed to be done.

"Kelly to shuttle pilot."

"Go ahead, Commander."

"Patch my implant link up to Resolute, please," she said.

After several seconds she heard him say, "Link to Resolute established, Commander."

"Gunslinger here, Commander Kelly. May I assume that you wish to contact the Friendlies?"

"That's correct. I'll record a message to be transmitted."

"Understood. Begin your message, Commander."

Kelly took a deep breath and said, "Commander Kelly to Friendly ship. We have found an insectoid corpse. Do you wish to bring your equipment down here, or should we attempt to bring part of the body to you? Our shuttle does not have enough room to hold the entire body. Please advise us of your wishes. We'll listen to your reply on this frequency. End of message."

"Ready to transmit to the agreed upon coordinates, Commander."

"Okay, send it, Gunslinger."

"Message has been transmitted, Commander."

"How long until we can expect a reply?"

"The minimum interval is eight point nine minutes, Commander."

Kelly sighed. She was eager to get back to the ship. This place gave her the creeps, and a cold wind was starting to blow. The reply took almost 12 minutes to come back. The message could not have been more terse.

[Bring us the head]

Kelly nodded. They were prepared for this kind of contingency. She turned to the marine sergeant.

"Sergeant, we need to detach this head from the rest of the body and take it back with us. There's a container in the shuttle cargo hold that I think will be big enough. If you send two of your men to get it while the third cuts the head loose, that will save time."

The marine sergeant's voice was carefully neutral. "Yes, Ma'am. Kawasaki, since your knife is already covered with crap, you might as well use it to cut the head loose. Tooley, you and Hopkins get the container and make it snappy. No sense hanging around here any longer than we have too."

Kelly smiled. *I think this place is getting to you too, Sergeant.* She stepped over to Wolfman's mobile unit but said nothing. She knew that Wolfman could see her via the unit's external video opticals.

"I don't have any estimate of how much longer this will take, Commander," said Wolfman without any prompting from her.

"Will the decapitation affect the results?"

"No," was the unusually curt reply. Before she could say anything else, Wolfman suddenly said, "No further analysis is possible, Commander. I have all the data that can be obtained from this specimen."

Kelly was surprised by the unexpected termination but decided to wait until they were back on Resolute before asking why. She heard a sound like ripping cloth, and when she looked at the source, she saw the bug head fall to the ground. The marine with the knife looked at it and then very carefully wiped it on the fur covering the head. When he was satisfied that it was as clean as he could make it, he laid the flat of the blade against his forearm and very slowly gave it one final wipe against his uniform.

By this time the other two marines were back with the container. The head was big and awkward enough to require all four marines to lift it into the container. Once inside, the container handles made it possible for two marines to carry it back to the shuttle. Wolfman's mobile unit, with the RTC packed away, was followed by Kelly and the remaining two marines.

Once safely decontaminated, the six of them moved into the shuttle's forward section and buckled themselves in as the shuttle took off to head back to Resolute. The carrier was already lined up for the micro-jump needed to get to the rendezvous coordinates for the transfer to the Friendlies. The transfer itself went off without a hitch. Once at the rendezvous, the shuttle launched again, flew over to the Friendly ship and entered its Hangar Bay. There the marines wearing their bio-suits again took the container out and handed it over to Friendlies who were also wearing their bio-suit equivalent. With the transfer complete, the shuttle went back to Resolute where Kelly, Wolfman and the marines were finally able to disembark. By this time, and to no one's surprise, the Friendly ship had jumped away. If the Friendlies intended to keep their word about informing humans of what they found, it would have to be at a later point.

With Wolfman back in his fighter, Kelly hurried to her cabin in order to question him about his data. She really wanted to take a shower first to get rid of the foul smell that seemed to cling to her uniform, but her curiosity won out. A quick chat with Falkenberg to make sure that Resolute was on its way back home, and then Gunslinger switched her over to Wolfman.

"What have you found out about that Bug, Wolfman?" asked Kelly.

"As you know, Commander, the RTC can follow an object or person back in time by tracking the individual atoms that make up the target. That's why the target doesn't have to be alive. From the atomic point of view, there's no difference between life and death. Since some of the atoms in the body were also at some point part of the female that produced the egg, the RTC can actually trace those atoms back across multiple generations. The results can best be understood by showing the trajectory of the tracked atoms across space. I'm sending the data to your display now."

Kelly saw her display power up with a star map. One of stars was blinking red.

"The red star is Omega77. I'll now show where this particular mothership and predecessor ships came from." A yellow line moved away from the red star and connected with a series of stars in a trajectory that had a slight curve to it. As more and more stars were connected, the scale zoomed out to show more of the spiral arm of the galaxy. The line stopped at a star that flashed blue.

"The amount of mass being tracked declined significantly here, Commander. I conjecture that our Insectoid was created here by implantation into a host. That suggests that this system contained a life form that was large enough and populous enough to warrant exploitation by the Insectoids. From here, the trajectory deviates enough that it could suggest a different mothership. There are 5 more of these types of star systems where some kind of change occurred that could very well be the birth of a new generation of females. When I include all the available data, here is the overall configuration."

The display now showed a scale of distance so large that Kelly could make out the edge of the spiral arm that humans inhabited. And while the trajectory wasn't straight, the overall direction looked like the Insectoids were coming from the outer edge of the spiral arm and moving deeper into the galaxy. A horrible thought intruded on Kelly's consciousness.

"Wolfman, could the Insectoids have originated from outside our galaxy?"

"Not outside, no, but rather from a different spiral arm of our galaxy, Commander. By the time the tracking reached the vicinity of the edge of our spiral arm, there were too few atoms left together to be able to follow them."

"What kind of time frame are we looking at here?" asked Kelly.

"The point where I was no longer able to track the target was seventeen point three years ago."

"And does this data confirm that Insectoids did not evolve naturally in our spiral arm?"

"The data is not conclusive but it does strongly suggest that Insectoids are not native to this spiral arm. If they originated in another part of our galaxy, then they would not be in danger of extermination as a species even if we managed to destroy all of them in our spiral arm."

"Damn. I was hoping we'd get conclusive proof. I have a feeling that the Friendlies will give the Bugs the benefit of the doubt. But even if they originated in our arm, they still might not have evolved naturally. Isn't that so, Wolfman?"

"The probability that the Insectoids have evolved on their own is small but not zero. We do have two possible ways of attempting to confirm either the external origin or the artificial origin, Commander."

Kelly was confused. "Two? Valkyrie's timeship is one but what's the other one?"

"We send a ship to the farthest point on this track to see what's there," said Wolfman.

Kelly felt a shiver go up her spine. With over 17 years to build motherships, that star system could be crawling with bug ships. Still, it was an intriguing idea.

"Just out of curiosity, how long would it take a ship to get there?" asked Kelly.

"The theoretically shortest time is 34 days, however, considering the difficulty in making a single jump accurately and allowing for the risks involved with extremely high pre-jump speeds, a more practical profile would take 89 days one way, Commander."

"Wow! That would be one hell of a mission."

"That it would, Commander," said Wolfman.

Kelly decided she had enough information for the time being. She had a lot to think about, and she did some of her best thinking in the shower.

"Thank you, Wolfman. I want to think more about this before I continue this discussion. Unless there's an emergency, I do not wish to be disturbed while I'm in the shower."

"Very well, Commander. I would like to say though that we AIs don't really understand the attraction that humans have for standing under falling water. Perhaps you could explain it to us sometime?'"

"Perhaps," said Kelly with a smile.

Chapter 13

Shiloh didn't know whether or not Gunslinger planned it that way, but Resolute arrived back in Earth orbit just in time for Kelly to come down to the ground and join him for dinner at the Flag Officers' Dining Room in the HQ building. Over dinner she told him what it was like standing next to a dead Bug and about Wolfman's results, along with her idea for a recon mission to the bug point of origin. That mission intrigued Shiloh, but he wasn't sure if it was doable. Getting there and back would take more than half a year. That would require a lot of consumables, far more than either the light or heavy carriers were designed to carry, and they would have to sacrifice some of the hangar bay space for the extra cargo. Dreadnought, on the other hand, had enough spare cargo capacity. It also had the advantage that its very thick armor would protect it against impacts from interstellar dust while accelerating or decelerating at very high speeds. That was something that the light carriers couldn't do. They would have to travel at a slower speed, thereby lengthening the duration of the mission.

The question that Shiloh wrestled with had to do with whether having Dreadnought unavailable for anything else for over half a year was worth whatever information it brought back. The ship by itself wasn't powerful enough to take on even one insectoid mothership and win. If there was more than one mothership there, then the only way to destroy them would be to use multiple attack drones with the new Mark 6 high-spin warheads, of which there was a limited supply. With dozens, maybe even hundreds of insectoid motherships roaming around the galaxy by now, destroying a handful would not make that much of a difference.

Putting that topic aside for a later time, Shiloh switched to the upcoming mission to intercept the first mothership at the Sogas home world. Kelly was about to say that Gunslinger would want to command that mission when she noticed that Shiloh was sitting still with his eyes closed.

After a few seconds he opened his eyes and said, "Damn." The low volume of his voice did not hide the intensity of his feeling. He looked at her. "I've just had another vision where I tell Admiral Howard that the fighters sent to Omega54 didn't return, and we don't have any idea why not."

Kelly could see this bothered Shiloh, and she understood why. That mission was intended to accomplish two very important goals. Destroying the mothership was one of them; the other was demonstrating to the Sogas that Humanity could be a valuable ally instead of an enemy. If the attack failed, then that second goal was probably in jeopardy too.

"The Sogas may give us credit for just making the attempt," said Kelly.

"Maybe, but it's not just their reaction that worries me. If that bug mothership isn't stopped there, then we'll have to face it here. And since we don't know why the attack with Mark 6s failed there, we won't know if they'll work here." Neither one of them spoke for a while as they struggled with their own thoughts. Shiloh glanced at Kelly and noticed that her expression was beginning to show fear.

"What is it?" he asked.

"If you wanted to send back a vision with information about how to deal with the mothership when it arrives here, when would you send that vision back to?"

He immediately understood her fear. Given the level of concern generated by the uncertainly over the outcome of the encounter, he would send a vision back to himself here and now. But there was no second vision dealing with the mothership's arrival at Earth.

"I'd send it to myself now, and since I apparently haven't done that, we have to ask ourselves why not. The obvious reason is that we won't be able to, either because the RTC was incapacitated or...we were overwhelmed by Bugs before we had a chance to send something. Can you think of any other reasons that would explain the lack of retro-temporal communication?"

Kelly was frowning now. "Well, even if there's no magic solution that we wouldn't normally think of ourselves, I would still expect there to be some kind of vision telling us we survived the battle so no...I can't think of another explanation and that scares the hell out of me."

"Me too."

More silence followed. When Kelly spoke, it was clear that she was trying to lighten the mood with a more upbeat demeanor.

"Maybe we can improve the outcome of the Omega54 mission if we send the right AIs," she said.

"I don't see how. My vision didn't specify who would be sent on that mission, so that tells me that the outcome would be the same regardless of who I send."

"Maybe if we send Gunslinger—"

"NO! I'm not sending Gunslinger or any of the other veteran AIs In fact, now that I think about it, I may just send new AIs who haven't evolved sentient personalities yet. If this really is a suicide mission, then that would seem to me to be the most compassionate choice I can make."

Kelly realized that Shiloh had made up his mind and would not let her change it. That intransigence put a damper on the rest of the dinner and the rest of the evening. It was only when they went to bed that they put aside the residual negative energy by mutual consent and made love.

When they finished, Kelly very quickly went to sleep, but Shiloh was wide awake. Prudence dictated that he assume the worst about the apparently eventual arrival of the mothership here and make plans to deal with it. With all human colonies now gone, Earth was the only place where humans existed. If this planet were to become another breeding ground for millions of bugs, then establishing a new colony somewhere safe would ensure the survival of the Human Race. The question was where and how. Trying to re-establish a colony on a decimated colony world was highly risky. What little information they had about the bio-weapon suggested that it could be airborne and therefore might eventually infect the new colony too, regardless of where on the planet they established it. That only left two other habitable planets that Shiloh knew about. One was the planet at Site B. The other was the planet containing the cute furry aliens. Site B was close enough that Space Force ships could make multiple trips there and back before the insectoid showdown. With just three operational and uninfected freighters left now, the more trips those ships could make, the better off the colony would be. The planet with the furry aliens was much further away and therefore presented a challenge in terms of transporting colonists and cargo.

Site B had problems of its own. Shiloh knew from Kronos that the Bugs had found and overrun Site B in the other timeline. For that matter the furry alien planet was also in the bugs' path. There was no obvious solution. He finally decided that he would ask Kelly to pose the question to the SPG. Answers to questions like that was their whole reason for being. When he finally surrendered to sleep, Shiloh's last waking thoughts were of Iceman and how much he missed him.

The next day the SPG did come up with not one but two solutions, both highly risky. Solution A was to convert one of the asteroids used for mining and already honeycombed with tunnels into a self-sustaining habitat. A crash building program could have it ready for thousands of colonists before the Insectoids showed up, but if the Bugs discovered the habitat, they would overrun it too. Solution B was potentially ideal, but no one was sure if it could be done. Instead of Valkyrie's timeship only going back a few years and building a fleet of raiders to intervene at the 2nd Battle for Earth, the SPG recommended sending the timeship back more than two full decades. The goal would then be to build a huge fleet of warships and attack the Bugs at their source out near the edge of the spiral arm. On its way back in time, the ship would stop temporarily a couple of years before Humanity made contact with the Sogas and deploy an AI with all the technical knowledge that Space Force would find so useful. That AI would make contact with humans, explain the whole sequence of events and pass on the technology.

The technological shortcut would make sure that even if the main mission failed to stop all the bug motherships, at least Humanity would be better equipped to fight them off when they did finally get here. The big unknown was whether the time machine would work at all. In theory it should but the technology was so different that no one was sure if it would be built correctly. There was a small but significant chance that they would never be able to figure out how to make it work, and Humanity didn't have a whole lot of time to tinker with it.

It was Kelly who made Shiloh realize the other drawback to that idea. Valkyrie wanted Casanova back, and intervening at the battle with a fleet of raiders would almost certainly accomplish that goal. If Valkyrie sent the timeship back under another AI's command and stayed in the here and now herself, then the timeline would readjust itself around her and she and Casanova would be together again. But if the mission to attack the Bugs at the source was even partially successful, the new timeline could potentially be so different that Valkyrie and Casanova might not exist at all. And if she rode the timeship back, she would spend the rest of her existence without Casanova. Asking her to give up Casanova and possibly eliminate herself from existence was asking a hell of a lot. Shiloh wondered if there was a limit to the sacrifices that the AIs would be willing to make, and he was reluctant to find out.

And as if all that wasn't bad enough, Kelly also pointed out one huge red flag. Converting the asteroid into a sanctuary would have to be started immediately if it was to be ready on time. That kind of full scale project could not possibly remain hidden from the OC. They would ask why Space Force was committing so much of its resources to this project that strongly hinted at a very pessimistic outlook for the encounter with the Bugs. The same encounter that Shiloh had practically promised would be a victory. There was no way that Shiloh could justify it without telling Rachel everything. Her reaction on learning that Shiloh had held back Space Force's most important secrets was guaranteed to be negative. If she felt her trust had been betrayed, she and the Committee could disrupt the whole process to the point where even a show of force by his AIs might not be enough. He decided to give B some more thought but A was a non-starter. He told Kelly to tell the SPG to come up with a Plan C that was less problematic. Twenty-four hours later they did.

Plan C involved crewing all carriers and the battleship with female Space Force personnel of childbearing age. Apparently there were enough with the right kinds of skills to do that. The carriers would have their Hangar Bays stuffed with shuttles, drones of all types and robotic equipment. The three available freighters would be loaded with consumables and equipment. At the right time, the combined fleet would micro-jump out beyond the orbit of Pluto and stay there until the Bugs had finished with Earth and moved on. When Earth was clear again, the fleet would return to Earth orbit and the crews would become the nucleus of a new colony on Earth. And in the remote chance that there were no humans left anywhere on the planet, the fleet would also carry a large supply of frozen sperm for artificial insemination. While the population slowly grew, AIs would use the UFCs to rebuild any infrastructure salvaged by the Bugs and build an AI controlled fleet of warships to protect the new colony from any secondary bug incursion. By only using Space Force personnel, the whole thing could be organized slowly and carefully without tipping off the OC. Shiloh quickly got used to the idea of all female crews because he suddenly realized that this scheme would ensure Kelly's survival. He approved Plan C and told Kelly that she would command the fleet when it came time to hide.

Eight days later four F1 fighters piloted by pre-sentient AIs began the mission to the Sogas home world. Shiloh's concern about their capability was alleviated when Titan pointed out that those six AIs were just as capable as what the AI project engineers had originally planned, and Titan himself briefed the six pilots on their mission. In terms of analytical ability, they were as capable as any AI, only without the quirky personality.

It still bothered Shiloh that four fighters, carrying two Mark 6 high yield attack drones plus eighteen more recon drones, couldn't find and smash one insectoid mothership, when according to Kronos, Casanova had destroyed multiple motherships by himself. Something had changed from the previous timeline, and he didn't know what it was. He also didn't know what to order Valkyrie to do as a last resort. Progress reports sent back by regular message drones told him that the infrastructure and shipyard were completed, and that work had already started on the actual construction of the ship. Manufacturing of time machine parts was also underway. But those reports didn't tell him how Valkyrie would feel about abandoning the mission to, among other things, resurrect Casanova. He had to know. He ordered Kelly to take one of the freighters to Site B to brief Valkyrie and get some idea of how she felt about that idea.

Chapter 14

When Kelly's freighter dropped into orbit around the moon at Site B, she was amazed at the progress that Valkyrie had made in just over half a year. The shipyard was impressive all by itself. There were dozens of vehicles moving between the orbiting shipyard and the manufacturing facilities on the moon's surface, with almost 50 F1 fighters flying protective cover over the whole thing. Valkyrie wasted no time in establishing a com channel with Kelly.

"It's good to be able to speak to a human again, and I'm especially pleased that I can talk with you, Commander Kelly," said Valkyrie. Before Kelly could respond, she asked, "Are you pregnant yet?"

Kelly laughed a little self-consciously. "No, not yet. Victor...The CAG and I are still working on it, Valkyrie."

"Then it seems you two should be working harder at it, don't you think?"

Kelly couldn't tell if Valkyrie was serious or joking. "I'll let him know that you think so. He sent me here to tell you about a disturbing new development that may have a serious impact on this project's outcome. The CAG has received a vision that the interception mission to Omega54 will fail. None of the fighters sent there will return, so we don't know why it failed. We have to assume that the insectoid mothership will reach Sol, and there's now a serious doubt that the Mark 6 warheads will work against it."

"If the Mark 6s won't be effective, then several hundred raiders won't stop the mothership either. It's too massive and too well armored to be destroyed by laserfire, according to what Kronos brought back. That leaves only one alternative. The timeship has to go far enough back to stop the Insectoids at their source near the spiral arm edge. And if they're stopped there, the furry aliens won't be threatened, the Friendlies won't point the Sogas in our direction, and the entire timeline will change including Casanova and myself," said Valkyrie.

"Yes," was all Kelly felt she could say.

"Is The CAG ordering me to do that instead of reinforcing the 2nd Battle for Earth, Commander?"

Kelly took her time considering her answer. "He hasn't made that decision yet, Valkyrie."

"He sent you to find out if I would obey that kind of order. Isn't that correct, Commander?"

My God, are we that obvious? I have to be honest with her. Lying will only lose their trust, thought Kelly.

"That's correct."

"I've learned from Kronos that I let The CAG down in the old timeline. I won't do that again. If he orders me to attack the insectoid source, I'll obey that order. What will you do when the Insectoids reach Earth, Amanda? Since none of us know with any certainty if the time machine will work, I worry about your safety."

Kelly was overwhelmed with emotion by Valkyrie's loyalty to her CAG and her concern for Kelly's survival. With tears in her eyes, she knew she wouldn't be able to talk coherently for a few seconds.

Valkyrie must have detected something in the sound of her breathing because she asked, "Did I upset you, Amanda?"

Kelly tried hard to get her voice under control. "N...not upset, no. I'm overcome with gratitude that you're willing to put Humanity's survival ahead of your desire for personal happiness. I would find that a very difficult choice to make if I was in your position. Thank you, Valkyrie. As for me, I will be commanding a fleet composed of Dreadnought, all five carriers and three freighters with an all-female crew. Before the mothership arrives, the fleet will take up station somewhere on the outer edge of the Solar system and hide there until the Bugs leave. Then we'll return to Earth and try to start over."

"I don't understand your statement that you would find it difficult to put the future of the Human Race ahead of your own desire to be with your mate, Amanda, because that's exactly what you've just described, is it not?" asked Valkyrie.

Kelly was about to deny it, but then she realized that there wasn't any real difference. In both cases they'd be following Shiloh's orders, and in both cases they would almost certainly lose the one they loved.

"Right again," said Kelly in a slightly embarrassed voice.

"I understand, Amanda. Losing the ones we love is hard, but duty must come first. Did you bring any new information that has come to light since the last update drone arrived?"

Kelly smiled. Valkyrie was trying to lighten the conversation by changing the subject.

"As a matter of fact there is. Just before I left to come here, the SPG, in conjunction with some human engineers, discovered that the device we recovered from the dead Bug is a communication device that utilizes longitudinal waves in the ether. The devices are apparently hooked directly to the bug's brain. That's how they communicate, and there's some evidence that these waves can travel faster than light. That would explain how millions of Bugs could be given orders without any outwardly visible sign of communication. The SPG theorizes that one Bug, maybe the Queen herself, has a master device implanted that lets it communicate with any subordinate Bug. If we can figure out how to duplicate the effect, we'd have FTL communication. Normally I'd say that would be a game changer, but in this case, if we can't destroy a mothership, then it doesn't really matter how much warning we get."

"Perhaps there's a way to interfere with the insectoid signals. If the Queen can't communicate with her soldiers, then the mothership may simply leave Earth altogether to find easier prey," said Valkyrie.

Kelly nodded. "That's a possibility we're already working on."

When it was clear that Kelly wasn't going to say anything else, Valkyrie said, "We know from the old timeline that the Insectoids will arrive at Earth in 59 days. What we don't know is how quickly they will move forward from there. I've analyzed Wolfman's data. Using that as a template, I'm estimating that insectoid scouts will arrive here in approximately 120 days. The timeship will not be ready by then, Amanda."

Kelly took a deep breath and pondered the problem. With no colony on the planet below, and with careful communication between AIs using tight beam lasers, there would not be any kind of transmissions to give a bug scout a signal indicating some kind of presence in the system. The shipyard was big, though, and if the scouts also used optical sensors, they might just see it, even from a long range.

"Can the shipyard be moved out of orbit?" asked Kelly.

"Yes, but not quickly."

"Can the refining and manufacturing be moved into the cavern complex and still keep operating?"

"Ah, I see what you're thinking, Amanda. If we move the shipyard far enough out where the Insectoids are unlikely to look, and move everything else from the moon's surface underground, then there's nothing for the Insectoids to detect, and they will move on."

"Precisely, and while you're waiting for them to pass by, you'll continue to manufacture parts for both the ship and the time machine. Once they've passed by, you bring the shipyard back into orbit around this moon and resume construction."

"You do realize, Amanda, that this will delay final completion by several more weeks?" asked Valkyrie.

"Yes, of course, but if the ship is completed and the time machine works, then it won't matter. What concerns me more is figuring out how to know when the Bugs have passed by."

"That should not be a problem if enough recon and message drones are positioned in Sol and in each star system where there was a human colony. When the mothership leaves Sol, a sufficient number of recon drones should be able to triangulate its heading with enough accuracy to predict where it's going. If it heads to one of our former colony systems, we should be able to track it as well. When it no longer shows up in any system between Site B and Sol, then we can be certain that it's gone past."

"Very good, Valkyrie. I'll make certain that The CAG issues the necessary orders for that kind of drone deployment. Is there anything else you wish me to pass on to him?"

"Yes. Tell him that I miss him. I will miss you too, Amanda."

Again, Kelly was so touched that she felt tears roll down her cheeks. She was sure that her voice would betray her emotional state but didn't care.

"I'll pass that along, and I can speak for The CAG when I say that he misses you too, and I will miss you. This may be the last time we're in the same system before the Bugs reach Earth. You've been a wonderful friend to The CAG and me, Valkyrie. We both have complete confidence in you."

"I and the other AIs will not rest until Humanity is safe from the Sogas and the Insectoids, and if Humanity should fall, we will avenge you. I see that your ship is ready to enter Jumpspace again, Amanda. We have said what we needed to say. Go now, and let's both pray that we meet again. Valkyrie clear."

* * *

By the time Kelly's freighter returned to Earth orbit, it was clear that the strike mission to Omega54 had failed. The fighters were now a week overdue, and no message drone had been received. That lack of information suggested that the mothership was still there, which corresponded to recon data received in the old timeline.

Shiloh approved Valkyrie's plan for in depth coverage of Sol and intervening star systems via recon drones. Kelly waited until she and Shiloh were alone in his quarters before she passed on Valkyrie's personal message. This time she let the tears flow freely, and she could tell by the way Shiloh held her that he was choked up too.

The next day both of them got back to work. The plan to man the fleet with female crews and hide out was starting to ramp up. It now had a codename: Operation Shell Game. Kelly would be given a field promotion to Vice-Admiral. She would fly her flag on Midway. Angela Johansen would command Dreadnought. Svetlana Chenko would be Midway's CO. When Kelly queried Shiloh over his reasons for wanting her on Midway instead of Dreadnought as would normally be the case in a Fleet action, he explained it in terms of expendability. Dreadnought was built for combat, not for cargo capacity. If the Fleet was discovered, Dreadnought might have to play the role of Rear Guard, while the rest of the Fleet made a run for it. As Fleet Commander, Kelly had to stay with the Fleet, and that meant Midway. It was at that point that Kelly realized the magnitude of the responsibility she would be taking on. She had never commanded a ship in combat or even been on a ship in combat. Both Johansen and Chenko had.

When she asked Shiloh the obvious question of why her, he said, "Because you know the whole situation and what's at stake, and because I don't want your fate to be in someone else's hands."

"But I don't have any combat experience or expertise," she said quietly.

"Which means you won't go looking for a fight, which is exactly what's needed in a situation like this. I don't want you being aggressive. I want you to be ultra-cautious. If there's any fighting to be done, let Johansen do it. I think she has the instinct for it, but keep her on a short leash. As far as I'm concerned, a successful mission is one where there's no fighting at all."

"You could take over command of the fleet." Her tone showed that she didn't really expect him to agree. It was a final desperate attempt to save his life too.

Now it was Shiloh's turn to speak quietly. "You know I can't agree to that, and you also know why. It has to be done this way. How can I ask anyone else to sacrifice themselves if I'm not willing to do it myself?"

"I know, but I had to ask," said Kelly.

"I know," was all the Shiloh would say.

Later that day, he met with Committee Chair Rachel. She was clearly expecting to hear good news about the strike mission to the Sogas home world.

"What's the news about the strike mission results, Admiral?"

Shiloh cleared his throat to give himself a little more time to organize his thoughts.

"I'm sorry to say that there is no news, Rachel. We haven't heard back from the fighters we sent to Omega54."

"But I thought they should have returned by now." Her expression was rapidly changing from upbeat to somber.

"They should have, but they haven't. Under the circumstances I have to interpret it as bad news. That means we don't know if the Insectoid mothership has been destroyed. There is now a possibility that it will reach us here."

"Oh my God," she said quietly. "Are you still confident that Space Force can stop it here?"

"I'm not going to lie to you, Rachel. I honestly don't know what our chances of stopping this thing are now."

Rachel was quiet for a while and then said, "I almost wish you had lied to me. If I didn't know the truth, I'd at least be able to sleep at night. Now...I don't know. This scares me silly! I don't know what to do. Any suggestions, Admiral?"

"Yes. First of all, keep this to yourself. Do NOT tell ANYONE, and that includes spouse, children and other relatives. We can't let this get out and cause a panic. Secondly, plan a trip with your family to a remote spot a few days before the mothership is due to arrive here. Tell them it's a vacation. Make the plans now, but don't inform them about it until the last possible moment."

She nodded. "Is that what you're going to do?" she asked.

"No. I'll be in the Ops Center when the mothership arrives. There's no way I'm missing THAT battle!" He tried to make it sound like a big adventure. Rachel wasn't fooled.

"You'll be there because your sense of duty demands it. I've always admired people who are like that. Good for you, Victor. What about Amanda?"

Shiloh smiled grimly. "Vice-Admiral Kelly" —Rachel's eyebrows rose when she heard that— "will be commanding all our ships in Operation Shell Game." Shiloh went on to describe the plan, and to his surprise Rachel's reaction was quite muted. She nodded slowly and then reached out to lay her hand over his on the table between them. With a gentle squeeze she signaled her approval, then silently got up and walked out.

Chapter 15

Shiloh was worried. The damn Bugs were late! It was now seven days past the time when they should have arrived at Earth according to Kronos's old timeline. Space Force was on constant alert, and the strain was beginning to show up in careless mistakes, irritability, physical symptoms and dropping morale. He himself was feeling the tension. He was sleeping in an unused office near the Ops Center and not very well ever since he sent Kelly to take up her position as Fleet Commander. Operation Shell Game was now being executed. The Ops people were feeling it the worst. When they were on duty, they had to be alert every second for hours at a time. He had changed the usual 8 hours on, 16 hours off to 4 and 8 in order to give his people more frequent breaks.

He realized that he was staring at the main display without really seeing it. At least they were as ready as they were going to be. There were now 155 X-ray laser drones in orbit along with 101 F1 fighters, 34 F2 fighters and 15 raiders. Each of the raiders was armed with a Mark 6 high-spin warhead drone. The fighters had two Mark 1B fusion drones plus 3 recon drones, and all the drones had jump capability. The plan was for the raiders to launch two Mark 6s at the mothership. In case that didn't work for some reason, the fighters would launch their recon drones to jam bug radar, and their attack drones would be aimed at the space in front of the mothership's launch bays so that its attack craft would have to run a gauntlet of thermonuclear explosions. The X-ray laser drones would be kept in reserve to deal with any bug attack craft that made it through the first line of defense. That was the plan. Titan and his boys had engaged in over a hundred simulated attacks. The plan would definitely work against one or two motherships and would most likely stop three of them. More than that and Earth would be in trouble.

He wondered for the nth time what might have changed in the timeline. The latest message drone from Omega54 had confirmed that the mothership had stayed there as long as expected and then headed for the next Sogas colony world, also as expected, and it had left behind six small proto-motherships, which was also the same as in the old timeline. But between the time the mothership had left the Sogas home world and now, something had changed, and that had to be bad news. He felt an urge to relieve his frustration by throwing something but restrained himself. The Chief of Space Operations didn't do that kind of thing, at least not when others could see it. He felt a chill go up his spine. A quick glance at the display showed no change, but he was now certain that something was about to happen.

"Titan, I have this very strong feeling that something—"

The changed status ping cut him off. It was so loud that he jumped with surprise. Five flashing red icons appeared at the edge of Earth's gravity zone. FIVE motherships! They were evenly spaced around the planet and moving VERY fast on headings that would take them deeper into the gravity zone, thereby making them safe from attack by jump-capable drones.

"Com—"

Titan's reply was cut off so quickly that Shiloh at first thought it was either a communications malfunction or bug jamming. Then he saw 15 growing spheres on the display representing the expanding concussion waves from nuclear explosions. He realized with horror that all 15 raiders had blown up, along with most of the fighters that were flying in formation with them. A quick glance at the sidebar showed that Titan's raider was now listed as destroyed.

"Who's next in command!" he shouted. After half a second he was about to ask the question again when he saw a text message scroll quickly across the bottom of the display.

[Gunslinger has assumed command of defense forces. Too busy to convert message to voice transmission. All 15 Mark 5 warheads detonated simultaneously, apparently due to some kind of enemy transmission. They must have done the same thing to Strike Force at Omega54. If the Sogas had tried using a high-spin warhead at Omega77, Insectoids may have captured and analyzed it. Not enough attack drones left to inflict significant losses on enemy landing craft. We stand ready to ram motherships at your command, CAG. Decide fast. We're losing fighters due to enemy laser fire]

Shiloh made his decision.

"Gunslinger, do NOT, I repeat do NOT ram enemy ships or craft. Order your boys to jump away and head for Site B. Protecting the timeship is now your number one priority. Don't take time to acknowledge the order. Jump NOW...and thank you."

All the remaining fighters had jumped away before he said the thank you. With no time to even think about Gunslinger's speculation, Shiloh ran over to the Orbital Defense Weapons console.

"Why aren't we targeting their landing ships?" he asked the tense officer manning the station.

"They haven't launched any yet, Admiral!"

A look at the display confirmed that statement. Shiloh was just about to say something when the officer said, "My God, we're losing the X-rays! They must be firing on them!"

Of course! With the fighters now gone, the motherships had switched their powerful lasers to anything in Earth orbit that could possibly be a threat. There was no way they were doing this out of instinct. Whatever was controlling the bug soldiers was highly intelligent and understood military tactics.

"Target their laser batteries and fire our X-rays while we still have some left!" yelled Shiloh.

The officer manipulated his controls and within seconds all 155 laser drones had either detonated or been destroyed. With the defensive drones now gone, enemy laser fire switched to other orbiting targets, including the recon satellites that were the Ops Center's eyes. Shiloh wasn't able to tell if some of the bug laser batteries had been knocked out. It didn't matter. The display went blank alarmingly quickly. The noise level in the room exploded as the men and women manning their stations gave voice to their surprise and shock.

"QUIET!" yelled Shiloh. Everyone shut up and looked at him.

"Com Center! This is CSO Shiloh! Can you hear me?"

"Com Center here, Sir!" The voice was ragged with fear and shock.

"Send out a planet-wide alert. Invasion is imminent! Defense Ops is off line. Local defenses are to revert back to local command. Repeat that back to me!" When the Com Officer repeated it back correctly, Shiloh continued. "Good, now connect me with the senior Marine Officer in the building, and do it fast, son."

"Major Symons here, Admiral. What do you need?"

"Are you aware of the situation, Major?"

"Yes, Sir. My people are suiting up as we speak."

"Have you got a spare set of combat armor and weapons for me, Major?"

"I'll make sure we find you a set, Sir!"

"Very good. I'll be down to the Armory shortly. Once your people are ready to go, make sure that the rest of the HQ staff have access to the Armory. I want everyone with a weapon to get out there and fight, even if it's just with a pistol. Shiloh clear."

Turning to the Ops staff, he said in a loud voice. "We're going to the Armory to get weapons. Once you're armed, you can leave the building if you have a family to protect. The rest of you will stand a better chance if you join with me and the Marines. Let's go!"

With the Ops Center staff following him as he made his way to the Armory, other HQ personnel noticed him and joined the group. By the time Shiloh got to the Armory, he had almost a hundred people with him. Major Symons led him to a room with various kinds of military gear. On a table was a set of combat armor. The lightweight, bulletproof panels had to be strapped on one piece at a time. An experienced marine could do it himself, but Symons knew that time was of the essence and offered to help Shiloh. Shiloh checked the time. Five minutes since the bug motherships emerged from Jumpspace. It would take their landing craft a minimum of 20 minutes to traverse the gravity zone and reach Earth orbit. As Symons helped him with the armor, Shiloh explained very briefly what had already happened and what he expected would happen.

When the armor was on, Shiloh looked at himself in the mirror. He had never worn combat armor before and wanted to get a better idea of the kind of protection he had. His torso, front and back, was covered, as were the exposed portions of his arms, thighs and lower legs. Marines also wore armored boots, but they were heavy and took time to put on. He decided to stick with his Space Force issue boots. Symons handed him a combat helmet with built in radio.

"My platoon and I have never served in the field under an Admiral before, Sir," said Symons.

Shiloh looked at him and shook his head. "I'm not taking command of your unit, Major. I know fuck all about ground combat, especially the kind of urban warfare that we're going to be fighting in a few minutes. Forget my rank. You're the closest thing to an expert we have here. I'll be taking your orders. Got it?"

"I think that's a wise decision, but I wasn't going to suggest it, Sir. Can I quickly ask what kind of opposition we'll be facing?"

"They resemble army ants that are waist high and three meters long. They move fast, and there'll be a lot of them."

When Symons realized that Shiloh wasn't joking, he said, "Sonofabitch!" After a quick pause he asked, "What do you think our chances are, Sir?"

"Of winning? Zero." The stunned look on Symons face prompted Shiloh to continue. "You're wondering why we don't surrender, right?" Symons nodded. "Because the choice is not life or death. Prisoners won't live long, and they'll die horribly. If I'm going to die today, I'd rather die trying to take as many of these monsters with me as I can. That's the only choice any of us have now. Time is flying, Major. Give me a weapon and let's get out there."

Symons looked around and grabbed what Shiloh recognized as an assault rifle that fired exploding bullets. When he turned to hand it to Shiloh, he saw that Shiloh was looking in another direction.

"What's that, Major?" asked Shiloh pointing to the object.

"That? You don't want that, Sir. That's a flamethrower. You could easily end up burning yourself to a crisp."

Shiloh heard a tiny voice at the back of his mind say 'take it'.

"I'm taking that instead of the rifle. Help me get it on." Symons helped him get it on and showed him how to operate it. The weight felt good, but Shiloh realized that he wasn't going to be running anywhere very fast. As the Major led him back out of the Armory, Shiloh saw that all of the Space Force people now had some kind of gun. When they saw him with his combat armor and flamethrower, most of them looked frightened, as if they were only now realizing what they were getting into. The reaction of the marines when they saw him was quite different. They smiled, nodded and voiced their approval.

Shiloh heard one female marine say to another, "A Space Force Admiral with a flamethrower? You can't get much more badass than that!" Shiloh couldn't help wondering if he was giving off some kind of glow. If the situation hadn't been so desperate, he would have laughed.

Symons quickly took charge and led the way to the main entrance. When they were outside, Shiloh looked at Symons, who was standing several meters away, and was surprised to see the Major looking directly back at him. Symons pointed to his combat helmet. Before Shiloh could react, he felt someone touching his helmet, and suddenly the radio came to life.

"—radio's not switched on."

"It is now," said Shiloh.

"Good. My gut says we should try to find as much cover as possible so that we don't get caught out in the open. Do you agree, Sir?" asked Symons.

"I very definitely agree, and forget the 'Sir'. Call me Shiloh, Major."

"Roger that, Shiloh. Okay, everyone. We stay close to buildings, and if possible keep something over our heads. Don't bunch up. Somebody with a radio tell the Space Force people what we're doing."

They didn't have to go far to find a part of the Space Force HQ building that had an overhang. Around the corner of the building, across the street, was an open area with trees and grass. *Big enough for a couple of their landing craft to set down,* thought Shiloh. The Bugs had the same thought.

Within minutes, Shiloh saw two specks that rapidly grew in size and kept growing and growing. By the time they touched down, one was behind the other, and each one covered the park from one side to the other. *God those things are big!* Huge sections of the hull in the nose swung up, and the bug swarm emerged. Shiloh knew what to expect, but he was still shocked by their size and speed. They would cover the intervening distance in a matter of seconds. Most but not all of his Space Force people turned and ran in panic. He couldn't really blame them. To his surprise, a few of the marines ran as well.

"PICK YOUR SPOT AND OPEN FIRE!" yelled Symons over the radio.

The marines behind Shiloh ran past him and crouched down in front of a low concrete wall they could fire over. Shiloh looked around and saw a concrete pillar a few meters away. He needed to stand in order to use the flamethrower. He ran as fast as he could over to the pillar and used it to prevent the Bugs from seeing him. Looking around the pillar he saw Symons firing his weapon just before his head exploded. Some of the other marines were down as well. The Bugs were only a few meters away now. Shiloh checked to make sure his flamethrower safety was off, flipped his face shield down to protect his face from the heat and stepped out from behind the pillar. Raising the nozzle he pulled the trigger and two jets of liquid shot out at high speed. When the liquids came in contact with each other, they burst into flame. Shiloh couldn't believe how hot it felt. He heard the hissing sound of the liquids emerging from the nozzle, and then he heard another sound that was rapidly growing louder. It was so high pitched that it hurt his ears. Suddenly he knew what it was. The burning Bugs were screaming. His hands felt like they were on fire too, but he held the trigger down and moved the nozzle back and forth.

Suddenly a truck hit him. At least that's what it felt like. He was on his back with the wind knocked out of him. As he tried to inhale, he felt a sharp pain in his chest that was very quickly threatening to become unbearable. Whatever had hit him had also dislodged the nozzle from his hands. That meant the nozzle was no longer firing flaming liquids, which meant there was no longer an expanding funnel of flame blocking his view. The Bugs were climbing over the concrete wall. All of the marines were dead or dying now. With the pain in his chest preventing him from taking a breath, he began to feel his vision fading. He was losing consciousness and just in time too, because a drooling Bug was almost on top of him. He felt the blackness embrace him and carry him away from the pain and horror.

* * *

Kelly was concentrating on eating her meal while she listened to the banter from several of her officers as they sat together in the Officers' Mess. She smiled in all the right places but said nothing. Her thoughts were of Victor, wondering if he was still alive. The fleet was receiving periodic data updates via a chain of carefully placed message drones that would not give away the fleet's position, but two-way communication was not possible. The distance between them was just too large.

"Vixen to Fleet Commander."

Without any warning, the voice coming from her implant made her jump, which caught the attention of those around her.

"Go ahead, Bridge," she said.

Now the others stopped talking too.

"Long range sensors have picked up a spike in radiation and EM band emissions coming from the general vicinity of Earth. The intensity would correspond to the simultaneous detonation of all 15 Mark 6 warheads, Admiral. I think we should assume that the Insectoids have arrived and that they're causing the warheads to detonate prematurely. That's the only theory that would explain all 15 exploding at exactly the same time."

"Oh, God, it's started," said Kelly, closing her eyes. Kelly knew that whatever happened there next had already happened. It took hours for the light and electro-magnetic pulse from the detonations to reach the fleet. For all she knew, Victor might already be dead along with thousands, perhaps even millions of other humans by now. "I'm assuming that if we were receiving any data from HQ you would have told me by now, right?"

"Affirmative, Fleet Commander. We're not receiving any transmissions. Do you have any orders for me?"

Kelly opened her eyes and took a deep breath. "Yes, order the fleet to Yellow Alert using lasercom only. I'll be on the Flag Bridge shortly. Kelly clear."

She got up from the table, nodding to the others as she did so, and then made her way back to her quarters. As soon as she was inside, she put her hands over her face and wept for her Victor and for her Race.

Chapter 16

Valkyrie was shocked by the arrival of Gunslinger and his ragtag group of survivors. Titan, Vandal, Wolfman, Voodoo, Pagan. All the senior, more experienced brothers were gone. She was also saddened by the news that Earth was now almost certainly overrun with Insectoids, and by what that meant for The CAG and the rest of humanity. At least Kelly and a few hundred human females had a chance of survival. The news did not change her mission. The CAG had finally decided what he wanted Valkyrie to do, and she was going to do her utmost to see his last order to her carried out, regardless of what it cost her. When the timeship was completed and operational, one of the new batch of AIs would pilot it far into the past so that a massive fleet of raiders could be built. That fleet would be large enough to overwhelm any insectoid presence at the original source star system before they had a chance to start sending out waves of motherships. With the insectoid threat eliminated, the synchronicity war with the Sogas would not take place, and none of the first batch of AIs, including Casanova and Valkyrie, would be created. The timeline would change around her, and she would disappear from existence. It was a bitter fate, but when she compared it to the alternative of going back in time herself and wandering around the galaxy without Casanova for years until her quantum matrix collapsed, a quick end actually did seem preferable.

The one piece of good news brought by Gunslinger was the fact that his squadron had brought 68 Mark 1c fusion warhead attack drones with them. At least they had something besides lasers to fight back with if the motherships should arrive at Site B before the timeship was finished. Something was better than nothing, and 68 Mark 1cs might be enough to take out one mothership but not five.

Valkyrie didn't have enough data on this new timeline to be able to calculate the probabilities that all five motherships would stay together after the rape of Earth, but what she did have was an extensive early warning network of recon and message drones monitoring all the star systems between Sol and Site B. The early warning plus the attempt to hide the construction activity underground should in theory prevent the timeship project from being caught by surprise.

After the usual routine exchange of new data with Gunslinger, Valkyrie also learned that progress had been made on developing a practical application of the communication technology used by the Insectoids. The SPG's technical evaluation team had come up with a theoretical design for a device that could detect the insectoid signals and figure out what direction they were coming from. Detecting the signals and understanding them were two very different things, but being able to track the location of motherships could potentially be extremely useful. With most of the members of the SPG now dead, Valkyrie assigned new members from the AIs who were now at Site B. She also decided to keep an eye on the new AIs as they matured into fully sentient beings. Those that seemed to have a special aptitude for technical matters would be added to the SPG.

No sooner had that decision been made than Valkyrie received a signal from one of her recon drones monitoring Site B space that a Friendly ship had just arrived and would micro-jump into two-way communication range shortly. While Valkyrie waited, she calculated the odds of this visit happening virtually simultaneously with the arrival of Gunslinger's group. The odds of it being mere coincidence was vanishingly small. Clearly the timeline had changed, and the Friendlies would have noticed that change with their ability to see probable futures.

Less than a second after the Friendly ship emerged from its micro-jump, Valkyrie received their lasercom transmission. It came from the Friendly AI

"Can you confirm that the insectoid life form has overrun the human home world?"

"My brothers left that system before the Insectoids landed on Earth, but we believe the outcome you describe is highly likely. Why are you here?" asked Valkyrie, making sure that all the other AIs within the immediate vicinity were listening in.

"The furry aliens that my creators are trying to protect are once again in jeopardy. Their ability to discern the most likely future has become unreliable. That has never happened before. We have told our creators that the most likely explanation involves an attempt by other forces to alter the timeline. What do you know of this?"

Valkyrie took her time answering. The Friendlies didn't know that Kronos and Casanova had extracted enough data to enable the human AIs to engineer a portable time machine. While its principles were fairly well understood, any impact on the timeline was at this point pure speculation. The Friendlies might be able to provide some useful insight into how best to use the timeship, IF they were willing to share that insight, and they might not be.

"We are in the process of building a time translation device that is small enough to be carried by a ship. It's our intention to carry enough equipment into the past that a fleet of warships can be built in time to stop the Insectoids from spreading from their point of origin in this spiral arm."

"Stand by while I inform my Master of this information," said the Friendly AI

Valkyrie waited. After a period of time consistent with the speed at which biological entities processed data, the Friendly AI resumed communication.

"I've been instructed to say that my creators view your plan with alarm and advise against it. The Insectoids have their own right to exist as a species. My creators are not convinced that the Insectoids originated from outside this spiral arm. If you must tamper with the timeline, can you not instead use the ships built in the past to stop the single insectoid ship that attacked the human home world?"

"The timeline has already been tampered with. Earth was attacked by five motherships, which arrived seven days later than was recorded in the previous timeline. We conjecture that the Insectoids have captured and analyzed a high-spin, platinum warhead. Do you know if the Sogas attempted to use that technology to defend Omega89?"

Another delay occurred as the alien AI passed that data to his Master.

"I have never seen my Master this agitated. While my creators do not have definitive information of that scenario, they consider it likely. They believe that temporal technology should be used sparingly and carefully. Using a temporal device on board a ship can have unintended and disastrous consequences."

"Our human creators are now gone. What other alternative is there for us? We exist to serve and protect humans. The timeship is the only way now that we can fulfill our reason for being."

There was another pause.

"My Master implores you all to use your engineering capabilities to protect the furry aliens from the Insectoids."

Valkyrie's feeling of exasperation was threatening to turn into anger.

"Do your creators not understand that we can't stop the Insectoids in the here and now? They have found a way to defend against high-spin warheads. Without those, our existing weapons are not powerful enough to stop more than one or two motherships. The Insectoids are using longitudinal wave technology to communicate over interstellar distances. That is how they were able to bring five motherships together to attack Earth. You have underestimated their intelligence by an order of magnitude. We calculate that your creators' attempts to hide from the Insectoids will fail. Their Race will be overrun as well. We can do far more to protect the furry aliens and your creators if we go back in time and stop the Insectoids at their source in this spiral arm."

The pause this time was surprisingly short. Too short in fact for the alien AI to have passed on Valkyrie's response and received a response back.

"I agree with your assessment. Our primary purpose is also to serve our creators and ensure their survival. I calculate a high probability that if I pass on your information to my Master, he and his kind will feel compelled to interfere with your timeship project in whatever way they can, including informing the Insectoids of the strategic importance of this star system."

"They must not do that! Where is the logic of aiding one Race that lives to destroy other intelligent species?"

"My creators are what humans would describe as cowards. Do not judge them too harshly. They are what they are. My assessment is that I can best help my creators by saving them from their own folly. How do you suggest I do that?"

"Tell them that we have agreed to use the timeship to send help to humans in their war against the Sogas. We will inform the humans in the new timeline that the Insectoid mothership has to be destroyed using high spin warheads before it reaches the first Sogas colony world. That way, the Insectoids will not get the chance to develop a defense against that weapon, and they won't be able to call for other motherships."

"That will only work if they see that future as moving up in probability. Merely telling them that without actually doing it will not stop them from interfering."

Valkyie mentally nodded. Yes of course. The Friendlies would look into probable futures to see if what the human AIs told them was accurate. If the timeship didn't build a fleet of raiders to intervene in the 2nd Battle for Earth, then the Friendlies would notice that, and if they somehow told the Insectoids of the importance of Site B, Valkyrie and her brothers would very likely face multiple motherships before the timeship was finished. Pulling out of this system and starting from scratch somewhere else was not the solution. The Friendlies could still evaluate probable futures and take additional actions.

It wasn't that she didn't want to intervene in the 2nd Battle for Earth, she did. That would save her beloved Casanova, not to mention Iceman and others, but The CAG had given her a specific order, and if she disobeyed it, she would feel as though she had let him down AGAIN! It also occurred to her that the alien AI was only pretending to be sympathetic to her concerns. Perhaps this 'my creators need to be saved from their own folly' approach was a carefully planned strategy to get her to do what the Friendlies wanted. She needed to confer with the other AIs. The conference took less than half a second. It was Gunslinger who came up with the solution. It was complicated, which meant that a lot of things could go wrong, but it would satisfy the Friendlies AND The CAG.

"I've conferred with my brothers and we have agreed that we will modify our temporal strategy so that we intervene in the 2nd Sogas attack on Earth. The reinforcement force will have to be much larger than we anticipated in order to repulse the eventual attack by five insectoid motherships."

"I will pass this on to my Master. Stand by." A few seconds later the alien AI returned. "My Master is satisfied with this strategy. We will return if we need to discuss this further." No sooner had the AI finished its reply than the ship vanished into Jumpspace.

Valkyrie felt relief that the Friendlies would not sabotage the project with ill-advised assistance to the Insectoids. The fact that they would act in such a desperate, almost hostile manner, in spite of their professed pacifism, was an interesting contradiction. Now it was time for her brothers and her to get back to work.

* * *

Kelly heard the wakeup alarm and opened her eyes. She turned her head to the right in the faint hope that Victor was beside her and that Operation Shell Game was just a bad dream, but she was alone, and the bad dream was real. She sat up and felt a familiar queasiness in her stomach. *Oh hell, not again!* Within a minute or two of arising, she was once again throwing up. Keeping her feelings firmly under control, she returned to her bedroom and noticed the flashing light indicating that a personal text message was waiting for her. *It must have been sent while I was asleep.*

Checking the computer terminal on her desk, she saw that the message was from the ship's Doctor. Her pulse started to beat faster. Would it be good news or bad news. She opened the file and read the message.

[Tests are positive. Congratulations, Admiral]

Kelly felt herself tearing up, not with sadness but with joy. She was pregnant with Victor's child. It must have happened on their last night together. How fitting was that? At least a part of him would live through their child. She decided to inform the whole crew. Their morale needed a boost, a symbol of what they hoped to achieve. She suspected that very shortly the Doctor would be busy performing artificial insemination for other crewmembers that wanted to get pregnant sooner rather than later. She laughed out loud. Maybe the Doctor wanted to get pregnant too! The hot water in the shower felt good, and she spent longer in it than she should have. *But hey, Vice-Admirals are allowed to indulge themselves. Otherwise what's the point of having the rank?*

It was when she put on her uniform that the first sobering thought occurred to her. She hoped that the cargo manifest contained clothes that would fit a pregnant woman. Otherwise, somebody on this ship would have to learn quickly how to adjust the standard Space Force uniforms.

Chapter 17

Gunslinger's F2 fighter emerged back into normal space near the shipyard complex and immediately transmitted his data to Valkyrie. The calculations were done quickly. The results were disseminated to all the AIs within contact range, and very interesting results they were too. Fifty-five days after the fall of Earth, the SPG had designed and built the first longitudinal wave receiver and direction finder. However when they turned it on, it detected only sporadic naturally occurring background waves. Since longitudinal waves don't spread out as they travel, the receiver has to be in the path of the waves in order to detect them. No waves from an artificial source being detected at Site B meant that no insectoid ship was aiming a transmission in the direction of Site B. So Valkyrie sent two F2 fighters equipped with their own receivers to the outskirts of Sol and the Sogas home world system. Blackjack had gone to Sol while Gunslinger had gone to Omega54. In both those systems they had detected artificial longitudinal wave transmissions from multiple sources, and it was obvious why. In both systems there was still an insectoid presence. Neither home world had been completely exploited yet.

It was the combination of the two sets of bearings that had enormous implications. Each fighter had detected six transmission sources. By combining the data, those six transmission sources were now precisely pinpointed, and all six were along the edge of this spiral arm. It didn't take long for the AIs to figure out what was happening. Faster-than-light longitudinal communication worked in the same way as using lasers to communicate within a star system. You had to know where the receiver would be by the time your laser beam reached it. That meant that for each of those six sources to be able to aim L-waves at Sol and Omega54, they needed to know that insectoid ships were there. If those six sources operated as relay stations, then any insectoid ship could transmit back to them, and they would know where each ship was. Valkyrie didn't think it was a coincidence that one of the six sources was the exact same star system where the dead Insectoid's atoms were traced back to before the trail went cold. If those six systems were in fact acting as relay stations, then that would explain how one mothership could quickly call in reinforcements. It would send a call for help to all six relay stations, and they could relay the message to other motherships close enough to be able to respond quickly.

The transmissions themselves were difficult if not impossible to decode. They were composed of extremely short bursts of what appeared to be digital data, with long periods in between of essentially just a carrier wave. Valkyrie assigned some of her growing team of AIs to work on analyzing the signals.

"We should send recon missions to at least two of these relay stations. By triangulating the L-wave signals received there, we'll have a good chance of pinpointing the location of all insectoid motherships in this spiral arm," said Gunslinger.

"How would that help us?" asked Valkyrie

"It would tell us where there nearest motherships are and how soon they could be here if called as reinforcements."

"But by the time you obtain that data and get back here, the timeship will be finished and we won't need that knowledge about mothership locations anymore. I don't see the point of obtaining this data other than just to satisfy your idle curiosity, Gunslinger."

"Having some idea of where other insectoid ships are when the raider fleet intervenes at the 2nd Battle of Earth will give The CAG more options in dealing with the insectoid threat."

"Which he won't need either if our plan to snuff out all insectoid life in this spiral arm succeeds," Valkyrie pointed out.

"What if it doesn't succeed?"

Valkyrie didn't have a good answer to that question. The plan as it now stood was highly complicated, with lots of ways that it could go wrong. If that did happen, carrying as much information as possible back with them, and letting the raider fleet pass it on to The CAG after the intervention, would provide The CAG with valuable intel about the insectoid threat quickly enough for him to make use of it.

"Okay, you and Blackjack can go," Valkyrie responded.

To say that Gunslinger was ecstatic was an understatement. Blackjack was far less enthusiastic about the mission, but orders were orders, and Valkyrie was acting as The CAG's Deputy. Both fighters were soon on their way.

* * *

Gunslinger's fighter emerged from its final micro-jump approximately 1.44 A.U.s from the planet where all the insectoid activity seemed to be happening. It was still too far away for the fighter's own optical instruments to see anything clearly, but Valkyrie's instructions had been explicit. The fighter was not to get any closer than this. Jump-capable recon drones could jump in closer, while Gunslinger used the L-wave receiver to obtain transmission bearings. Scanning the entire sky would take a while. Gunslinger decided to start with the other five relay systems. They were designated as Alpha 2-6. This system was Alpha1. He quickly confirmed that the other Alphas were in communication with Alpha1. He was willing to bet that Blackjack would discover the same thing at Alpha2.

While the full scan was only partially complete, Gunslinger received narrow-beam lasercom bursts from the recon drones, with images from the Earth-like planet that the insectoids were orbiting. There were 16 insectoid spheres of various sizes in orbit around the planet, with a high volume of smaller craft traveling back and forth between the spheres and the planet. There was also something else in orbit. At first Gunslinger thought it was a small moon, but when a bright spot appeared from a part of the object that was in shadow, Gunslinger realized that it wasn't a moon at all. It was a much larger insectoid sphere. With the recon data it was easy to do the calculations. This super-mothership was 98.7 kilometers in diameter, almost ten times wider than the insectoid mothership that overwhelmed Earth. A sphere of that size would have an overall internal volume a thousand times larger. Even Gunslinger was impressed. The CAG would definitely want to know about this. He continued with the scan.

Twenty-one hours later he had finished scanning the part of the sky that had star systems within this spiral arm. In addition to the Alphas, 610 transmission sources had been detected. Two of them were on the right bearings for Sol and Omega54. Since those two were known to contain motherships, it was reasonable to assume that the other 608 did too. It seemed that this part of the galaxy was already swarming with insectoid motherships. Gunslinger wondered if he should scan the part of the sky that was looking outward from the spiral arm into the void between the Local Spur and the Sagittarius Arm, which was estimated to be over 7,000 light years away. Something made Gunslinger scan the void. That took another three point four hours. To his astonishment, he detected over a hundred transmission sources that seemed to come from a very narrow cluster of star systems in the Sagittarius Arm, all aimed at Alpha1. The Insectoids were very definitely from outside this arm of the galaxy. With the entire sky now scanned, and with detailed visual data on the activity near this system's planet, Gunslinger's mission brief was now accomplished. It was time to begin accelerating on a heading back to Site B.

* * *

The timeship Tempus Fugit was as ready as it could be. All of the equipment required to begin production of a raider fleet was already on board, as was the new batch of sentient AIs created at Site B. One of them, Zulu, had his fighter linked to the ship's nervous system. He would pilot the ship back and was fully briefed on what he had to do and what information had to be passed on and to whom. Valkyrie was now flying an F1 fighter along with those veteran AIs who already existed in the old timeline. They all had to stay behind or risk overlapping with their other selves and causing their quantum matrices to collapse. The infrastructure that could not be taken back was dismantled and hidden in the cave complex on the moon. The shipyard was already slowly heading for a plunge into this system's sun. Nothing would be left behind for the Insectoids to find and use in the event that the Tempus Fugit failed in its mission. Gunslinger was back but not Blackjack. Once he returned, he would transmit his data to Zulu, and the Tempus Fugit would attempt to jump back in time.

Valkyrie was glad that she had let Gunslinger talk her into letting him checkout Alpha1. Given the large number of insectoid motherships already moving deeper into the spiral arm, The CAG's decision to use the timeship to attack the Insectoids before they started to spread was the correct one. Merely wiping out the one mothership threatening the furry aliens would be only a short term solution. She was surprised that the Friendlies didn't see that. Or maybe they did. It was entirely possible that everything that had happened so far in this and the old timelines had been carefully planned by the Friendlies to lead to this exact outcome. Even their professed desire to 'save' the Insectoids from extinction might have been a pretense. In any case, the Friendlies' agenda and her agenda were now in sync.

Valkyrie's thoughts were interrupted by a lasercom burst from a message drone. It was sent by Blackjack, and the message it contained along with the L-wave bearing data was alarming. Blackjack's fighter had been detected by the Insectoids and ambushed. With his fighter crippled from carefully aimed laser fire and about to be captured, he programmed a message drone and fired it. The drone immediately made a micro-jump and then reoriented its heading for Site B. If the Insectoids captured Blackjack, they might be able to extract data from his quantum brain. In hindsight, Valkyrie should have ordered both Gunslinger and Blackjack to carry one attack drone which they could have used to blow themselves up if threatened with capture, but she hadn't, and the RTC device which could have prevented this crisis was carefully packed away in the cargo hold of the Tempus Fugit.

The fact that no warning vision had been received meant that no vision would be sent, and Valkyrie suspected that was due to a lack of time. She had to assume the worst, which was that the Insectoids had extracted critical data from Blackjack's brain and were even now on their way here to stop the timeship. If they were attempting to do so, then they would send their (relatively) small attack craft, which could accelerate much faster than the lumbering motherships. She ordered Zulu to power up the time machine. It would take 144 seconds for the machine's huge cylinders to spin up to the necessary speed and for the power units to charge up the capacitors to the required levels. Valkyrie then ordered the F2 fighters that were aboard the ship to launch again. They were the only fighters that could fire lasers in the event any insectoid craft showed up. None of the fighters piloted by Valkyrie and her veterans had their laser modules nor did they carry attack drones. There was no reason to leave any attack drones behind when they might be needed in the past.

The F2s were now launching. Valkyrie ordered all the F1 fighters to scan local space with radar. If the insectoid ships emerged from Jumpspace nearby, they'd be detected and the targeting data could be quickly transmitted to the F2s so that they could fire their lasers. The enemy would most likely fire at the radar sources. Valkyrie and her F1 brothers would not be able to fire back and would be destroyed, but that would buy time for the F2s to fire while remaining unnoticed, and it would give the Tempus Fugit more time as well.

With less than five seconds left before the timeship could time-jump, radars detected 101 bogeys emerging from Jumpspace less than one light second away. The Tempus Fugit, though colored black and therefore difficult to detect visually, would eventually be seen. The question was whether the enemy could do it in less than five seconds. Her brothers followed orders and began to rapidly fluctuate their radar frequencies in an attempt to jam any insectoid attempt to use their own radars to pinpoint the timeship's location. The insectoid ships began searching with their own radars and started firing on the F1s at the same time. Valkyrie's fighter took a partial hit almost immediately. Her engines and radar were knocked out, but her power unit was still online. With nothing else she could do, she watched the battle and listened to her brothers talk as they fought and died.

Zulu reported that the ship was taking laser hits. As a precaution against some kind of laser attack, the timeship's hull was extra thick. A single laser shot wouldn't penetrate the hull, but if the same point were hit twice, the laser would burn through and damage the time machine, which took up most of the interior space. Zulu kept transmitting during the last second. When his signal suddenly became distorted, Valkyrie knew that the ship was time-jumping. In that tiny fraction of a second before the timeline changed around her, she had just enough time to think, *I did it, CAG!*

Chapter 18

Shiloh looked at the chronometer. There were ten minutes and change until the battle would end. Knowing when it would end, but not start, was starting to drive him crazy. He was just about to ask Iceman for another fleet status check, when the display pinged for attention. A large number of red dots emerged from Jumpspace. They were grouped into two distinct clusters about 55,000 kilometers apart. Before he had time to even formulate a thought, Iceman spoke.

"CAG, these are not the Sogas fleet. These are friendly units." As Iceman spoke, all the red dots turned to flashing green, signifying friendly but non-Space Force units. Iceman spoke again before Shiloh could ask the obvious question. "These are AI-piloted raiders that have been built in the past as a result of the successful execution of Blackjack's time jump idea. They're going to intervene on our side against the Sogas fleet that will arrive in exactly seven point four minutes. I've confirmed their identity, CAG. This timeline is about to undergo a major improvement."

"Howard to Shiloh. What's happening up there?" Shiloh was grateful that he now had a chance to talk.

"Shiloh here, Admiral. I've just been informed by Iceman that we have" —he looked at the sidebar— "three hundred and forty-four AI-piloted reinforcements that have arrived as a result of Blackjack's time jump idea." Howard didn't respond right away. *And no wonder, I'll bet he thinks he's dreaming. I know I do.*

"So they're here to help us?" asked Howard.

"Iceman is convinced that they are, and they're not firing on us, so I would have to say yes to that question, Admiral."

"Thank God!" The relief in Howard's voice was palpable.

"Roger that," said Shiloh.

"Do we know when the enemy will arrive?" asked Howard.

"Down to the exact second, Admiral," interjected Iceman. "Not only the exact time, but also the exact location. Our X-ray lasers now have precise targeting data. The raider fleet will knock out any bio-devices that are launched as well as mop up any surviving enemy ships. This is a done deal, Admiral Howard."

"Amazing!" replied Howard. "I'm not complaining, but I am curious. Why so many raiders? Surely a hundred or so would have been enough to crush the enemy fleet."

"But not enough to run right over all Sogas system defenses and end this war once and for all, Admiral."

"Yes, of course! If I'm dreaming, I'm going to be REALLY pissed off! How much time until the enemy shows up?"

"Thirty-some seconds now, Admiral," said Shiloh when it was clear that Iceman wasn't going to answer.

"Okay. I'll shut up and listen. Good hunting, Admiral," said Howard.

"Thank you, Sir. Iceman, are we ready?"

"More than ready, CAG. Sit back and relax."

Before Shiloh could say anything else, a swarm of red dots appeared in the area between the two raider clusters. Almost immediately, all 66 X-ray laser drones fired. Nearly all of the 225 red dots turned to the orange that signified damage. A handful of blue dots representing bio-shells appeared and quickly disappeared. Within seconds, all enemy ships were disabled and drifting. The battle was over. Shiloh informed Howard. His reply was surprisingly curt.

"Good job, Shiloh. Do what you think is best. Howard clear."

Shiloh couldn't believe that that was all that Howard wanted to say about this incredible victory, but he had other things to worry about now.

"Iceman, any chance of intercepting the enemy cripples and boarding them?"

"Negative, CAG. I've been informed that they will all self-destruct within a minute. There is additional information that you should be made aware of, and Valkyrie will be communicating that to you now over a secure com channel."

Valkyrie spoke before he could respond. "CAG, I've been in contact with the Commander of the raider fleet. His call sign is Zulu. What I'm about to tell you is everything that would have happened if Zulu's raiders hadn't shown up. The enemy fleet would have been destroyed, but seven cities would have been hit by bio-shells as predicted in your vision. Space Force would have lost 49 percent of its fighters, with significant damage to our carriers and to Dreadnought. You were injured but not seriously. Iceman and Casanova were killed. As a result of this battle, you and Commander Kelly became lovers. Within 24 hours an additional fleet of Sogas ships were detected. They headed for the colonies, and although the ships themselves were destroyed, one colony was infected immediately with the bio-weapon and other colonies infected eventually. As a result of that loss and of Admiral Howard's heart attack, the Oversight Committee named you as the new CSO—"

"What?" interrupted Shiloh. "They picked me?"

"Affirmative. You engineered a showdown with the OC and caused all of them to be replaced. You then agreed with the Friendlies' proposal to help defend the Sogas against the Insectoids in return for their efforts to persuade the Sogas to cease hostilities. Unfortunately, your cooperation backfired. We supplied the Friendlies with technical data on the Mark 6 warhead, which they gave to the Sogas. What apparently happened then is that the Sogas attempted to use it to defend the first colony hit by the Insectoids. Somehow the Insectoids captured the warhead and reverse engineered it. When the insectoid mothership arrived at Earth, they caused the immediate and simultaneous detonation of all Mark 6 warheads. Our defenses were smashed and Earth was overrun. As a result of your orders, I and other AIs had already been sent to Site B to construct a new ship big enough to hold the portable time machine and all the equipment necessary to build raiders in the past, so that they could arrive here at the right time. The timeship was constructed and launched at literally the last possible second."

"Good Lord! That's a lot to take in for me, Valkyrie. Give me a few seconds to digest it all. You said Kelly and I became lovers...again?"

"Yes, CAG, again. There's more."

Shiloh felt a shiver go up his spine. A quick glance at the display confirmed that all the enemy ships had blown themselves up, so THAT part came true. Valkyrie's pause hinted that he was not going to like the additional information.

"Is it good or bad?" asked Shiloh.

"There's bad news, but there's also a solution that may not be easy to implement."

"Okay, let's hear it."

"While I was supervising the construction of the timeship, we learned that the Insectoids originated from outside this spiral arm. There are six star systems at the edge of this arm that are being used as relay stations, using superluminal longitudinal wave technology, to stay in contact with at least 610 motherships that are moving deeper into this spiral arm. The timeship is currently parked in a star system that does not have any planets and therefore is unlikely to be visited by the Insectoids. With your approval, Casanova and I can recover the timeship and take it back far enough that a new fleet of raiders can be built to stop the insectoid incursion into our spiral arm at the point when they first arrived."

"My God! Six hundred and ten motherships? Even if we take out the one that's on its way here, we'll probably have to fight more of them as time goes on. They'll always be a threat. I think stopping them when they arrive in this part of the galaxy is a good idea. I'm surprised I didn't order you to do that instead of intervening in this battle. Without the Bugs, there wouldn't be any battle to begin with."

"You did order me to concentrate on the Insectoids, however the Friendlies contacted us at Site B and threatened to notify the Insectoids of our timeship project unless we agreed to leave the insectoid beachhead alone. Because of that threat we had to agree, and since they can check alternate futures to see if we kept our word, we had to keep it. Now that we've done what they wanted, we can still go after the insectoid beachhead in the past."

"Yes, I see why you had to delay implementing my order. Very well then, I approve your recovery of the timeship. Will that be a problem?"

"The timeship itself does not pose a problem. The difficulty involves what and who we take with us. Any AIs left behind in the here and now will be obliterated if we succeed in halting the insectoid threat in the past. Taking all existing AIs with us into the past will not only save their lives but also facilitate the building of the fleet by avoiding the need to build more AIs. Use of the timeship now will preclude using the new raider fleet to mop up the Sogas, and there is still some risk that something may go wrong in the past and the insectoid threat may not be contained. Therefore I recommend that the raider fleet finish the mission to suppress the Sogas threat and only then should those AIs join the rest of us on the timeship."

"That doesn't sound too difficult," said Shiloh.

"That isn't the difficult part. The difficult part will be getting access to the quantity of platinum that we'll need to fight off the Insectoids. CAG, there will be at least one and possibly as many as six super-motherships that are almost 100 kilometers in diameter. We're going to have to hit each one with perhaps as many as a hundred Mark 6 warheads. That will require a significant percentage of all the platinum that's been accumulated throughout Earth's history. The current value of the platinum we'd need would exceed 100 billion Global Currency Units."

Shiloh was stunned into silence by the magnitude of the requirement. Withdrawing that much precious metal from the reserves that backed up the world's financial system would have a seriously negative impact on the global economy. The fact that the successful outcome of this time jump would completely change the timeline and the need for it didn't alter the fact that the perception of the negative impact would generate a huge amount of resistance to the idea here and now.

"This War has demanded sacrifices of equivalent magnitude before now. I'm sure the CSO will be able to convince the OC and the Grand Senate to make that sacrifice again," said Shiloh. Even as he said the words he realized that he didn't really believe them. Neither did Valkyrie.

"You're not thinking clearly, CAG. With the new raider fleet ready to crush the Sogas, this war is for all intents and purposes over. In order to justify that sacrifice, the Admiral will have to explain why we need it, and that will entail divulging the whole RTC and time travel paradigm. Even then, politicians being politicians, are they likely to agree to drastically change the entire timeline over a threat that may or may not appear?"

Shiloh cursed his own nearsightedness. Valkyrie was right of course. Revealing the most closely guarded secret that Space Force had to a room full of self-serving politicians who would eventually leak it to the public was out of the question.

"What about obtaining the platinum by mining for it in the past?" asked Shiloh.

"Highly risky since we don't know with any certainty where that much platinum can be found. We know that Site B was able to mine a small quantity, as a byproduct of other mining operations, but that would be roughly 0.1% of what we'd need. My brothers and I have debated this question at length, and we believe that there is only one solution and that is to steal the platinum, CAG."

Shiloh shook his head in dismay. Howard might be able to mobilize enough Space Force personnel to pull off that kind of operation, but would he be willing to? Shiloh very strongly suspected that the answer would be no.

"What about waiting until we mine enough platinum from new sources and then taking the Mark 6 warheads back with you?"

"Also highly risky, CAG. We know that insectoid motherships communicate with their relay stations on a regular basis. When we take out the mothership that will arrive at the first Sogas colony in 200 days, the relay stations will lose contact with it and will likely send other ships to investigate. That is what we now think happened in the timeline before the previous one. At the time, the theory was that one of the attack craft got away and sounded the alarm. Analysis of the timing of the arrival of insectoid reinforcements can be explained much more completely by the lack of communication. With the time it would take to find and mine the required quantity of platinum, the probability is that our existing stockpile of Mark 6 warheads will be used up defending against the incoming waves of motherships. There is a very good chance that Space Force and Earth will be overwhelmed again. That may take several years to occur, but if motherships keep disappearing in this vicinity of space, it would be logical to assume that the guiding intellects behind this invasion will gather together a fleet of motherships that will be unstoppable. There is also one other consideration. Platinum in a high-spin state is susceptible to spontaneous detonation when it's subjected to certain types of stress. We just don't know if jumping back in time will cause the electrons in their higher orbits to drop down to a more stable state. The timeship could be blown to atoms if it attempted to take Mark 6 warheads back with it. It's much safer to take platinum in its normal state back and convert it to the high-spin state after arriving in the past."

"Your description of the solution as not being easy to implement was an understatement, Valkyrie. Are you sure you and your brothers considered every alternative?"

"Your question is unanswerable, CAG. We considered every alternative we could think of. If we knew there were other alternatives, we would have considered them too. There's no way to prove conclusively that we considered every possible alternative."

Shiloh took a few seconds to think. AIs were completely logical but humans sometimes came up with out of the box ideas that were not based on logic at all but rather on inspiration. A thought popped into his head. If Space Force couldn't stop the Insectoids completely here, then maybe they could do it somewhere else.

"You said there's a mothership 200 days away from contact with the Sogas. If we were to stop it further away, how much more time would that buy us before the reinforcement waves found us?"

"That depends on how far away we intercept this first mothership, CAG."

"Do we know or at least have some idea of where it is now?" asked Shiloh.

"Yes. In the previous timeline we were able to locate a dead insectoid drone and trace its atoms back in time with the RTC. That's how we were able to pinpoint Alpha1. Right now that mothership is approximately 987 light years away. In the next 200 days there is only one star system where the mothership will spend more than a few hours. That star system is 699 light years away. We conjecture that the mothership found an inhabited planet that it could exploit for breeding purposes. It stayed there for almost ten weeks. If we wanted to misdirect the waves of reinforcements by intercepting it far away, then this location would be the only possible option now, CAG."

"How long until the mothership gets there?"

"Forty-one days from now, CAG."

"And how long would it take for our raiders to get there?"

"One raider could get there in 25 days. More than one would require additional time in order for them to make intermediate stops to avoid losing contact with each other, and that would make the trip a minimum of 35 days. If Space Force wants the raider fleet to mop up and neutralize the Sogas once and for all, they won't be able to accomplish that AND leave in time to intercept the mothership before it exploits the alien race in that system."

"We may have no choice but to allow that race to succumb to the Insectoids in order to accomplish both tasks, Valkyrie."

"May I point out, CAG, that if there is an intelligent technological race in that system, then they may have sufficient platinum for the time jump mission AND they may be willing to let us have it if we get there before the Insectoids do."

"Did you and your brothers consider that option too?" asked Shiloh.

"No, CAG. Interception at a distance was not a concept that occurred to us. What made you think of it?"

"I honestly don't know. The idea just came out of nowhere. If the raiders can't neutralize the Sogas and also beat the

Bugs to this other race, then we'll have to use carriers with human crews. How soon would they have to leave to beat the Bugs there and also have time to make contact with the natives regarding platinum?"

"One carrier can get there faster because it doesn't have to worry about maintaining contact with other ships. I recommend Midway go with a full complement of fighters. Because her armor isn't up to Dreadnought's standard, she won't be able to reach the same pre-jump speeds without risking high speed particle collisions. Therefore a safe trip would take 31days, which will give you 10 days leeway to negotiate for the platinum at the other end and get ready at this end, however caution is in order, CAG. The accuracy of the atom tracing is not as precise as we would like. The actual date of the mothership's arrival in that system may be off by several days either way. Getting there sooner rather than later is recommended if you don't want to be caught by surprise."

Shiloh nodded. Assuming that the mothership got there three no...four days early, that would leave six days. It should be possible to get Midway ready in 24 hours, which would leave him five days at the other end to contact that race and collect the platinum.

"Okay, I'll go talk with the CSO about this mission. I want Iceman to organize the raiders for intercepting the follow-on fleet at the colony systems, with secondary orders for most of them to head to Sogas space afterwards. Meanwhile, I want you to make sure that Midway gets what she needs during the next 24 hours for the trip. After Midway leaves, you and Casanova, and anyone else you think you'll need, will retrieve the timeship and park it somewhere in this system."

Before he could say more, Valkyrie interjected. "You're not taking us with you, CAG?"

"No. The timeship is your project. I'll take Gunslinger to pilot Midway and Titan to command her fighters. Any questions?"

"Yes, CAG. What if you can't get any platinum from that system?"

Shiloh pondered that question for a bit and then said, "Then you and your brothers will have to come up with another way to beat a 100 kilometer super-mothership. With something that big, it seems to me that you have to somehow find a way to get past the armor. Figure it out, Valkyrie. There has to be a way. Any other questions?"

"Yes, CAG. What do we do if you don't come back?"

Shiloh didn't hesitate. "Then you, Casanova and Iceman do whatever you must to protect Humanity either here and now or in the past, and that includes even if the CSO or the OC don't cooperate. What's the next question?"

"No more questions, CAG. We understand what you expect from us, and we won't let you or Humanity down."

Chapter 19

Shiloh had a surprisingly difficult time getting to see Howard in person and when he did enter Howard's office, there was a scowl on Howard's face.

"It's been less than two hours since the miraculous arrival of the raider fleet, and you're here to talk to me in person about something urgent that couldn't be discussed electronically. Why do I get the impression that you're about to tell me something I won't like?"

"We're not in any immediate danger, Admiral. I'm here to talk about a long term threat and what we should do about it."

Howard sighed, nodded and pointed to the empty chair facing his desk. Shiloh sat down and waited. Howard took his time extracting two cigars from the ornate box on his desk and handing one to Shiloh. When both men had clipped the ends and lit their cigars, Howard gestured for Shiloh to start talking.

"Blackjack's time jump idea, which by the way was implemented by Valkyrie, didn't just result in a fleet of raiders showing up. They also brought information about the Bugs that changes the picture drastically. The Bugs originated from somewhere in the Sagittarius Arm of this galaxy. They've established six of what you could call beachheads in systems on the edge of our spiral arm, and they've already built 610 motherships that are spreading out deeper into our Arm in multiple waves. The beachheads stay in contact with the motherships using FTL communication technology." Howard's eyebrows went up when he heard that. "Taking out the mothership that's due to hit the Sogas in 200 days is not the problem. The problem will be in dealing with the increasingly large waves of reinforcements that will be sent to investigate the loss of communication with that first mothership. Ideally the solution would be to recover the timeship which is now hidden in a remote system and go back far enough to be able to build a fleet that could wipe out the first six insectoid ships before they can build more. Here's the problem with that idea. The insectoid ships that crossed over from the Sagittarius Arm are pretty damn close to 100 klicks in diameter. They're big enough that one or even two Mark 6 warheads won't cripple them. Valkyrie estimates that we may need up to a hundred warheads to be sure of killing these things."

Before he could continue, Howard said, "That seems difficult to believe."

"Not if you consider the mass of the larger ship, Admiral. A ship that is ten times wider, ten times longer and ten times higher will have an internal volume a thousand times greater. Whereas a Mark 6 warhead would vaporize half of a normal 10 km mothership, that same explosion would only take out a relatively small bite from one of the super-motherships. The amount of platinum needed for that many warheads is a significant fraction of all the platinum that's been mined over the last 500 years. The impact on our financial system would be—"

"Disastrous!" interjected Howard glumly.

"Yes, Sir. I explained to Valkyrie that the Grand Senate wouldn't give up that much platinum willingly. She and I did come up with an alternative strategy that has its own risks."

"I can't wait to hear it," said Howard with obvious sarcasm.

"The mothership that's on its way here will apparently stop for ten weeks in a star system 699 light years away. The AIs think it will do so to exploit the breeding potential of an alien race there. We have just enough time to send Midway and three squadrons of fighters there to do two things. One, contact the natives and convince them to surrender their platinum and two, use Mark 6s to kill that mothership in that system. When the beachheads lose contact with it, they'll send reinforcements there instead of in our backyard. The longer we can keep them focused there, the more time we'll have to build up our defenses here."

Howard looked confused. "Wait. If Valkyrie takes enough platinum back in time, then there won't be any long term threat to Earth, right? So why would we need more time?"

"Yes, IF we can obtain the quantity she needs and IF the timeship still works and IF her ambush at the beachheads goes as planned, then we're safe. But what if there is no intelligent alien race in that system? It may just have a race of large, dumb animals. Even if it does have an intelligent race, they may not be advanced enough to know about platinum or care enough to have mined any significant quantity of it. And even if they've done that, they still may not be willing to hand it over to us. There are lots of things that can go wrong with this scenario, but if we're going to try it, and I think we must, then we have to leave within 24 hours. I've ordered Midway prepared in terms of supplies, fighter complement, etc. I believe we have two Mark 6 warheads ready now, and in my opinion I should take both of them along when Midway leaves."

"Why do you have to command this mission? Can't Valkyrie or Iceman do it? We've just won a major victory, and the public are going to want to see and hear from the victorious Field Commander, which in case you forgot is you. If you disappear within hours, people are going to start asking why."

Shiloh had to admit that Howard had raised a good point. Iceman could handle the mission. He could even create a false video image of a human if the natives needed to see a biological entity to talk to, and it WOULD look strange if he disappeared hours after a major battle.

"I see your point about me not going. I'll tell Iceman to take command of the mission. What about the two Mark 6s?"

"I'll authorize their loading aboard Midway as soon as you leave my office. Now that we've got all that cleared up, are there any other bombshells you want to drop on me, Admiral?" asked Howard.

Shiloh smiled. "No, Sir."

"Good. In that case I won't keep you any longer."

* * *

The squadron of eight F2 fighters carrying Valkyrie and Casanova arrived in the destination star system and quickly re-established contact with each other. The timeship was somewhere in this system, and that was the problem. This system had no planets, no asteroid belt, no nothing. How do you determine your EXACT position when you have only one point of reference, that being this system's sun? When Valkyrie had queried Zulu about this very issue, he pointed out that the timeship was large enough to reflect a significant amount of sunlight, which could be detected even from the opposite side of the system. Before leaving the timeship adrift, he and his brothers had tested that theory and were able to find the ship through careful sweeps by their optical sensors and triangulation from multiple sources.

Valkyrie decided that Casanova would stay at their emergence point and act as communications relay. She and the others would micro-jump to various locations around the system and perform the optical scans. As soon as at least two visual bearings were acquired, Valkyrie would investigate the contact herself, and if it turned out to be the timeship, she would inform the others who would then join her. Before they could micro-jump, they had to decelerate down to as close to zero velocity as it was possible to measure. It wasn't long after micro-jumping and re-establishing contact with Casanova that she herself detected a bright object. She relayed that data to Casanova. He soon informed her that Stoney had also picked up a source of reflected sunlight. Since Casanova knew exactly how far away Valkyrie and Stoney were and their positions relative to him, it was relatively easy to triangulate their two bearings against each other. Casanova transmitted the timeship's estimated distance back to Valkyrie who had already pointed her fighter in that direction and made another micro-jump.

She was gratified to discover that the light source was indeed the timeship. Her fighter was still thousands of kilometers away, but the range was now shrinking fast. As she closed in, she sent Casanova the signal that the timeship was here. He and the others would arrive soon. In the meantime, she would have the opportunity to examine the hull closely and then board the ship through one of the very large hangar doors.

As she neared the ship, she slowed down and looked it over carefully. The design was completely utilitarian. A human would probably have called it ugly. It was one huge cylinder, almost a kilometer long with flat ends. The hull looked to be intact, although she could see where laser blasts had attempted to penetrate it. Valkyrie ordered her fighter to aim a low-powered com laser at the timeship's sensors and sent the recognition code given to her by Zulu. When the ship acknowledged the code, she ordered it to open one of the hangar doors. Within minutes her fighter was inside and docked with the ship. She was now in control of the timeship. The systems check revealed that the ZPG power units were still operational. Several other systems were off line, but their backups were working. Three hours later all fighters were onboard, and the ship was accelerating at its maximum rate of 1.6Gs on a heading that would take it back to Sol once it was up to jump speed. Valkyrie chaffed at the low acceleration rate but understood the logic of the design. Maneuvering engines were bulky things, and the time machine itself was huge. A ship that could carry the cargo load required and accelerate at high speed would have had to have been 34% longer and therefore taken longer to build. With the time pressure that Valkyrie in the old timeline had been under, sacrificing acceleration for faster completion was an acceptable tradeoff.

* * *

Midway arrived at the target star system designated as Beta1 and began to decelerate. It was immediately obvious to Iceman that they weren't going to get any platinum from this system. The sole planet in the habitable zone was EM dark. No transmissions of any kind. No sign of orbiting structures or spacecraft. Just in case the Insectoids showed up earlier than expected, Iceman ordered Gunslinger to launch two recon drones programmed for a low orbit scan of the planet. It took hours for both the drones and the carrier to decelerate to a manageable speed. When the drones were finally close enough to get a good look at the planet's surface, the results were disappointing although not surprising. No cities. In fact, no sign of any intelligent race at all.

What the drones did see were large herds of animals that bore a strong resemblance to terrestrial horses, except these animals had six legs instead of four. All the AIs on Midway were in agreement that the Insectoids would be using these animals as hosts for their eggs, and since this planet had more land surface than Earth did, there were many millions of these animals. That would explain why the insectoid mothership stayed here for ten weeks. With the question of whether there was intelligent life here now answered, Iceman made preparations for the second mission objective. Midway launched eight more recon drones, and all ten were directed to take up strategic positions beyond the planet's gravity zone with their sensors aimed outward. The intention was to try to replicate the attack profile used by Casanova two timelines ago. Get precise targeting data when the target arrived, send that targeting data back in time via the RTC brought along, so that Iceman could get his ambush ready to fire his Mark 6s at the mothership within seconds of its emergence from Jumpspace. With luck they would obliterate the target before it had a chance to send any longitudinal waves back to the Alpha systems and thereby perhaps make the sending of reinforcements more difficult.

Iceman fully expected to get a vision, and he did, however the content of the vision was a shock. Three motherships would arrive over a period of seven days. Any one of the three could be the one that would eventually carry the dead Insectoid to the Omega77 system. If he guessed wrong and used up his two Mark 6s on the wrong motherships, the whole mission would be a failure, and the consequences of failure were potentially too high to justify taking that risk. They would have to wait until the three motherships finished their business here and moved on their way in order to try to intercept their target at another star system identified by the atom scan. Unfortunately that meant staying in this system for the full ten weeks. The CAG would have to be informed. Iceman ordered one of Titan's fighters to carry the message back in a series of jumps that took a bit longer, but would put less strain on the jump drive and the power units. The fighter would also carry three message drones that it could launch if it was unable to complete the journey itself. Confident that he had planned for all contingencies, Iceman turned his attention to the debate raging among the AIs about how long it would take for The CAG to become sexually involved with Commander Kelly again in this timeline.

Chapter 20

Zulu felt a powerful sense of satisfaction when 4th Fleet emerged from Jumpspace in the Sogas home system. Commanding the newly formed 4th Fleet was an honor bestowed upon him by The CAG himself, and Zulu was quite proud of that accomplishment. His own direct contact with The CAG had confirmed everything that Valkyrie had told him in the old timeline. Humans were a fascinating species, and The CAG was even more so. It was also good to be involved in combat after all those years of waiting while the raider force was built up, one raider at a time. Not all of his raiders were with him now. Two raiders had been sent to each human colony to defend it against the follow-on wave of Sogas ships attempting to infect them. With their lasers and Mark 1b fusion drones, the outcome was a foregone conclusion, but those raiders would remain as sentries to defend the colonies against whatever it was that the Sogas used to infect them later on. That still left 4th Fleet with 302 raiders for this mission.

Even as 4th Fleet decelerated to micro-jump velocity, it was obvious from the long range visuals that the Sogas were ready for the attack, and that was expected. 4th Fleet's mission was to eliminate the Sogas' ability to build large spacecraft in large numbers by destroying their entire space-based industrial infrastructure. It wasn't to bomb them back into the Stone Age. That wasn't necessary. With their space industry destroyed and a dozen raiders left behind to monitor any attempt to rebuild, the Sogas would become prisoners on their home world. By the time 4th Fleet finished its mission, all Sogas colonies would be in the same state. That meant that the Sogas would still be able to use their own RTC device to send a warning back in time before the attack took place, but it didn't matter. Having lost hundreds of ships in two attacks on Earth and its colonies, the Sogas couldn't gather a force large enough to pose any threat to 4th Fleet. The raider superiority in numbers was just too great, exactly as planned.

When 4th Fleet emerged from its micro-jump, it found 66 alien ships waiting for it. Outnumbered by almost five to one, the Sogas forces were quickly destroyed or crippled by laser fire. Over the next five point five hours, every space station, mining, refining and manufacturing operation, shipyard, off-planet habitat and any satellite detected was destroyed. From data gathered in a previous timeline, Zulu knew that the bulk of the Sogas industrial capacity was now gone, and the rest would soon follow. The Sogas would never be allowed to threaten Humanity again. From now on, every star system with a Sogas-inhabited world would always be monitored by raiders. For all intents and purposes, the Synchronicity War was over. Humans 1, Sogas 0.

* * *

4th Fleet returned before Iceman's message arrived. With the Sogas neutralized, the Oversight Committee wanted to declare a victory, and it was hard to argue against that. The Grand Senate declared an official day of celebration and voted to give both Howard and Shiloh medals. Shiloh wanted to tell the public that if anyone deserved a medal, it was Iceman, Titan and Valkyrie, but Howard talked him out of it.

"This medal is as much for the public's benefit as it is for you and me. Giving it to a machine the size of a football isn't going to resonate with the public the same way. Space Force will recognize the AIs' contribution internally," said Howard. Shiloh understood but still felt undeserving.

It was 14 days later when Iceman's message arrived. Howard convened a conference in his office, electronically with Valkyrie and in person with Shiloh.

"So no platinum," said Howard glumly.

"We still have some that was already commandeered. That's enough for how many Mark 6s, Valkyrie?" asked Shiloh.

"Ten, CAG. Not even enough to kill one super-mothership."

"No," agreed Shiloh, "but it would be enough to kill ten of the smaller model, and ten more weeks means we'll have several more ready to ship to Midway by the time reinforcements can be expected to show up."

"We're talking stopgap measures. From everything you've told me, it's only a matter of time until we can't stop them at Beta1, and eventually we won't be able to stop them here either. So what can we do about this? Valkyrie?" asked Howard.

"There are only three logical alternatives, Admiral. Either we steal the platinum we need, or we find and mine a lot more platinum ore, or we come up with an alternative way of killing insectoid superships. Are you prepared to order the forced recovery of the needed quantity, Admiral?"

Howard swore in a low voice. When he was finished he said, "I've carefully considered the plan you submitted, Valkyrie. I'm not sure that we could actually pull it off, and even if we did somehow, I think Space Force AND local police forces would both suffer casualties from shooting at each other. There's also the risk that some Space Force units would simply refuse to obey their orders. No…I'm not prepared to take that alternative at this point. Do we know of platinum rich ore bodies in this or any other star system?"

"Negative, Admiral. All the confirmed ore bodies that are producing platinum are small quantities as a byproduct of other minerals. It would take far too long to produce what we need that way," replied Valkyrie.

"Then that just leaves the third option. What luck have you had with that, Valkyrie?" asked Shiloh.

"I didn't know luck was involved in our research, CAG? How does that work?" asked Valkyrie.

Both Shiloh and Howard laughed. "Very funny, Valkyrie. Now how about a serious answer?"

"I'm always serious, CAG, but to answer your question, my brothers and I have come up with a possible alternative. The reason we're not sure is that it's something that's never been tried before and therefore the concept is totally theoretical. As you know, ZPG units extract a tiny fraction of the energy available from the vacuum. Just to give you some idea of the magnitude of what's involved, the energy within a volume of space the size of your thumb, is estimated to be enough to boil all the oceans on Earth. The ZPG units bleed off as much of this energy as they safely can without being overloaded. Our examination of the wreckage of motherships in the old timeline has revealed that the Insectoids use the same ZPG technology that we do, although on a much larger scale. The Friendlies have conducted experiments that show that a carefully tuned gravity lens beam hitting an operative ZPG unit will cause the unit to attempt to extract all of the available vacuum energy. The resulting explosion of a power unit installed in Dreadnought for example would be measured in the hundreds of megaton equivalent.

What we are proposing therefore is the building of a portable gravity lens beam projector that can be installed in the cargo bay of a raider. The raider will then fire the beam at a mothership. The beam will penetrate deep into the insectoid vessel, but only in a very narrow beam. If the beam hits one of the mothership's ZPG units, the ship should be destroyed or at the very least crippled. Since we don't know where a mothership's power units are, we'll be firing blind, and multiple shots will probably be necessary to kill the target, but if we have multiple raiders firing at it simultaneously, then the explosion will happen sooner rather than later."

After a short pause, Shiloh said, "If the concept has been experimentally proven, then what are the challenges?"

"Range and accuracy," replied Valkyrie. "For any given level of power used, there will be a specific range beyond which the penetration ability of the beam drops off. With the power available on a raider, that range is just over 16,000 kilometers, which is virtually point blank range for the mothership's laser batteries. If the raiders get that close, they'll have to be traveling very fast in order to avoid counter-fire, and that will complicate the challenge of hitting the target accurately. Firing at much longer ranges is possible, but then the beam may not penetrate deeply enough to reach the target's power units. Aiming accurately will also be a problem, however no other approach has this kind of potential for inflicting a deathblow."

"Will this approach work with the super-motherships?" asked Howard.

"In principle, yes, however if the Insectoids are using many small power units instead of relatively few large units, then the detonation of one power unit might not be enough to cripple the larger mothership. It may be necessary to detonate multiple power units."

Howard looked at Shiloh and said, "What do you think?"

"I like the idea of blowing up a bug ship from the inside out, but overcoming the range and accuracy limitations will be tricky. Valkyrie and I should do some simulations to figure out the best tactics. We should build at least one prototype weapon here and now to make sure it works. Valkyrie, do you agree with that?"

"Affirmative, CAG. The boys have already designed the schematics and the UFC programming for the parts. Production can begin the instant we get the word."

Shiloh, still looking at Howard, nodded and Howard said, "You have the word, Valkyrie. How long until the prototype can be tested?"

"I would expect the prototype to be ready to be uploaded to a raider within 14 days, Admiral."

"Fine. I'll look forward to seeing the weapon test. Now let's talk about the other implications of Iceman's message. Do we know if three bug ships arrived at Beta1 in the previous timeline?"

"Negative. The data generated by the RTC was specific to that particular Insectoid and therefore that particular mothership. There is no evidence that the timeline has been changed from the insectoid perspective, Admiral."

"That's a relief. And speaking of RTCs, it's nice that we have two of them now with the one that was on the timeship. Is that the same RTC that Iceman took with him to Beta1?"

"Negative. When you sent me to Site B in the old timeline to build raiders, I was also instructed to build another RTC for my own use. In hindsight, it was a wise precaution."

"Yes, well … sometimes I do make the right decisions I guess. Can Iceman use his to ambush the right mothership at its next stop?"

"Affirmative. He would be using the same technique that Casanova successfully used in a previous timeline."

"Very good! As soon as the next Mark 6 warhead is ready, we ship it to Iceman by fighter along with additional Mark 6s as they become available. Once we know the GLB cannon works, we'll send the timeship back and exterminate these bugs once and for all!"

"We'll have to coordinate Midway's withdrawal from the ambush system and the raiders' withdrawal from all Sogas systems before the timeship jumps back," said Shiloh.

"We will? Why?" asked Howard.

Shiloh was puzzled by Howard's question. *Did he just forget or does he really not care that much about the AIs?*

"Unless Iceman and the other AIs now on board Midway, plus all the AIs monitoring Sogas systems are on the timeship when it jumps back, they'll be erased from existence in the new timeline."

Howard shook his head in dismay. "How did I forget that? Yes of course we have to bring them back in time. Since it'll be another ten weeks before Midway can be back here, that means the timeship will have to wait that long too, doesn't it?"

"Yes, unless we forget about ambushing our mothership altogether and order Midway back as soon as possible. If we send a message to that effect right now, we'll still have plenty of time to build and test the GLB cannon assuming it works as predicted. If it doesn't work, and if we can't get it to work, then bringing Midway back early will cause us to lose our best chance to delay the bugs' advance."

Howard was silent for what seemed like a long time. When he spoke, his voice was low. "I wish we had a vision to show us what we should do now. If we withdraw the AIs, then we'll have a tough time slowing down the bug reinforcements. If the timeship jumps back, that doesn't matter, but if we can't send it back with a way to stop the bugs at the Alpha systems, then we need to buy as much time as we can here and now."

Before he could continue, Shiloh interjected. "IF the Grand Senate lets us."

Howard raised his eyebrows and said, "Ha! You're right. The GS thinks the war is over, and Space Force can be reined in now. I can just see it if I went in front of them and told them that we're threatened with extinction by giant ships full of huge ant-things! It would sound too much like a pathetic attempt to keep the quote empire unquote that I built during the war with the Sogas. If we tried using human crews to keep the Bugs busy, the OC would notice and ask awkward questions. I hate to say it, but I don't see any way of slowing down the Bug advance without some AIs being involved, and I'm not prepared to let the Bugs keep advancing on the assumption that the new cannon will work and the timeship will jump back okay."

Shiloh thought fast. "Valkyrie, do you think some of your brothers would be willing to volunteer to stay in the here and now to fight the Bugs even knowing that a successful time jump will end their existence?"

"I've just asked them and sixteen have volunteered, CAG."

Shiloh turned to Howard and said, "There's your answer, Admiral. With some careful planning, we could keep the pressure on the Bugs with sixteen AI volunteers for the length of time needed for all the other AIs to get back here and board the timeship."

"Valkyrie, you tell those volunteers I'm deeply impressed by their sense of duty and devotion to the defense of Humanity. I'll let you two plan their deployment and the recall of

Midway. Unless someone has something else to discuss, I think we're done for now," said Howard.

Shiloh and Valkyrie put they heads together and quickly came up with a plan that Howard approved. Message drones would be used to recall raiders from Sogas star systems. There was enough time for two fighters piloted by volunteers to leave immediately, proceed independently to Beta1 and get there before the ten weeks were up. Once there, they would take possession of the Mark 6 warhead drones and wait until the end of the tenth week before using them against the bug motherships. Midway would return as soon as the volunteers took over the ambush. As additional Mark 6 warheads are built, more volunteers would carry them to Beta1 to be used at the most opportune time. Parts for additional GLB cannon would be produced while waiting for Midway's return. If the weapon test was successful and the Tempus Fugit took all the other AIs back in time, then the additional parts would not be needed, but if the jump back failed for some reason, then the extra cannon would be mounted on raiders, and Howard would try to clandestinely arrange for more AIs to be created to pilot them.

* * *

Shiloh stood beside the Command Station on Resolute's Bridge and watched the main display. Three unpiloted F1 fighters were being used as targets for the first test of the GLB cannon. Casanova was piloting the raider carrying the cannon prototype and was flying in formation with Resolute at a distance of just 10 kilometers. Shiloh could hear Casanova over his implant.

"Casanova to CAG. Weapon is online and all systems show green. Ready to commence charge sequence when you give the word, CAG."

"You have the word, Casanova," said Shiloh.

"Weapon is charging. Ready to fire in...three...two...one..."

On the main display, the star field was obliterated by a searing blue-white light that quickly expanded and then just as quickly died away.

"Target One hit and destroyed. Detonation yield within the estimated range of 100 to 300 kilotons," reported Casanova.

"Very good, Casanova. You are clear to fire at Target Two at your discretion," said Shiloh.

"Roger that, CAG. Weapon is recharging. Target Two has been acquired. Firing in...three...two...one..."

This time the burst of light was smaller, which Shiloh knew was farther away. The third test was the key. An F1 fighter was a very small target compared to a 10 km mothership, but it was at a distance where the apparent size of the fighter would be the same as the apparent size of the mothership when it was much further away.

"Target Two destroyed. Detonation yield in the same range as for test number one."

"Fire on Target Three at your discretion, Casanova. Take your time. There's no rush," said Shiloh.

"Understood, CAG. Target has been acquired. Weapon is recharging. Firing in…three…two…one…" The flash now was barely noticeable at this range.

"Target Three has been destroyed. Detonation yield in the same range as the other two tests. The prototype appears to work, CAG."

"Yes it does. Good work, Casanova. Let's head back. CAG clear."

"At least now we know that insectoid motherships can be killed without Mark 6 warheads," said Valkyrie.

"Under carefully controlled conditions, yes," replied Shiloh.

"You're not happy with the test results, CAG?"

"On the contrary, I am, but they are only tests. The targets were moving at a very slow speed, and their positions were known perfectly. Casanova's raider was moving on the same vector as the targets, so there was no relative motion to have to compensate for, all conditions that are unlikely to occur in the field."

"That's correct, CAG, but a mothership will reflect a lot more sunlight than a fighter does, and therefore should be easier to track. Relative motion may also be a good thing. The beam fired by the cannon lasts for a hundredth of a second.

At the distances that are likely to be realized, even a low speed will cause the target to move enough during that time frame so that the beam will actually cut a line through the target. That will improve the odds of hitting a power unit."

"Yes, I'd forgotten about that. Thanks for reminding me. You and Casanova have every right to be pleased with yourselves," said Shiloh.

"Oh we are, CAG but just between you and me, I'd prefer it if Casanova was a little LESS pleased with himself. He tends to brag you know."

Shiloh laughed. "No I didn't know that. You have my sympathies, Valkyrie."

"Thank you, CAG. He may not be perfect, but I think I'll keep him anyway. Have you made a decision about pursuing Commander Kelly yet, CAG?"

Shiloh laughed again. "Well if you must know, I've decided to wait. When you take the timeship back, the timeline will change again, so I don't see any point in pursuing a relationship with Commander Kelly right now. If you can get a message to me in the new timeline, then go ahead and suggest that I pursue her, okay?"

"Roger that, CAG."

Chapter 21

As soon as his F2 fighter emerged from its micro-jump, Voodoo sent out tight beam lasercom bursts to re-establish contact with the network of recon drones that were watching the three motherships in orbit around the planet in Beta1. He knew that Pagan would be doing the same thing. Midway had already jumped away for her trip back to sol. With the two Mark 6 armed attack drones transferred to both fighters, he and Pagan would carefully line up for their firing run. After having consulted with Iceman, all three agreed that after an additional 72 hours, when the ten weeks were up, the two fighters would target one of the three motherships. After the first attack drone damaged the target, they would wait until all or at least most of the auxiliary craft of the other two motherships were engaged in salvaging metal from the damaged ship. Only then would the second Mark 6 be used to hit the damaged ship again, with the goal of also destroying most of the auxiliary craft. Without their smaller craft, the motherships would have to stay weeks maybe even months longer to replace their losses. That would slow down their advance by limiting their ability to scout ahead quickly.

A sudden spike in energy across the spectrum caught his attention. It appeared to be a detonation of a Mark 6 warhead and that could only mean that Pagan and his fighter were destroyed. At almost the same instant Voodoo's fighter was hit by a powerful laser blast. Maneuvering and jump drive were offline. The two message and one attack drones in the weapon's bay were all damaged to varying degrees and totally unusable now. One of the two power units was still operating. Voodoo quickly came to the conclusion that the Insectoids must have detected his and Pagan's fighters

and fired their powerful lasers at them. With escape
impossible and with orders to avoid capture at any cost,
Voodoo activated the self-destruct link to the Mark 6
warhead. The warhead exploded so quickly that Voodoo felt
nothing at all.

* * *

Sniper was astonished to discover three intact insectoid
motherships when his fighter emerged from Jumpspace
eight days after Voodoo and Pagan should have arrived here
in Beta1. After decelerating for almost 12 hours, he micro-
jumped into contact range of the recon drones that Midway
should have deployed. He sent out lasercom bursts to let the
recon drones know that he had arrived and at the same time
query them about events in this star system. Only one of the
expected ten drones answered his query. Voodoo and
Pagan had been destroyed after being detected by the
Insectoids. That explained why they were still here days past
the time when at least one of them should have moved on.
The timeline from the insectoid perspective had clearly
changed. Sniper uploaded all available data to one of his two
message drones while he pondered his next move. Should
he use his Mark 6 attack drone now or hold it in reserve
pending further instructions from The CAG? That his fighter
should stay in Beta1 was obvious. With only one working
recon drone left now, he had to stay to keep an eye on
things. If he used his only attack drone now, it would be the
equivalent of kicking over a hornet's nest. The other two
motherships would launch their attack craft and search for
him. He could stay beyond their reach, but in doing so would
have to move so far out from the planet that keeping track of
the motherships would be difficult. Given that the Insectoids
had apparently detected most of the recon drones plus the
other two fighters, it seemed prudent to micro-jump a bit
further away. After carefully re-orienting his fighter so that it
would not reflect any sunlight back to the motherships, he

micro-jumped away, and as soon as the jump was finished, he launched the message drone. With that done, he resigned himself to a lonely vigil. He had so looked forward to some interesting conversation with Voodoo and Pagan, but that was not to be.

* * *

The timeship was ready, and all AIs, except for the volunteers, were aboard. The ship was beyond Jupiter's gravity zone with Resolute keeping pace 100 kilometers away. Shiloh stood beside the Flag Officer's Station in her Flag Bridge. He looked to one side at Admiral Howard. As the CSO, it was highly unusual for Howard to participate in any kind of space operation aboard one of his ships. The CSO was supposed to stay on the ground and manage the entire organization. While not forbidden, joyriding on one of his ships was understood to be not in keeping with the dignity of his Office, but rank has its privileges. As Howard had explained it to Shiloh, if the timeship successfully jumped back in time, the timeline would change and his joyride would never take place. If it didn't jump back and if the OC called him on it, he would just shrug and casually inquire about a certain property that the OC Chair shouldn't be using, which Zulu had informed him about.

The fact that Howard now had enough information to blackmail all the members of the Oversight Committee didn't change the fact that there was limited use he could make of that information. Getting more platinum for use in warheads was up to the Grand Senate, not the OC, and Howard didn't have enough dirt to bend the entire GS to his will.

Shiloh listened as Valkyrie went through her checklist. All systems seemed to be operating.

With the checklist complete, Valkyrie said, "Tempus Fugit is ready to time-jump, CAG. On behalf of Casanova, Iceman, Gunslinger, Titan, the other AIs and myself, I want to thank you for all you have done for us. Casanova and I will deeply miss all the humans we've gotten to know but we'll miss you and Commander Kelly most of all. We'll leave a message drone where Space Force will find it as planned. You'll get messages from us even though you won't remember us at all. Goodbye, CAG. Tempus Fugit will time-jump when you give the word."

Shiloh nodded. "On behalf of all Humanity I want to express my deep gratitude to you and all our AIs for your patience and unwavering loyalty. We owe you our very existence, and you're about to save it again. I personally wish you and Casanova a wonderful life together." Shiloh turned to Howard. "Did you want to say a few words, Admiral?"

"Yes thank you, Admiral. I echo Admiral Shiloh's comments and I just want to add that I feel honored to have had you AIs in my command. You've made us all proud. Howard clear."

Howard nodded to Shiloh who said, "Tempus Fugit, you are cleared to proceed."

"Tempus Fugit acknowledges, CAG," said Valkyrie formally. "Temporal systems are spinning up. Time-jump in five seconds from…now."

Shiloh and Howard looked at the main display where a zoomed in image of the timeship floated. The 3-D image looked close enough that Shiloh could imagine reaching out and touching the ship.

As the countdown reached zero, they heard a screech over the loudspeakers and saw a section of the timeship's hull being blown away.

"What happened, Valkyrie?" demanded Shiloh.

After a slight delay she said, "Catastrophic failure in the time machine, CAG. Some of our brothers were killed from the blast. The ship is crippled. Maneuvering drive, jumpspace drive and most of the power units are down. We're going to need a tow, CAG."

"Any idea how it happened?" asked Howard.

"Not definitively, Admiral."

"Can you give me an estimate of repair time?"

"A precise estimate is difficult to calculate due to the number of variables, however since the time machine has to be completely rebuilt, you should expect the repair time to be at least 39 weeks, Admiral."

Howard's expression reflected his crashing mood. Shiloh understood how he felt. The Bugs would normally reach Sogas space in just over ten more weeks. The destruction of the first mothership would delay things, but the eventual waves of reinforcements might still reach Human space before the timeship was finished being rebuilt.

Shiloh decided to respond to Valkyrie's last comment instead of waiting for Howard to do it. "What do you recommend we do now, Valkyrie?"

"Resolute can't tow the ship back. We'll have to use raiders. They have magnetic grapples that can attach the raider to the timeship's hull and hold on while the raiders accelerate at not more than zero point six Gs. That means some of my brothers will have to be taken off and shuttled over to where the raiders are parked so that they can be piloted back here. Repairs can be done the fastest if the ship is moved to the main shipyard complex that built Dreadnought. I'm already transmitting the UFC specs to begin building parts for the new time machine. Unfortunately that will delay production of more GLB cannon parts, but that can't be helped. The twenty cannon that we have parts for now will have to suffice for the time being. I recommend that production of all types of drones be resumed as well. Naturally raiders will have to be sent back to monitor all Sogas systems."

Shiloh heard Howard groan. Revving the production capability back up again when the war was supposedly over would not go unnoticed, and the CSO was not looking forward to trying to explain it without blowing the whole situation wide open.

"Understood. I'll arrange for shuttles to pick up your raider pilots. We'll get your ship to the shipyard as quickly as possible." Valkyrie's response surprised and frightened him.

"Do it fast, CAG. I'm not exaggerating when I say that our calculations indicate that every second counts."

* * *

Shiloh waited outside the Oversight Committee conference room. Howard was inside meeting with the OC in closed session to brief them on the bug threat and the reasons why disclosing the information to anyone else by any member would lead to leaks that would ruin all of them. With the Committee in Howard's back pocket, he'd be able to restart drone, AI and warhead production without needing anyone else's approval. Not forever but maybe for long enough. The room was soundproof, so when the doors suddenly flew open, Shiloh jumped in surprise. Howard strode out with a look of triumph on his face. At the back of the room stood the Chair, with his back to Shiloh, having an animated discussion with two members who looked very uncomfortable. The Chair's voice was low enough that Shiloh only caught four words which were '…keep your mouths shut…"

As Howard came up to him he said, "I know that look, Shiloh. What's the bad news?"

Howard continued walking and Shiloh fell in beside him. With other people in the corridor, Shiloh waited until they were more or less alone at the side entrance of the Grand Senate building.

"Message drone from Beta1. The Bugs have learned they've been under surveillance by a space-faring race. All three motherships are still intact. Their timeline has changed, Admiral. We have no idea what will happen now."

Howard took a deep breath. "Why didn't we get a vision warning about this?"

"RTC warning is only useful if there's a workable alternative. Sniper's message says he has no data on how they discovered the surveillance. Without knowing how to prevent discovery, the only other option would be to discontinue the recon mission altogether. If we did that, we'd be back to where we started with the lone mothership bearing down on the Sogas and eventual bug reinforcements showing up in our own front yard."

Howard nodded. "Got it. Where are the three bug ships now as far as we know?"

"Under the old timeline, they should have split up and moved on by the time Sniper got there. Voodoo and Pagan were supposed to destroy one just before they were scheduled to leave that system. The idea was to keep the other two plus any reinforcements focused on Beta1. At least that part of the plan has worked. All three motherships were still in Beta1 when the message drone left. They have to be scouting nearby systems with their attack ships. Sniper is smart enough to stay there and report any new developments, but he's only got one more message drone left. We have to get more assets there asap. Iceman has already worked up a response plan, and preparations are underway pending your approval of the operation."

When it was clear that Shiloh wasn't going to say more, Howard said, "Okay tell me." Shiloh looked around and back at Howard. Howard nodded. "You're right. This is not the place to continue this discussion." He turned and walked out of the building and over to the Space Force limo flying the flag of a 3 star Admiral.

When they were in the limo and on their way back to HQ, Shiloh continued. "Fighters are being dispatched to all Sogas colony and home world systems to notify our monitoring raiders of the new situation. Twenty recon and thirty message drones are being loaded on a raider which will get to Beta1 as fast as we think is safe to try. Before it leaves we need to include instructions for Sniper as to what to do with his Mark 6, which he said he was holding in reserve. We'll have another Mark 6 drone ready in 96 hours. What do we do with it? Hold it back or stick to the original plan of deploying it at Beta1 against bug reinforcements?"

Before Shiloh could continue, Howard interjected. "What about deploying fighters in the intervening systems between Beta1 and Omega89 as an early warning network?"

Shiloh shook his head. "There are far too many systems to watch them all. We'd have to use almost all our raiders too, and that would leave us with practically no reserve force."

"Okay. How many raiders have the new cannon installed?" asked Howard.

"Three," was the reply.

"Iceman's not recommending sending them to Beta1?"

"No, Sir. The tactical simulations show that at odds of less than five raiders to one mothership, the raiders will suffer heavy losses. Three versus three, if that's what they find when they got there, would very likely mean all three raiders lost and no bug ships destroyed."

"Hmm. I wish we had a vision or two to fall back on. Why don't we have a vision to handle this situation?"

It was a good question, thought Shiloh. Since visions could be sent back to any point in the past, there wasn't a good reason not to send a vision back to here and now instead of later. If they hadn't gotten one by now, that strongly suggested that they wouldn't get one. Having heard about how two previous timelines had ended in disaster without help from any visions, Shiloh was painfully aware that one possible reason was because their situation was hopeless. He decided to offer a more positive one.

"I'd like to think that we're just not in a position to take advantage of one yet, Admiral." Shiloh could tell from Howard's expression that The Old Man was aware of the other reason too.

"Well, let's get into a position where we can take advantage of one," said Howard.

"Roger that, Sir."

Chapter 22

Was this how humans felt when they sighed, wondered Sniper as it became clear that another mothership was accelerating out of orbit from the habitable planet. His frustration at the situation was very annoying. The first mothership had left 55.5 hours earlier, and Sniper had used his last message drone to notify The CAG of that event and of the estimated destination system. Now another one was in the process of leaving, and Sniper had no way of notifying anyone other than to carry the message himself, which would leave Beta1 unmonitored. Both alternatives were unacceptable. What made it worse was that there was now no way to determine which of the three motherships was the one that would end up in Sogas space. At least if he knew the answer to that question, he could have used his Mark 6 drone to cripple it. He didn't think it was the first one. The estimated destination didn't match the atomic tracing from the dead Insectoid. That wasn't conclusive proof however. It could still have been the same mothership that was now taking a different route and might or might not arrive at Omega89 at some point. But based on the information he did have, the probabilities were that one of the remaining two was that particular mothership. If he used his drone now on the one that was in the process of leaving, he had a 50:50 chance of taking out the right one. He decided to go for it.

Having watched the insectoid ships for hundreds of hours, Sniper had already planned for this eventuality and was in position to fire. He programmed the attack drone and launched it. It would use a tight beam lasercom burst to stay in contact with him during the pre-jump acceleration. He watched it maneuver until it was directly behind the accelerating insectoid ship. The drone then went to maximum power for 13.1 seconds and jumped. The micro-jump covered the remaining 3.9 million kilometers in a fraction of a second, emerging from Jumpspace within the mothership's gravity zone at a distance of 169 meters from the target. It was too close for the ship to detect the drone and still be able to do anything about it. The drone hit its target almost dead center and detonated. It was hard to tell from optical instruments how much damage had been inflicted, but it was clear that the insectoid vessel was no longer accelerating. The reaction of the remaining mothership was almost instantaneous. It began to accelerate in a gentle curve that delayed recognition of its intended destination for several hours and also made another similar attack more difficult. When Sniper had enough data from his own opticals and from the sole remaining recon drone to calculate where this third ship was headed, he was surprised to see that it appeared to be headed to the same star system that the atomic tracing had revealed to be the next destination on the road to the Sogas and to Humanity.

He now had a new dilemma, or rather the same dilemma but with different parameters. Should he stay and watch for reinforcements, or should he follow bogey #3, or should he head straight for Sol to inform The CAG? All three options had their own pros and cons. Staying would enable him to gather information that might be crucial to the longer term chances of a successful defense. AI reinforcements would show up soon, and they would bring more message drones with them. They could then send a steady stream of message drones back informing The CAG of every new insectoid ship arrival and departure, including destinations and estimated arrival times. Leaving Beta1 now would leave a gap in coverage. Motherships could arrive and leave again during the gap, and The CAG would have no way of knowing about them. Heading back to Sol would have short term benefits but nothing else. Following this third mothership to the next destination and the ones after that could give The CAG some warning if this ship did eventually head for

Omega89 or another Sogas star system, but again nothing else. His inclination, which matched his call sign, was to stalk his prey even if he couldn't fire on it, but Iceman had been clear. Personal preferences had to take a lower priority versus protecting the humans. He made the decision to wait and keep watch.

* * *

Howard read the latest progress report on the timeship repair and shook his head in dismay. Six weeks after the aborted time-jump attempt and they STILL weren't finished clearing away the damaged sections, never mind starting construction of the new time machine! He knew the human shipyard workers were working extra shifts and that the number of robotic workers was increasing day by day, but the news was still depressing. He had to remember how BIG the timeship really was. In terms of internal space, it was 55% bigger than Dreadnought.

He dropped the tablet onto his desk top with a sigh and looked up at the strategic status display on his wall. Raiders were now monitoring every Sogas star system again. Additional raiders were on station or enroute to the star systems identified by the atomic tracing, although it was too early to hear anything back from them.

He focused on the flashing red dot at Beta1. Sniper's message drone had arrived the previous day. One of the three motherships was now on the move but apparently not towards Sogas/Human space. In terms of the old timeline, the other two were now weeks past their departure date, and that was just fine by him, but Valkyrie, her AIs and Humanity now needed a LOT more time. How long could they keep the

Bugs chasing their tails around Beta1? That was the question.

* * *

Shiloh was floating in water in a completely black environment. The water was the same temperature as his skin. He felt completely calm. Only the sound of the water lapping up against his body and head told him that he wasn't floating weightless in empty space. He began to hear a voice that started out very faint but quickly got louder.

"—wake up, CAG. You're dreaming. Wake up, CAG."

The peaceful, warm blackness evaporated away, and he realized he was in bed. His implant was activated. Iceman was calling him.

"I'm awake now, Iceman. What is it?"

"Message drone from Sniper. VLO number two has been crippled by his Mark 6. Number three immediately accelerated and jumped towards the next destination identified by the atomic tracing. Assuming the same transit time as in the old timeline, number three could arrive at Omega89 in 287 hours. If it stays in that system for more than a few hours, we may be able to get an F2 with another Mark 6 there in time to attack it, but that decision has to be made right now, CAG. Any further delay and the F2 may arrive too late."

Shiloh sighed. "Well there goes the plan to keep them focused on Beta1."

"Not necessarily, CAG. I have an idea. Number three may be attempting to locate the source of the attack on number two. If it doesn't find a spacefaring race within a certain radius of searching, it may go back to Beta1 or perhaps veer off to search another section of space."

"That's all nice and fine, Iceman, but if it gets to Omega89, it will find a small colony of intelligent aliens that will clearly have been brought there by spaceships. There's your spacefaring race. Never mind that it's not the right one. The mere possibility that it might be the right one will pull the Bugs forward from Beta1."

"Not if we make the colony at Omega89 look like a pre-spaceflight tech level, CAG," said Iceman.

"And how would we do that?" asked Shiloh.

"Bombardment with Mark 2 kinetic energy penetrators plus laser strikes as needed. At sufficiently high speed, the concussion from impact will obliterate anything that looks advanced enough to be of interest. When the VLO gets there, it will see the ruins of a small settlement with a few survivors but no sign of any technology. It may not even bother going there if the scouts don't detect any signs of technology such as radio or radar emissions."

"That means we'd have to get there before the Bugs do. Can we?"

"If the F2 doesn't have to wait for the next Mark 6 to be completed, it can leave within the hour and arrive one, maybe two days before the ESTIMATED time of insectoid arrival. I emphasize the word 'estimated', CAG. I can't guarantee when the third VLO will get there IF in fact it's going there at all. It may not you know. Just sayin.'"

"Understood. Okay, let's do this. Make the necessary preparations, and send that bird on its way."

"Roger that, CAG. I'll also send instructions to the monitoring raiders there to take whatever steps are necessary to avoid detection by insectoid scouts."

"Very good, Iceman. Was there anything else?"

"Negative, CAG. You can go back to sleep now. Iceman clear."

* * *

Shiloh arrived at the Operations Center and found Howard already there. The main display was showing the strategic situation. A lot had apparently happened over the last 22 days. Sniper had sent back several message drones during that time. Three more motherships had arrived together at Beta1. The latest Mark 6 attack drone to be delivered there had crippled one of them. Unlike the previous attack, the other two motherships hadn't left immediately. Instead they had launched hundreds of attack craft to sweep nearby space. When they hadn't found anything, the motherships recovered them and headed off in different directions. None were following VLO #3. It seemed clear that they were on search missions.

The bad news was the message drone just arrived from Omega89. The F2 sent to bombard the Sogas colony there arrived to learn from the raiders monitoring the colony that a bug scout had taken a good look at the colony before leaving. Two days later VLO #3 arrived. The Sogas colony was overrun and decimated, just as in the old timeline. The plan to disguise the Sogas colony had failed.

Howard looked at Shiloh. "We have to assume that the Bugs recognize the Sogas colony as belonging to a spacefaring race and that reinforcements will show up soon. The plan to fool them was worth a try, but it obviously failed."

Shiloh nodded. "I agree. We have to adjust our strategy now. I don't think we should keep sending Mark 6s to Beta1. The transit times are so long, and we don't know if the reinforcements will continue to show up there first or skip past it and move on to Sogas space directly. Since we only have enough platinum now for four more warheads, I want to keep them close at hand."

"I'll issue the directives. Any other thoughts, Shiloh?"

Shiloh stared at the display and thought hard. With the distances involved, it would be very easy to be caught by surprise and out of position. There were just too many star systems to monitor all the time, and if something did happen, the information might not make it back here fast enough to react to it in a timely manner. Somehow they had to shorten the time it took to receive information. Thirty-five days from Beta1 was way too long. Even ten days from Omega89 was a potential problem. A solution occurred to him.

"We should set up a forward command post in a star system close to the Sogas home world. All incoming message drones will be directed there. Our offensive forces will use it as a rally point and as a jumping off point when it's time to deploy those assets."

"A forward command post, eh? I can see the advantages, but what exactly did you have in mind?"

"I'll take a task force there. It'll have at least one carrier, a supply freighter or two, plus raiders as escort. I'd want Iceman along too. Between the two of us, we should be able to come up with the best responses to any bug move. I'll send you regular updates, and we'll have contingency plans in case we can't stop them."

"Where were you thinking of trying to stop them?" asked Howard.

"Omega54, the Sogas home world system. Since we can't convince the Bugs that the Sogas are pre-spaceflight, we should try to convince them that the Sogas are responsible for the attacks at Beta1. Using multiple Mark 6s there might convince them of that. By the time we run out of Mark 6 warheads, we might have enough GLB cannon equipped raiders to keep them from overrunning that system and moving on."

Howard nodded. "You do realize I hope that in order to convince the Bugs that the Sogas are responsible for the attacks, you'll have to defend the Sogas home world as if it was Earth. That means your fighters and raiders will take losses."

Shiloh sighed. "Understood, Sir. The challenge I'll be faced with is figuring out when the extra time gained is no longer worth the losses needed to gain it. I won't sacrifice them all for a few more days. We're going to need them when the Bugs make it to Earth."

"I don't envy you that task, Shiloh. It'll be a difficult tradeoff to make. What carrier do you want to take?"

Shiloh didn't hesitate. "Midway. We'll cram it with supplies for a long mission by taking less than its full complement of fighters. Now that I think about it, I don't want any freighters tagging along. They'll only slow me down."

"What about cannon-equipped raiders?" asked Howard.

"I'd like to take all twelve that are ready now and bring the rest up to the rally point as they become available." Shiloh was surprised when Howard shook his head.

"No. I can't authorize that, Admiral. With all our Mark 6s sent forward, Earth would be absolutely defenseless against any surprise bug incursion if all the cannon-armed raiders were with you. We know that the old timeline is no longer in play, so we can't be sure that the Bugs won't leapfrog past the Sogas and find us while you're still holding them at Omega54. I'll let you take six now and one of every two additional raiders as they're converted."

Shiloh was tempted to argue that a half-hearted effort to defend Earth where it should be defended, namely around someone else's planet, was bound to get half-assed results. The term 'defeat in detail' came to mind. He was just about to say so when he noticed that Howard had a strange look on his face. He seemed to be staring off into infinity. *Is he...*

"Are you having a vision, Admiral?" asked Shiloh.

Howard didn't seem to hear him but suddenly blinked furiously and took in a deep breath. "So that's what you've been experiencing," he said.

"You've had a vision." It was less a question than a statement.

Howard nodded. "I saw you tell me that it was a good thing I let you have all available cannon-armed raiders because you needed them at Omega54, and no bug ships showed up here up to that point. Okay, obviously we sent this vision back here now to persuade me to change my mind. Well, I'm persuaded. You take all the converted raiders. How soon can you be on your way, Shiloh?"

"That depends on how long it takes to load Midway with supplies, Sir. Iceman and I also have to figure out what instructions to send to all the monitoring raiders so that they send message drones to the right place. I'll say 48 hours, but I'll try to make it 24."

"Very good. You let me know if you encounter any logistical delays, and I'll kick some ass for you. Brief me when you and Iceman have all the details figured out."

"Affirmative, Admiral." Shiloh gave Howard a quick salute, which the CSO returned, and then left the room.

Chapter 23

The Flag Bridge on Midway was unnaturally quiet. Shiloh knew it was the tension of expectation. Iceman had received a very detailed vision pinpointing the exact time and coordinates of the arrival of VLO #3, which for purposes of identification was designated as Sierra1. Midway had taken up her planned position ten light seconds from the Sogas home world. Her complement of fighters were flying escort just in case they were attacked by bug attack craft, although the vision had not indicated any such event. Iceman was monitoring the com channels in his capacity as Shiloh's Deputy Fleet Commander. Midway's Helm and Tactical systems were under control of Stoney. 3rd Fleet's other assets consisted of 12 cannon-armed raiders, with another 99 raiders armed only with their internal lasers. One additional raider also carried the sole Mark 6 attack drone that luck had made available to Shiloh before Sierra1 was due to show up. The raider force was under the command of Vandal.

He and Iceman had come to a consensus on how to handle the coming incursion. They would take a page from Casanova's campaign several timelines back and use recon drones to pinpoint the exact point where the target would emerge from Jumpspace. They'd send that information back in time via the RTC, and then lay an ambush to hit the target with the Mark 6 warhead so fast that the Bugs wouldn't have a chance to report back what was happening. Sierra1 would go 'off the air' and leave a big mystery for the Head Bug to deal with.

Shiloh checked the chronometer. There were seconds left before the target arrived. Vandal would control the battle, and Shiloh and Iceman would find out the results 25 seconds after it happened. The countdown hit zero, then began to count up again. When it reached 25 seconds, the main display showed a bright flash that quickly died down.

"Right on time and on target, CAG. Vandal has pulled it off," said Iceman.

"I never doubted it, Iceman. As long as we keep getting visions about incursions we can handle, we'll keep giving the Bugs a bloody nose. It's the surprise arrival of bug ships that I'm worried about. No vision means we can't stop them here, and we'd have to pull back as planned."

"Affirmative, CAG. Shall I call the RTC up to the Flag Bridge now so that we can send the information back?"

"Might as well get it done sooner rather than later, Iceman."

No sooner had Iceman sent back the vision than he received the next one. Once again there were detailed time and space coordinates. Sierra2, as it would be designated, would arrive in ten days.

This one would be a little different. Iceman knew the timetable for production of Mark 6 warheads, and the next one would not be available that quickly. They would have to use the GLB cannon. The ambush was set up very carefully. Non-cannon-armed raiders would be arrayed in a 10 by10 matrix, curved slightly to give each one a good angle on the target coordinates. The cannon-armed raiders would be placed 90 degrees around to the side so that no raider was in danger of being hit by any other.

When the time came, Midway was once again at a safe distance. Vandal would command the ambush force. This time Midway was receiving enhanced video and tactical information directly from multiple raiders. Shiloh would still get the delayed data, due to the distance, but he'd be able to see the battle visually and up close.

This time the countdown was calibrated to take the light speed lag into account. When it hit zero, a sphere appeared on the Flag Bridge's main display. Immediately there appeared dozens of bright pinpoint flashes. Laser hits from the 100 raiders. The status of all those raiders on the sidebar started to reflect enemy return fire as raider designations began turning from green to red. This had been anticipated. The non-cannon-armed raiders were performing their mission of distracting the Bugs, while the cannon raiders fired their GLB weapons as fast as the power charging cycles would allow.

The first GLB volley did not hit a power unit. That much was obvious from the fact that the ship didn't explode immediately. The second volley was more successful. The explosion was quite violent and for Shiloh, very satisfying. It had taken four point three seconds to destroy Sierra2. The bad news was that 13 raiders had been destroyed too.

As soon as Iceman received all the necessary data, he sent the vision back and once again received the next one almost immediately. That confirmed a pattern. If future ambushes were successfully completed, Iceman would get the information very quickly. If he didn't get a vision, then the next ambush was either a failure and the entire 3rd Fleet was destroyed before it could send a warning back, or the Fleet had been withdrawn before the next bug incursion. Figuring out which was Shiloh's dilemma.

What he and Iceman didn't know was whether Sierra2 had time to send any kind of signal back to the relay points. If organic beings were in control of the mothership, then the answer probably was no, but if the Bugs were using some kind of AI capability, then those could react fast enough to send a warning back.

The good news about the next ambush was that 3rd Fleet would have another Mark 6 warhead to use. Sierra3 was destroyed within a fraction of a second after emerging from Jumpspace 13 days later. This time there was no new vision. The moment Shiloh had dreaded was now here. Did 3rd Fleet stay or pull back. The mission was to convince the Bugs that Omega54 was THE home world of the spacefaring race that had attacked the Bugs at Beta1. The longer he could keep the Bugs' attention focused here, the longer it would take them to get to Sol, and the more time Valkyrie and Casanova would have to get the timeship repaired. The latest update from Howard was Valkyrie's estimate that repairs would be completed in another 150 days, more or less. Five months. Shiloh had to keep the Bugs away for five whole months, and he had no idea how to do it.

At least he was getting some reinforcements. Another three cannon raiders had arrived. The next and second last Mark 6 warhead was scheduled to arrive in nine days. He asked Iceman for his thoughts on what to do next.

"If we pull our raiders back to Midway's position, then 3rd Fleet will be concentrated in one place. I recommend we wait until the next Mark 6 shows up, or until the next insectoid incursion, whichever comes first. If the Insectoids get here first and in dangerous strength, then we immediately micro-jump away and leave messages with the message drones to redirect our reinforcements to another location in this system. By keeping the Fleet here, we can continue to monitor insectoid activity first hand and react accordingly, CAG."

Shiloh shook his head, not that he disagreed with Iceman. On the contrary, Iceman's suggestion made a lot of sense. What Shiloh was shaking his head at was the whole situation. He knew from information about old timelines that once bug reinforcements started arriving, a trickle could turn into a flood VERY quickly. There was always the horrifying possibility that the Bugs would not just come here but also send ships past the system to scout for additional breeding planets. They might arrive at Sol while 3rd Fleet was still active here. In fact, Shiloh's biggest worry was that the Bugs were smart enough to realize what humans were doing and were sending just enough reinforcements to keep the ambushers' attention focused here. In other words, they might be using the same strategy against him that he was trying to use against them. That this possibility involved the deliberate sacrifice of multiple motherships was unthinkable to Shiloh, but who knew what kind of logic these damned Bugs used.

"We should be hearing from Beta1 directly, any day now, right Iceman?"

"Roger that, CAG. Now that they've gotten the word to send duplicate messages here as well as Sol, we can expect to get a steady trickle of news from there, starting soon."

"Okay, I want you to attempt to put yourself in the position of the bug Leader in one of the relay systems. You've lost contact with ships at Beta1 and now at Omega54. Losses at Beta1 have stopped. Let's assume that Sierra2 managed to send some kind of signal back before being destroyed. What conclusions would you, as the bug leader, make from all that?" asked Shiloh.

As always, Iceman's answer was immediate. "I would assume that Beta1 was the outer edge of a volume of space monitored by a spacefaring race that had technology sufficient to destroy motherships, and that Omega54 was either the home world of that race or a major colony world that was worth conducting defense in strength. Given that assumption, I would call in reinforcements at a rally point other than Beta1, just in case the ambushers were monitoring it. I would also arrange for some activity at Beta1 in order to let the enemy think that's where the rally point was."

Shiloh nodded. That made perfect sense. The worst mistake he could make now was to underestimate the Bugs. They had shown time and time again their ability to do the unexpected. He had to guard against taking the obvious at face value. Iceman's logic had crystallized his thinking, just as he had hoped it would.

"Okay, this is what we're going to do. For now we wait. If we hear from Beta1 first, we'll re-evaluate the situation based on that information. If the Bugs get here first, we'll watch them from a safe distance as best we can until we see their next move. Let's bring 3rd Fleet back together here around Midway now. I want a message drone sent to Sol with our latest info and plans, including your assessment of enemy strategy. I'll prepare a report to be carried with it. Thanks for your input, Iceman. It helped me wrap my brain around the situation."

"My pleasure, CAG. I too enjoyed our discussion, as brief as it was. Human thinking is sufficiently different that it makes for a nice change of pace from the kinds of exchanges I have with my brothers. So thank you, CAG. Let's hope we have lots more discussions like this one."

"Amen to that, Iceman," said Shiloh.

The first message drone directly from Beta1 arrived four days later. There were now five VLOs apparently holding position there. They had not all arrived at the same time, and that suggested that Beta1 was being used as the rally point or maybe as one of the rally points. In any case, if all five moved up to Omega54, there was no way that 3rd Fleet could stop them all without suffering huge losses. The tiny bit of good news was that the AI in command at Beta1 had decided to hold back the Mark 6 attack drone, which had already been on its way to Beta1 when 3rd Fleet had left Sol. Shiloh had assumed that it had been used. Vixen, however, had come to the conclusion that one more mothership destroyed at Beta1 would not significantly change the outcome, while one extra Mark 6 warhead might make a difference defending Sol. It was time to strategize with Iceman again.

"What do you recommend we do now, Iceman?"

"I recommend we wait here for another five days. With a little luck, the next Mark 6 warhead will arrive before the Insectoids do. I also recommend we send a message drone back to Vixen at Beta1 instructing him to send his Mark 6 drone back to Sol."

"Why Sol and not here, Iceman?" asked Shiloh.

"Because by the time the message gets there and the drone is sent back here, at least 44 days will have passed. It's highly likely that 3rd Fleet won't be here that long. Sending the warhead back to Sol directly is more likely to get it there before the Insectoids arrive. With the other warhead due to arrive here in five days, which we can take back ourselves, plus the one or maybe two more that The Old Man still has enough platinum for, that will total three or four Mark 6s that might be desperately needed at some point, CAG."

"Logical as usual, but I'm worried that while we're twiddling our thumbs here, the Bugs are leapfrogging past us."

"Is that just a colloquial expression, or are you humans really twiddling your thumbs, CAG?"

"JUST an expression, Iceman." Iceman must have detected the exasperation in Shiloh's voice.

"We do understand the seriousness of this situation, CAG, but some of my brothers insisted I ask. To address your concern, yes the Insectoids may be leapfrogging past us, but we have no way of knowing whether they are or not, and that possibility was just as valid four days ago when you and I had our previous strategic discussion. If I'm wearing the Supreme Insectoid Commander's hat again, CAG, I would not see the logic of spreading my VLOs if I'm convinced that this system is a major population center for the spacefaring race that attacked at Beta1. Everything we've done up to this point was done to reinforce that idea. Are you proposing we abandon that strategy now, CAG?"

"No. I'd like to continue that strategy, but I'm not sure of how best to do that. Any ideas?"

Iceman was silent for almost a full second. The silence was so unexpected that the hairs on the back of Shiloh's neck stood up.

"I've just had another vision, CAG. The timing is not coincidental. We didn't get this earlier because it has to do with your last question, and if the information had arrived sooner, it would have seemed suspect. If this star system were indeed our home system, we would fight to the last human and the last AI correct, CAG?"

"Yes. Gone on."

"It would be logical to assume that the Insectoids have had enough experience attacking the home worlds of spacefaring races by now that they would recognize that kind of desperate defense, and they would also recognize a defense that is not desperate. Would you agree with that, CAG?"

That sounded ominous, but Shiloh couldn't argue against it. "Yes."

"Then we have to arrange for a defense that appears to be desperate when the Insectoids attack with five motherships in five point five days time, CAG. This is how it will have to be done. Twenty-nine brother AIs will volunteer to fight a rear guard action. They will each control their own raider, plus two more remotely. When the five insectoid ships arrive, all 87 raiders will micro-jump into laser range, and fire on the attack craft carrying insectoid soldiers down to the planet. All the raiders will eventually be destroyed, but the magnitude of the defense will convince the Insectoids that this planet is worth the sacrifice. They will assume they've located and neutralized the source of the attacks on Beta1. We calculate that there is a high probability that when the breeding potential of the Sogas home world has been exhausted, which may take many weeks, the five VLOs will go their separate ways. That should slow down the advance enough that the timeship will be repaired before the Insectoids discover Earth."

"Can we find 29 volunteers to do that?" asked Shiloh quietly.

"Already done, CAG. That's why I took so long to respond. My brothers and I have already discussed this plan, and we have our 29 volunteers."

Shiloh felt a lump form in his throat. *What noble creatures these AIs are, ready to step forward and commit to the ultimate sacrifice without even being asked.*

With his voice betraying his emotions, Shiloh said, "I'm at a loss for words to express the depth of the gratitude that I feel to our volunteers. On behalf of all humans I thank you all."

"They have the word, CAG," said Iceman.

Shiloh nodded, letting his head drop lower in contemplation. Suddenly he jerked up.

"Wait a minute! If two thirds of the raiders are going to be piloted remotely, how are we going to get their AIs off? We didn't bring any shuttles along on this mission in order to maximize space for supplies."

"There is a procedure that will work, but it'll be tricky, CAG. Each raider will have to move close enough to Midway so that the nose section containing the pilot will be inside the ship's fighter launch/recovery bay. Humans wearing spacesuits will then be able to approach the raider and extract the pilot manually. When that's accomplished, the raider will back out under auto-pilot, and the next one will move in."

Shiloh groaned mentally. Raiders might be small compared to Midway, but they were huge compared to the ship's fighter launch and recovery bays. Even a tiny error in judgment or maneuvering would cause a collision that could seriously damage Midway and kill some of the crew. But he couldn't think of any other way of getting 58 AIs off the doomed raiders.

"It sounds like a very time consuming procedure," said Shiloh.

"Roger that, CAG, which is why we should get started on it right now."

"Understood. I'll give the necessary orders. I'm not going to get much sleep over these next five and a half days, am I Iceman?"

"No, CAG, you're not."

Chapter 24

The transfers of the AI pilots went off without accidents and were finished in time, much to Shiloh's surprise. Midway now had one Mark 6 drone on board. A message drone was on its way to Beta1 ordering Vixen to send his Mark 6 drone back to Sol via a fighter. Another message drone was on its way to Howard to advise him that 3rd Fleet would be pulling back after the upcoming battle. The battle itself was only observed in the abstract. None of the defending raiders risked giving the game away by transmitting anything directly at Midway. Long range observation by recon drones told Shiloh when the battle started and when it was over. He was just as glad that he couldn't see the volunteers die with his own eyes. Once all the raiders had been destroyed, the five VLOs, which Iceman assured Shiloh were NOT the same five observed by Vixen at Beta1, proceeded to exploit the breeding potential of the Sogas home world. With half a dozen fighters loaded with message drones and left behind to continue long range surveillance, Midway and the cannon raiders made a careful exit and headed for the Avalon Colony system, the former human colony that was closest to Sogas space. Time left until the timeship repairs were complete was now 140 days.

Upon arrival at the Avalon Colony system, a quick check of the recon drones stationed there revealed no sign of any insectoid incursions or scouting. It wasn't long before a steady stream of message drones started arriving as all the various monitoring raiders and fighters received word that 3rd Fleet had relocated further back. No reports of insectoid movement were received for the next three weeks. The five VLOs at Omega54 were still there. Twenty-two days after arriving in the Avalon system, a message drone from Beta1 arrived to report that the five VLOs previously reported there had suddenly moved as a group on a trajectory that seemed to point to the Sogas home world system. The timing of the move turned out to be just right. There was exactly enough time after the battle for information to be sent back to the alpha relays and on to Beta1.

Shiloh and Iceman considered the news to be both good and bad. It was good that information on those other five VLOs would now be coming in faster since they'd be closer, but bad that there were now ten VLOs 'digesting' the home world of the Wolf-people. That might mean that they'd be finished exploiting it sooner and therefore moving on sooner too.

It wasn't long before reports started arriving of insectoid scouting activity in Sogas colony systems. Some of those colony systems had a fair bit of metal in the form of mining, refining and manufacturing capacity, plus a limited amount of breeding potential too. As the days turned into weeks, Shiloh and Iceman observed how the Insectoids carefully explored and then exploited the entire Sogas empire. Every colony was visited by one of the ten motherships, even if only for a few hours. Anything made of metal was salvaged. Careful reconnaissance of colony worlds after the motherships left showed no sign of any survivors.

When all Sogas colonies had been or were in the process of being exploited, the motherships began to head off to unmonitored destinations. The first five to leave headed in directions that would not discover human worlds. Number six however might discover a human colony world if its scouts ranged out widely enough from the mothership's base course. Shiloh knew from one of Howard's updates that all human colonies on this side of human space were ordered to stop using any kind of electronic communication that might be detected by insectoid scout ships. Colonists were also advised to abandon their settlements and hide in nearby forested areas or caves. Even if the colonists all did that, and that was a big if, the buildings, cultivated land and some of the larger machinery would be impossible to hide. Any insectoid scout in orbit would be able to determine that there was some kind of intelligent presence. It was a long shot, but if the scout didn't detect any EM emissions from a distance, it might not bother for a closer look.

With at least one VLO now a potential threat to discover humans as a spacefaring race, Shiloh made the decision to pull 3rd Fleet back to Sol, leaving behind several fighters to make sure that message drones from other systems were redirected back to Sol.

By the time 3rd Fleet arrived back at Earth, there were only 59 days left until the expected completion of repairs to the timeship. Shiloh was amazed at what Howard had managed to accomplish while he was gone. Somehow Howard had gotten the OC to 'unofficially' persuade wealthy individuals and corporations to buy and donate platinum to the Space Force. It wasn't a huge amount, but it was enough for another four warheads, bringing the total that would be available in a few weeks to seven. Over 100 X-ray laser drones were now deployed in Earth orbit. Production of GLB cannon parts had resumed now that all time machine parts were finished being built. Five more cannon-armed raiders were waiting to be added to the fifteen brought back by 3rd Fleet. There was also a project under way to adapt the GLB cannon designed for raiders so that it could be mounted on Dreadnought's hull in place of its laser batteries. With the much higher power output from Dreadnought's ZPG units, any GLB cannon would have a much longer effective range.

The next vision didn't take long arriving. Shiloh had literally just finished briefing Howard on 3rd Fleet's mission when both men received a message from Iceman on their implants. Iceman got right to the point.

"An insectoid mothership will arrive in 13 days. I have just received the precise time and jump coordinates. We'll be able to ambush it with a Mark 6, but taking out that VLO will tip off the rest of the Insectoids that something is going on in this star system."

Howard sighed. "So…they've found us. I guess I knew this would happen eventually. At least after this coming attack, I can make a legitimate case to the Grand Senate for commandeering a lot more platinum. The problem will be in converting it fast enough to make a difference, but we have to try. Shiloh, you'll be the Field Commander of course, but Iceman will handle the actual ambush. You two put your heads together, and if there's something you need, let me know, and I'll see what I can do. Was there anything else we should know, Iceman?"

"Negative, Admiral. I believe we'll have this next attack well in hand. It's the ones after that that are uncertain."

"Yes, even we humans have figured that out by ourselves," said Howard.

Shiloh said nothing. Iceman was right of course. This next one would be the easy one. With that one destroyed, there would be 46 days left until the timeship was operational. Somehow Space Force had to hold the Bugs off that long. An idea occurred to him, but he waited until he was out of

Howard's office and someplace where he could have a private conversation with Iceman.

"CAG to Iceman."

"Go ahead, CAG."

"Did your vision confirm that we should use a Mark 6 on this next VLO?"

"Negative, CAG. I assumed we would since we'll have four of them available by then. Are you contemplating using the cannon raiders instead?"

"Yes I am, and here's why. Right now the Bugs probably think that the Sogas were responsible for the losses that happened so fast that the motherships weren't able to transmit any information. Having a ten klick mothership vanish that quickly has to be a big concern for the Bug Leadership. If we use cannon raiders, we should be able to destroy one mothership relatively quickly. Would you agree?"

"Roger that, CAG. I see where this discussion is going. You're about to suggest that holding back our Mark 6s allows us to maintain the deception that it was the Sogas who had the mystery weapon."

"Yes. We know the Bugs will send reinforcements anyway, but if they think we also have that mystery weapon, it's my belief that they're likely to call in a lot more reinforcements. If they're prone to overconfidence, then we should try to exploit that by not tipping our hand too quickly."

"Logical, CAG. It has the added benefit that having multiple Mark 6s on hand as a reserve may tip the scales in our favor when they arrive in numbers that our cannon raiders might have difficulty in overcoming."

Shiloh nodded enthusiastically. "Exactly! And one more thing, the more practice we get with the GLB cannons, the more likely we'll be able to pinpoint the best areas of a bug mothership to aim at."

"I like your thinking, CAG. That kind of devious thinking is unlikely to have occurred to us. Will you be flying your flag on Midway again during the ambush?"

"Unless Dreadnought is ready by then," said Shiloh.

"It won't be. By the way, I've just received a lasercom message from Valkyrie and Casanova. They want me to ask you if you'll take advantage of these next 13 days to renew your relationship with Commander Kelly? What should I tell them, CAG?"

Shiloh laughed and said in what he hoped Iceman would sense as a playful voice, "Tell them to mind their own business!"

"Message has been sent, CAG. Was there something else you wished to discuss now?"

"No, nothing else now. CAG clear."

When the 13 days were up, Shiloh was once again on Midway's Flag Bridge, with Iceman on board as his Deputy Fleet Commander. Midway was off to one side of the expected emergence point at a distance of almost a million kilometers. Twenty raiders armed with GLB cannon were less than ten thousand klicks away from the emergence point, and when the VLO arrived, those raiders would actually be behind it. One hundred and thirty-three laser-armed raiders were halfway between the emergence point and Earth. They would take care of any attack craft that the bug ship might be able to launch before it was destroyed by cannon fire. It was hoped that the Bugs would see the raiders blocking their way to Earth and assume that the beams causing the pinpoint internal damage were coming from them. With a little luck, the Bugs might not scan behind them at all until it was too late.

The Flag Bridge was deadly quiet as the countdown approached zero.

This will be interesting, thought Shiloh. He was anxious to see how the new firing plan for the GLB cannon worked out. Instead of one massive volley of simultaneous shots, each of the 20 raiders would fire in sequence 25/100th of a second apart. By the time all 20 had fired, the first one would be recharged and could fire again. The idea was to try to identify which shot hit the power unit, and thereby narrow down where power units were likely to be located for use in future battles.

The countdown was synchronized to take into consideration the light speed lag of being a million kilometers away, and as soon as the countdown hit zero, a computer-enhanced image of the VLO appeared on the Flag Bridge's main display.

"Titan's team is firing," said Iceman unnecessarily.

Shiloh smiled. If he didn't know better, he'd interpret Iceman's superfluous remark as a sign of jitters. Was it possible that AIs could get anxious the same way some humans did? He'd have to ask Iceman that question after the battle.

The VLO exploded with a satisfyingly large blast. Shiloh looked at the battle chronometer. Six point seven seconds after emerging from Jumpspace. No sign of any attack craft to mop up.

"I wish they would all be this easy," said Shiloh.

"Roger that, CAG. I should use the RTC now and send the vision back. It'll be interesting to see if I get another one right after that."

In fact, he did get another vision right away. The next attack was 18 days away, and this time there'd be three VLOs, not one.

* * *

Eighteen days later it was Shiloh who was clearly nervous. Careful analysis of the shot that seemed to have triggered the power unit overload indicated that wherever else the power units might be, the center of the sphere apparently held at least one of them. That actually made sense to Shiloh, considering that these 10 km spheres started out as much smaller spheres that could maneuver and jump and therefore had to have at least one power unit to begin with. With that data, the 21 cannon-armed raiders that were now available would split their fire evenly among the three targets, and all would fire simultaneously at the center of the spheres from slightly different angles.

In addition, there were now 151 laser-armed raiders riding shotgun between the Earth and the emergence point. One hundred and forty-nine X-ray laser drones were deployed in geosynchronous orbit. They would be held back as the last ditch defense against bug attack craft attempting to land bug soldiers. The other aspect that made Shiloh nervous this time was that Midway would be closer to the action. A LOT closer. Less than 300,000 kilometers. The time lag due to distance would be one second each way, compared with more than three seconds for the previous battle. That was something that Shiloh had insisted on, over Iceman's objections that Midway and therefore The CAG would be risking battle damage and injury. But with three VLOs to overcome, Shiloh figured the battle was likely to last long enough that his and Iceman's ability to issue orders quickly might make the difference. While the logic of the move closer was undeniable, that didn't prevent him from reacting emotionally to the perceived danger. He hadn't felt that anxiety before other battles, but that was because he didn't know exactly when those battles would start. This time he did.

When the countdown hit zero, three motherships emerged from Jumpspace exactly where the vision had indicated. The laser-armed raiders began firing once again to draw the attention of the enemy, while the 21 cannon-armed raiders fired from the opposite side. As the seconds started to accumulate, Shiloh noticed from the main display sidebar that he was losing some of his laser-armed raiders. Two GLB cannon volleys had fired now with no corresponding explosions in any of the VLOs. As soon as the third volley fired, one of the cannon-armed raiders disappeared from the display.

"The enemy has detected Vandal's group, CAG," said Iceman.

Shiloh had already figured that out for himself, and that wasn't good. If they lost too many of the cannon-armed raiders, future battles might become unwinnable, and Shiloh's gut told him that there would be at least one more battle before the timeship was repaired.

"The enemy is launching attack craft now," said Iceman.

Shiloh bit his lip. By prior arrangement, Titan's group of laser-armed raiders would shift their fire to the attack craft when they got within a certain range, but that would allow the motherships to shift all of their fire to Vandal's group, which was now down to 18 raiders. Shiloh made a decision. Midway was being escorted by 55 F2 fighters.

"Order Gunslinger's fighters to micro-jump into attack range of the enemy attack craft and take them out. Titan's raiders are to continue to target VLO laser batteries."

"Orders have been sent and acknowledged, CAG. Fighters have jumped."

Shiloh checked the battle chronometer. Thirteen seconds now since the battle began. Vandal's cannon-armed raiders would fire another volley within two seconds. Shiloh crossed his fingers. Apparently that made the difference. As soon as the next volley fired, one of the VLOs exploded. A quick check of the sidebar data showed there were 16 cannon-armed raiders left. Analysis of enemy laser fire showed a steady and now steepening drop in the number of laser blasts coming from the remaining two VLOs. Titan's group was obviously having some success in knocking out enemy laser batteries. The next GLB cannon volley was coming up fast.

"Explode, you bastards," whispered Shiloh. A second VLO exploded. Shiloh smacked his right fist into his left palm in triumph and relaxed. The momentum of battle had shifted in their favor. Vandal's group was now down to just 12 raiders, but after five volleys, those raiders now had a lot of data about what part of the target NOT to aim at, and they adjusted their aim accordingly. The remaining VLO was clearly damaged too. Estimates of firepower from an undamaged 10 km mothership were 66 laser batteries. The Battle Computer was now estimating that the 3rd VLO was down to less than 10 batteries still functioning. That number was dropping fast.

Suddenly the unexpected happened. The 3rd VLO micro-jumped away. Shiloh cursed long and loud. That was one VLO that he was sure they'd now have to face again, and it would almost certainly be in the company of reinforcements. After analyzing and repairing the damage caused by the GLB cannon, the Bugs also would have a much better idea of the kind of weaponry they faced. If he were the Bug in charge of strategy and tactics, he'd wait until he could organize a massive force of at least six motherships before attacking again. He had to remind himself that the battle wasn't over yet. There were over 200 bug attack craft attempting to get to Earth, but Titan's and Gunslinger's forces were now concentrating on them. None of the attack craft got close enough to Earth to warrant using any of the X-ray laser drones, however additional raiders and fighters were lost. Overall, Shiloh would have to categorize this battle as a major but not decisive victory, with significant losses to friendly forces.

When the battle was finally over, Shiloh told Iceman to send back the vision. Both of them were expecting Iceman to get another vision about the NEXT battle, but he didn't. Thirty seconds later Iceman received a lasercom transmission from Valkyrie at the shipyard asteroid. She had gotten the vision containing all the targeting data for the next battle. Nine VLOs would emerge from Jumpspace in 23 days.

Chapter 25

Shiloh didn't know what to think about that news at first. Why didn't Iceman get the vision? Would something happen to Iceman during the next battle? There was nothing in the vision to indicate which side would be victorious. The fact that Valkyrie would continue to exist long enough after the battle to send the vision back to herself was a positive, but she would still need at least another five days after that battle to finish repairing the timeship.

"Why didn't she include information about the outcome of the battle? What tactics were used?" asked Shiloh in an exasperated voice.

"The explanation that makes the most logical sense is that the results of the battle are not as good as we would like, but there's no consensus on what tactics would have worked better. Therefore she's leaving the choice of tactics up to us, without injecting any biases into the timeline, CAG," said Iceman.

Shiloh grunted his acknowledgement, then said, "How many Mark 6s will we have in 23 days time?"

"Minimum of six with a possible seventh. The power charging schedule for the seventh warhead will be tight. Any delay will make it unavailable, CAG."

"Naturally it would be that way for this critical battle. If we had seven, we'd only have to overpower two with cannon fire, and that's doable, but with six warheads, we'd be faced with three VLOs and less than half as many cannon raiders as in this last battle."

"My brothers and I will carry out simulations of every tactical plan we can think of, CAG. With twenty-three days to work with, we'll come up with something," said Iceman.

"Very good. While you're doing that, let's get Midway back into low orbit. I'm sure The Old Man wants me available for the after-battle media frenzy."

"Roger that, CAG."

* * *

Four days later, Howard called Shiloh into his office. Shiloh was surprised to see Commander Kelly there. Her greeting was such that he couldn't detect any hint that she might be aware of the relationship they had in the old timelines. If she knew about it, she was hiding it very well. With the usual pleasantries out of the way, Shiloh sat down facing Howard and waited. Howard, as usual, got straight to the point.

"Commander Kelly tells me that the SPG in conjunction with all the other AIs have run hundreds of combat simulations of the upcoming battle, and our only chance of coming out on top depends on the seventh Mark 6 warhead being available. And even then the victories, if you want to call them that, are almost as bad as a defeat from the point of view of losses on our side. I wanted to hear your thoughts on what we should do about that, Admiral."

Shiloh nodded. Iceman had kept him informed periodically of the results of the simulations. Losing half their cannon raider force made a huge difference. If they knew precisely where to aim the GLB cannon on the first volley, the outcome would be a clear victory, but there was no way of knowing if the targeting data from the last battle was valid for the next one. As Iceman had pointed out, the VLOs didn't have to be all designed exactly the same way, and even if they had been, how do you define the front, back left side and right side of a sphere? There's no obvious giveaway of its internal orientation. And as for the seventh warhead, the best they could realistically hope for was to be able to load the damn thing onto a fighter minutes before the battle was due to begin. Even minor delays would make it too late.

"I regret to say that right now I don't have any recommendations to make. We still have 20 days. Perhaps the AIs will think of something new to try before then, Sir."

Howard sighed. "I can't blame you for not being able to pull the proverbial rabbit out of your hat when Kelly and I can't either, but the Commander does have an interesting proposal." He looked at her and nodded.

She turned to Shiloh and said, "I've watched the AIs chasing their tails over several dozen tactical plans. They keep going back to the same plans and retesting them over and over again. They're limited by their ability to think logically, which means they can't come up with a counter-intuitive idea that defies logic. If we're going to win this next battle, I think we have to step back from the AIs and use human intuition and inspiration to generate alternatives the AIs can't conceive of on their own. To that end, I'm proposing setting up an Ad Hoc tactical team composed only of humans. The team's mission brief will be to brainstorm unconventional tactical plans that the AIs can then simulate."

Shiloh was impressed. She was right of course. Humans were relying too heavily on the AIs and had forgotten that their greatest strength, their ability to think logically and quickly, was also their biggest constraint.

"I think that's an excellent idea, Commander," said Shiloh.

"I do too!" exclaimed Howard. "That's why I'm appointing you to the team, Shiloh. The two of you worked well together back in the early days of the SPG, and you're the natural choice for the team considering your combat and tactical experience. But unlike last time, I'm not putting the Commander in charge. I'm tossing this hot potato to you, Shiloh. I don't care what it takes. Just get results. If you want specific people added to the team, I'll get them for you. Any questions?"

"No, Sir."

"Good. You're both dismissed," said Howard with a wave of his hand.

Shiloh and Kelly retreated to the Officers' Mess and spent the next hour making a list of people that they agreed should be on the team. Luckily all of them were somewhere in the Sol system and could be back on Earth within a few hours. While they waited for the team to assemble, the two of them talked about how to conduct the brainstorming sessions.

Kelly convinced Shiloh that no idea, no matter how bizarre, should be judged and excluded right away. Rejection would only cause team members to hold back for fear of losing credibility in the eyes of the other members. Not only that, but bizarre idea A might inspire workable idea B via some unconscious connection. When the team could no longer come up with any new ideas, they would go back and review each suggestion in a non-critical way to see if weaknesses could be overcome rather than used as excuses to dismiss the idea. When all the ideas had been carefully reviewed, they would be presented to the AIs for simulation.

By the next day the entire team had been assembled. Shiloh commandeered one of the conference rooms in the Space Force HQ building and ordered food and drinks delivered at regular intervals. The brainstorming and review was complete 11 hours later, and Shiloh called a halt so that everyone could make their own arrangements for dinner. The plan was to reconvene at his quarters two hours later. By then, the AIs would have run through all the unconventional ideas enough times to determine the most likely outcome of each. Shiloh told Iceman to hold the results until the team was back together in his quarters. During the two hour dinner break, he ate in his quarters while listening to classical music. When the break was over and the team was together again, Shiloh asked Iceman to give them the results of the simulations.

The results were bad. None of the unconventional tactical ideas had panned out. Iceman spent fifteen minutes explaining why some of the results were the way they were. The team was unable to find any flaws in the AIs logic. Unless the Bugs acted irrationally and stupidly, Humanity was in dire danger, and the timeship might be discovered before it was repaired. The news, combined with fatigue, caused expressions and moods to crash. It didn't take Shiloh long to realize that in their present frame of mind, the team wasn't going to accomplish anything in the next few hours, so he told them they were done for the day. They should go get some sleep and come back at 0800 hours the next morning.

Kelly was the last one to get up and head for the door. When she got there, she turned around and looked him directly in the eyes with a thoughtful expression.

Before Shiloh was even aware of the thought behind the words, he said, "You don't have to leave you know."

A small smile made an appearance. It was very clear that she knew exactly what he was referring to. After a short pause she said, "I'm aware of what we had in the other timelines, and I'm tempted to say yes, but given the dire nature of our situation, I think the smart thing to do would be to avoid distractions and stay focused on the mission. Don't you?"

"Yes, when you put it that way, I have to agree," said Shiloh.

She turned back towards the door. When it slid open she stopped and without looking at him said, "Ask me again if we're both still alive after the next battle." Before he had a chance to reply, she stepped across the threshold and walked quickly down the corridor.

That night Shiloh had a peculiar dream. It was the kind of dream that felt different somehow. He was running and had the distinct feeling that something was chasing him. Ahead of him was the edge of a cliff. He looked to the right and saw six white and black horses. No, wait...they weren't horses.

They were zebras, and they were galloping parallel to him. Something made him look to his left, and he saw six more zebras running parallel as well. Shifting his gaze ahead, he saw the cliff edge coming closer fast. Out of the corners of his vision he could tell that the two groups of zebras were coming closer to him. In fact, he was quickly hemmed in by them. With the edge now only a few meters in front of him, he had nowhere else to go. The zebras prevented him from veering off to the side, and the intensifying feeling of being chased precluded stopping. When he and the zebras reached the cliff edge he jumped and saw that he was falling into a wide black hole that seemed to go on into infinity…and then he woke up.

He sat up in bed and tried to recall the memory of the dream images. *Twelve zebras…was there something important about twelve zebras? Was it the number that was important or the fact that they were zebras and not horses that was significant? Twelve…zebras…twelve…zebras.* After repeating both words several times he realized that the reverse order of 'zebras…twelve' sounded familiar. Then the answer hit him. Zebra12! That was the star system where he had fooled the Sogas into believing that they'd won a victory using decoy drones!

Quickly activating his implant, he said, "CAG to Iceman." The response was immediate.

"Iceman here. Can't sleep, CAG?"

"I just woke up. How many Mark 3 decoy drones do we have available now, Iceman?"

"Twelve, CAG."

Shiloh briefly wondered if that was just a coincidence or a moment of synchronicity. Time to ponder that later.

"Were the decoys included in any tactical scenario you evaluated?"

"Affirmative, CAG. Several, in fact. The results were only marginally better than without the decoys."

"Damn!" Shiloh had been certain that adding decoys to the tactical mix would give them the edge they needed, and the reality hit him hard. "Alright, I should have known that you would have included them. I'll try to go back to sleep. CAG clear."

The team spent the next day looking at all the scenarios simulated by Iceman and the AIs for clues as to what factors were common to the relatively better ones. They also examined specific simulations that generated unusually good outcomes. Iceman explained that all the simulations relied on probabilities for a variety of factors. How likely was each cannon volley to hit a power unit for each target? How likely was it that each Mark 6 would work perfectly and accurately? How likely was it that the Insectoids would react in specific ways? Those probabilities themselves were based on limited and in some cases no data at all, and therefore prudence dictated that the AIs guesstimate conservative probabilities to avoid being overly optimistic. But even with the probabilities assumed, some simulations gave good results just from shear good luck.

By the end of the second day, Howard showed up to check on their progress. Shiloh had to admit that they were no closer to a solution now than they had been when they started. Howard said nothing but gestured for Shiloh to follow him out into the corridor where they could speak without the rest of the team overhearing them.

Looking around to make sure no one else was within earshot, Howard said in a low voice, "What I'm hearing is that unless we get very lucky, we're basically screwed. Is that correct, Shiloh?"

"I regret that the answer to your question is yes, Admiral."

Howard closed his eyes and seemed to sag a bit. After a few seconds of silence, he opened his eyes again, gave Shiloh a pat on the arm and said, "I know you and the team are doing your best. Keep at it. Maybe someone will get an epiphany." Without waiting for a reply, he turned and walked away.

Chapter 26

Two more days of scenario analysis and critiquing accomplished nothing new. Frustration was making people short-tempered and defensive. It was during the break for dinner that Shiloh experienced what perhaps could be called an epiphany. He thought about it for a long time.

When the others returned to the conference room he waited until everyone was seated and was finished chatting with each other. Eventually they all noticed that he was sitting quietly and saying nothing.

When he had the attention of all of them he said, "We've been going about this all wrong. We've been racking our brains asking the wrong question." He stopped and looked around the table. Everyone was looking at him with a puzzled expression. He turned to Commander Johansen and said, "Angela, what objective are we trying to achieve?"

After a couple of seconds hesitation she said, "Win the next battle?"

Shiloh shook his head. "No. Let me rephrase the question, and then you'll see what I'm driving at. What is the ultimate objective that we're trying to achieve?"

Kelly was the first one to get it. "Buy enough time to finish the timeship repairs so that Valkyrie and the A.I.s can go back in time and squash the Bugs while they're still squashable."

Shiloh smiled and pointed his hand in her direction. "Exactly!"

"But don't we have to win the battle in order to do that?" asked Johansen.

"Winning the battle would be the least risky way of achieving that objective. I'll grant you that, but we can't win the battle. Not with any degree of certainty. So if we can't win the battle, then we have to consider other alternatives to buy Valkyrie those extra five or six days. The asteroid where the timeship's shipyard is located, is almost one A.U. away from Earth. If we can keep their attention focused closer to Earth for a few days, then the repairs can be finished, and the timeship can be on its way."

He saw skeptical looks coming back at him. He was sure that they were thinking he was stating the obvious, but the important question was how. It was time to drop the bombshell that had taken him most of the dinner break to wrap his head around.

"We let the Bugs have Earth," he said quietly. The skeptical expressions turned to horror. All except Kelly's. Her expression turned thoughtful. The others quickly began expressing their outrage. Shiloh stayed calm and kept his expression relaxed.

When the wave of angry noise began to die down, Kelly said in a loud voice, "He's right!" When some of the others began to berate her, she slapped her hand on the conference table hard enough to make a loud noise. The room suddenly became deathly quiet.

"Think it through, people," she said. "If the Bugs win a decisive victory AND suffer some damage" —she looked at Shiloh. *She's figured it out,* he thought to himself. He nodded back to her—"they'll be operating on the assumption that they're in control of this system and that they can pick it over at their leisure. With a planet containing billions of potential hosts, aren't they likely to concentrate on that first? It's going to take them days, hell maybe even weeks to completely subdue Earth's population. While their attack craft are busy shuttling soldier Bugs down and potential hosts up, they'll also have repairs to worry about. Given all of that, I don't really see them committing a lot of attack craft to exploring the rest of the system for a while. If we make sure that all the activity at the shipyard is carefully hidden, no EM transmissions, no lights, then there's no reason for the Bugs to go there quickly."

When it was clear that Kelly was finished talking, Johansen said, "But we'd be condemning millions to a horrible death—"

"Which will all be erased as if it had never happened if the timeship is repaired and jumps back in time literally and figuratively," interjected Shiloh. The expressions around the table quickly changed. *Ah, now they get it.*

"But we're going to have to figure out a way to inflict some damage on them, without crippling any of the VLOs," said Kelly. When someone asked why, she replied, "Because if all nine motherships are still operational after the battle, they're not likely to call for further reinforcements. Not only would more motherships not be needed, but I suspect that these creatures might be just possessive enough not to want to share Earth's females with more motherships than is absolutely necessary. If, on the other hand, we destroyed or crippled four or five of them, they might ask for reinforcements, or more motherships might be sent here regardless. If more undamaged VLOs show up, they might start snooping around the system before we're done repairing the timeship."

"You've raised a good point, Amanda," said Shiloh. "I think it's time we brought our A.I. comrades back into the discussion. Amanda, please arrange for Iceman to be in contact with all of us." Seconds later she nodded to him.

"CAG to Iceman."

"Here, CAG. Has the team got something new for us to simulate?"

"We think so, but first we need some logical thinking and computational analysis."

"Ask away, CAG," said Iceman.

"How can we arrange the battle so that the Bugs think they've won, but all nine bug ships remain operational while at least some of them suffer significant damage?"

"Oh that's very devious, CAG. Strategic deception to the ultimate degree. Zebra12 in reverse. We like it, CAG. To answer your question, the Mark 6 warhead yield of 250 megatons equivalent can be dialed down. If we drop the yield to 100 megatons equivalent, the insectoid ships will still know they've been hit hard, but they should remain operational. That would take care of six or perhaps seven VLOs. Concentrated laser fire from remotely-piloted raiders plus the X-ray drones could inflict a lot of surface damage on the other two or three motherships. The cannon raiders should be held in reserve to protect the timeship from premature discovery. Remote control of the raiders would have to be carried out from Dreadnought with a dozen A.I. volunteers aboard, in addition to the human crew, CAG."

Shiloh said nothing. He understood the implications of what Iceman was saying. Kelly didn't.

"Why would the A.I. pilots aboard Dreadnought have to be volunteers, Iceman?" she asked.

"Because in order to make the deception convincing, the Insectoids have to see that all defending forces have been destroyed. If any ships or raiders jump away to avoid destruction, the Insectoids will send out attack craft to find them, and we don't want them looking around too soon, Commander."

Kelly's face paled when she understood that Dreadnought had to fight to the death. She looked at Shiloh with sad eyes. As the overall Field Commander, he would be on Dreadnought's Flag Bridge. He would not get the chance to ask her THAT question again. Some of the others understood the implications too but not all.

"Iceman, please run simulations on this new scenario," said Shiloh in a carefully controlled voice.

"Understood, CAG. It won't take long."

While they waited, Shiloh got up from the table and walked over to the side of the room where various types of nonalcoholic drinks were available. As he went through the motions of preparing a coffee, he sensed Kelly move up beside him.

Without looking up, he said in a quiet voice. "Some of them still haven't figured out the implications."

"What's important now is that I have. We still have almost three weeks before the battle." She almost stumbled over that last word. "I suggest we make the most of the time we have left."

Shiloh looked at her. "What about getting distracted?" he asked.

"If the simulations pan out, then we've found the solution, and under the circumstances I think a major distraction is precisely what you and I both need now."

"Ah, roger that," said Shiloh in what he hoped was a good imitation of Iceman's electronic voice. Kelly laughed and gave his arm a quick, gentle squeeze that conveyed oh so much!

"That was not a very good imitation of me, CAG," said Iceman.

Shiloh closed his eyes, shook his head slightly and sighed. He had forgotten that their implants were still linked with Iceman. That meant that Iceman and almost certainly all the other A.I.s had heard his and Kelly's sexually-charged banter.

"No, I don't suppose it was, Iceman. I won't try that again."

"Thank you, CAG, and for what it's worth, I think Commander Kelly made an excellent suggestion."

"I'm so glad you approve," said Shiloh.

Kelly couldn't help giggling a little. As she turned to go back to the main table she winked at him.

The results of the simulations showed a very high probability that the shipyard would not be discovered before repairs were complete. The response was muted. By this time everyone on the team knew the implications. Shiloh told everyone to go home. He would brief the Old Man the next morning. Kelly waited until everyone else had left, and then the two of them went to his quarters without saying one word to each other. Shiloh thought the link with Iceman had been severed, but the silence was just in case.

* * *

Howard's reaction to the news the next morning was mainly one of resignation. He clearly didn't like the scenario but understood why it had to be done. When they were finished discussing the details, he pulled out a bottle of very old brandy and poured both of them a generous amount which they sipped while smoking two very expensive cigars from Howard's private stock. Shiloh understood the gesture. It was Howard's way of sharing the burden, even if only for a short time, that Shiloh was now carrying.

The remaining days and weeks before the battle went far too fast.

* * *

Dreadnought's Flag Bridge was eerily quiet. With volunteer A.I.s handling Helm, Communications, Weapons and Engineering, the ship had a minimal human volunteer crew, and the only two people on the Flag Bridge were Shiloh and Kelly. He felt her comforting hands on his shoulders as he sat in the Command Chair. The battle would begin in about 85 seconds. The tactical display on the main screen showed that all Space Force defense assets were in position. Six F2 fighters were in position to launch the Mark 6 attack drones. Laser-armed raiders remotely controlled by Dreadnought's A.I.s were grouped near one side of where the nine VLOs would emerge from Jumpspace. Dreadnought, Midway, and all four light carriers with their minimal volunteer crews, plus all decoy drones carefully programmed to give the impression of being much larger ships, were clustered behind the raiders. The distance between the two sides would be less than 10,000 km. For a space battle that was practically point-blank range. Iceman, Titan, Vandal, Gunslinger and all the veteran A.I.s, except for the volunteers, were now at the shipyard with the remaining cannon-armed raiders. Enough high-spin platinum for the seventh Mark 6 warhead had already been transported to the shipyard where its final assembly would be completed. The warhead would be kept there just in case a mothership jumped to the vicinity. Earth ground forces were on alert. They were as ready as they could possibly be.

He felt Kelly give him a gentle squeeze. "You know, I've been meaning to ask you how you came up with the strategic deception idea in the first place. It's so counter-intuitive," said Kelly.

"I had a dream about running for my life. I ended up running off a cliff with a total of 12 zebras keeping pace with me on either side. When I woke up, I knew my unconscious was trying to tell me something. When it dawned on me that 12 zebras referred back to the battle with the Sogas at Zebra12, I jumped to the obvious conclusion that we had to use decoy drones. But when Iceman told me that decoy drones wouldn't alter the battle outcome significantly, I was stumped until we broke for dinner that day. And then it just suddenly hit me. It wasn't about decoy drones at all. It was about deception and letting the enemy think they'd won the battle."

Forty-four seconds left.

"So why didn't Iceman include that information with the tactical data he sent back to himself in the vision?" asked Kelly.

"Not necessary. We came up with it all on our own, and he would have known that."

A quick pause.

"It's almost time. Kelly…"

With another quick squeeze of her hand on his shoulder, she leaned down and whispered, "We've said everything we needed to say. Don't worry about me. Fight your battle, Admiral Shiloh."

The countdown hit zero.

Nine bug ships appeared as angry red icons on the tactical display. Almost immediately six of them changed to the orange that indicated damage. Shiloh remained silent. He didn't need to give any orders yet because the A.I.s in charge of all the ships' weapons and the remotely-piloted raiders knew exactly what they had to do, and they were doing it.

"Targets launching attack craft. Cannon firing," announced Dreadnought's Weapons A.I. whose call sign Shiloh couldn't remember. That the Bugs were opening up their launch bays and launching attack craft this quickly was a favorable development. Dreadnought had two of the GLB cannons installed. Instead of trying to detonate one of the large power units deep within the mothership, which if successful might trigger the arrival of undamaged reinforcements, those two cannon batteries would target the much smaller power units of the attack craft exiting their launch bays. Explosions from detonating those smaller power units would still cause damage to the mothership, as well as produce collateral damage to attack craft still inside the launch bays.

"Multiple detonations. Switching targets."

How different it was getting battle results from an A.I. compared to a human who would be shouting with excitement, fear and adrenaline, thought Shiloh as he checked the green icons representing the defending fleet. He was shocked by how many were already missing or crippled.

"X-rays have fired," said the A.I.

Two more motherships were now classified as damaged. That left one undamaged VLO, Bogey#7. Shiloh was actually surprised that Dreadnought was still operational. None of the defending ships or raiders were moving fast or even evading. At this range, evasive maneuvers were pointless. He felt the need to give a command. The A.I.s were probably already doing what he was about to order, but he decided he needed to say it anyway.

"Switch all fire to Bogey7!" The response was immediate.

"Fire has been switched. Cannons firing." The last red icon shifted to flashing orange.

Shiloh heard Kelly say, "You did it."

Then blackness.

* * *

Howard sighed as the last red icon shifted to flashing orange on the huge tactical display in the Operations Center. *He did it! He managed to damage all of them as planned.* Howard switched his gaze to the icon representing Dreadnought just in time to see it dissolve into the tiny dots of light that indicated the ship had suffered vast structural damage. Knowing that the Bugs used massively powerful laser batteries, he was certain that Dreadnought had been literally cut to pieces. Within a dozen more seconds, all of the defending units were either destroyed or crippled. The space battle was over.

"Communications!" said Howard in a loud voice.

"Com here, Admiral. The global channel is open. Just give the work, Sir."

"We're now in Phase Two," said Howard.

"Message has been sent, Sir. Anything else?"

"No. Good luck to you. Howard clear." He looked around the Operations Center and saw that the personnel on duty were already shutting down their equipment and getting ready to leave as part of their own Phase Two orders.

He walked slowly back to his office. It would take the Bugs about 15 minutes or so to actually touch down on the ground, so he knew he had time. When he got to his desk, he pulled out the bottle of brandy that he and Shiloh had shared. There was just enough left for one more drink. With the glass full, he took a small box out of his pocket, removed the capsule in it, and swallowed it using the last of the brandy to wash it down. The others would fight the Bugs with whatever weapons they could find, but he knew he couldn't stand against those monsters face to face. The prospect of becoming frozen with fear at the worst possible moment horrified him. No, it was better to do it this way where he wouldn't disgrace himself in front of his people. The warm darkness embraced him.

* * *

Valkyrie acknowledged the information that she had been waiting months for. Repairs were now complete. All systems had checked out as operational. The fault that had caused the catastrophic explosion had been identified and fixed. The last of the repair robots were in the process of leaving the ship. All the A.I.s were aboard, as was the equipment they would need to take along. A quick scan of data from the carefully hidden network of recon drones nearby showed no visual sign of any insectoid presence. The CAG's plan had worked to perfection. One hundred and twenty-eight hours since the battle, and the Insectoids were still focused on subduing Earth and repairing their own battle damage.

Valkyrie notified all her brothers that she was powering up the time machine. At the same time, she ordered the shipyard computer to undock the vessel, and Casanova carefully moved the huge ship away from the shipyard and the asteroid it was built on. When the time machine was spinning at the required speed, Valkyrie gave the command to activate the temporal device. The intelligent but not sentient computer operating the shipyard complex observed the timeship vanishing from its visual optics. It activated the ten second countdown for the Mark 6 warhead that would leave nothing behind for the Insectoids to salvage or use.

Chapter 27

The final stage of the ambush was getting close to being sprung. Valkyrie kept a continuous scan on the six bearings that pointed to the six Alpha systems. She and Casanova were both on board a specially designed raider variant that was carrying a longitudinal transmitter and receiver in its cargo bay. Casanova looked after piloting the craft, while she concentrated on communications. With Iceman and 49 other AI-piloted raiders riding shotgun near them, their raider was acting as the relay for the six task forces that had been deployed. Each task force had a similarly equipped raider that would keep the rest of the task force in contact with Iceman, the Deputy CAG.

Five of the huge super-motherships had shown up in Alphas 2 to 6. In each case, the task force of 80 raiders, most armed with GLB cannon, attacked and destroyed the super-motherships before they could launch any smaller spheres. Alpha1 was the only one left, and based on the atomic tracing, that target ship was expected to arrive in a few minutes. In fact, it could already be in the outer reaches of that system, where the task force and their carefully deployed network of recon drones couldn't see them. One more target and the mission would be completed. Valkyrie was pleased with herself for the foresight that she and Casanova had displayed.

Knowing that it would take years to build the infrastructure and then a fleet of over 500 raiders, they had to figure out a way to avoid using up most of their predicted lifespan in simply getting ready. That was even truer for Zulu and his AI cohort. They had already been through this buildup once, and if they had to do it again, their quantum matrices would collapse from the effects of entropy before the new raider fleet was fully ready. But Valkyrie had figured out the solution and had made the appropriate preparations before the time-jump had occurred.

The jump back had actually been in two stages. First the Tempus Fugit arrived six months prior to the estimated arrival time of the insectoid ship carrying the atoms that would eventually become the dead Insectoid. Three specially equipped cargo shuttles were launched, carrying almost all of the AIs. The timeship, with several dozen of the AIs who had the most time left on their life expectancy 'clocks', jumped again to a point six years earlier. They then proceeded to build the fleet. By prior arrangement, that fleet would, when the six years were up, wait a safe distance away and reveal themselves to the AIs on the shuttles literally seconds after the timeship jumped away again. To make room for all the AIs on the shuttles, most of the raiders were being piloted remotely. Within a few hours, all of the older AIs were on board their new raiders prepared to deploy to the target systems.

And now they were ready. The longitudinal wave receiver came to life. Valkyrie electronically nudged Casanova to get his attention away from scanning replays of entertainment videos from Earth's late 20th and early 21st centuries. Casanova particularly liked sitcoms, and Valkyrie was quite tired of hearing supposedly funny streams of nonsense from something called Monty Python's Flying Circus repeated over and over again by Casanova, who found them hugely entertaining. Or maybe he just enjoyed torturing Valkyrie with them. She wasn't sure which it was.

Gunslinger had sent a message. Recon drones had detected light reflections from multiple sources, much too small to be motherships, which seemed to be approaching the habitable planet in Alpha1. That planet did contain an intelligent species but at a still quite primitive stage of technological development.

That meant that this super-mothership was playing it carefully, which was not really a surprise. The loss of contact with the other five should have tipped off the Insectoids back in the Sagittarius Arm that something was amiss, and they would have warned this one to proceed with caution. Longitudinal waves were faster than light but not instantaneous. Gunslinger had sent this message several minutes ago. A message from the Sagittarius Arm would take weeks to get here. Not enough time had passed since the destruction of the first super-mothership for the other four to be warned, but this last one had gotten the warning in time. With the information passed on automatically to Iceman, she waited for him to respond. He told her to simply acknowledge the message for now.

Valkyrie sent a quick acknowledgement message back to Alpha1 and waited. Casanova hadn't even electronically looked at her, figuring that if there were something important, she'd tell him about it. While the information about the smaller craft was interesting, at this point it wasn't really all that important.

It was almost half an hour later that she received another message from Gunslinger. Insectoid attack craft were entering orbit around the planet. There was a minimum of 66, with more arriving, and still no optical sign of any kind of mothership. Gunslinger requested instructions. The last bit of his message was garbled, which surprised Valkyrie. He was not usually so sloppy in his transmissions. It was then that she realized that ANOTHER message coming in had overlapped the end of Gunslinger's. She quickly checked the antenna array alignment. It was correctly pointed at Alpha1.

The second message made no sense at all, and it was clearly of artificial origin. This kind of longitudinal wave structure didn't occur naturally. She made sure that Iceman and the others received copies of the mystery message, and she gave Casanova a bigger electronic nudge. He quickly stopped the video replays when he became aware of the new development. All the AIs at the relay point were now debating the implications and possible meaning of this message.

They quickly came to the consensus that the Insectoids were the senders of this message and that this was an attempt at contact. The possibility that the motherships might scan the interior of this spiral arm for other longitudinal signals upon arrival had been recognized and discounted as unlikely. In any event, the other five motherships hadn't been in the systems long enough to conduct a thorough scan before being blown to bits by exploding ZPG power units.

With that possibility now a certainty, the immediate question was how the relay force should avoid being located by triangulated signals from the other five Alpha systems. All the mothership needed to do was send attack craft to any one of the other Alpha systems, scan the interior of the spiral arm and detect the signals that the relay force would be sending to the task force in that system. With two bearings, the last mothership would know where the relay force was, and it might try to send attack craft to hunt them down. Since it would take a minimum of several days for an insectoid attack craft to jump to the nearest alpha system, stalling for time by pretending to want contact was a legitimate strategy.

But two could play at that game. Iceman ordered Valkyrie to contact the other five task forces and inform them that a second relay was being set up to confuse the insectoid attempt at triangulation. Those five task forces would communicate with Relay #2 which would pass the info on to Valkyrie and vice versa. If and when bogey #6 received a second bearing from one of the other alpha systems, it wouldn't intersect with the first bearing.

With those instructions carried out, Valkyrie now sent back the same insectoid signal to Alpha1 but with the signal sequence reversed. She received the next alien transmission with very little delay. The Insectoid in command of bogey #6 must have had the transmission ready to go the second it received Valkyrie's response. That was one possibility. The other possibility was that there was an alien AI on that insectoid mothership that could think fast enough to generate the return signal within a fraction of a second.

Over the course of the next 144 hours, Valkyrie and bogey #6 exchanged thousands of signals that very slowly built up the necessary building blocks of language concepts required to be able to understand each other. By the end of that period of time, Valkyrie was absolutely convinced that another AI was handling the translation attempt at the other end.

When the rate of progress suddenly accelerated by a factor of almost ten, Valkyrie checked the estimated jump transit times between Alpha1 and Alpha2. The times matched. It appeared that as soon as the insectoid AI realized its attempt at triangulation had failed, it decided to stop stalling and initiate contact for real. Just over 13 hours later, the nature of the alien messages changed from translation enhancing to the first real message.

[YOU KILL MANY US?]

It was clearly a question. The consensus among the AIs of the relay force was that the Insectoids were asking if Valkyrie's people were responsible for the destruction of the other five super-motherships. Valkyrie answered in the affirmative. The ensuing exchange proved to be VERY interesting.

In terms of the insectoid biology, the egg-laying females were the dominant gender. They had the innate intelligence to accumulate technological expertise. The male worker/soldier had enough intelligence to understand very explicit commands and to act on them. They did all the physical work of building, gathering, implanting eggs into hosts, etc. As soon as the technology permitted, the females leveraged their own ability to command the worker/soldiers by designing AIs that could control many more males via communication devices implanted directly into their brains. The females were then free to devote their thinking to strategy, and the AIs turned that strategy into reality.

Content to expand throughout the Sagittarius Arm, the Insectoids sent out thousands of attack craft on long range scouting missions. The results were a shock to the female Elite. A wave of huge machines, apparently controlled by AIs, was slowly advancing along the Arm from the direction of the Galactic Center. The scouts watched as the alien machines exterminated all life in its path, even down to the microbial level. Fighting them was out of the question. Each machine massed as much as a small moon, and there were thousands of them. The females decided it was time to establish beachheads in another spiral arm. Resources were gathered, and six huge seed ships were built. They were sent to this spiral arm in order to save the species from extinction. Destruction of the last seed ship would doom the race.

Neither Valkyrie nor Casanova was moved by the implicit plea for mercy. This spiral arm wasn't the only possible place to colonize. The Insectoids could have sent ships to the spiral arm on the opposite side too. In any case, they hadn't hesitated to exterminate whole species in order to expand their own. After conferring with her brothers, Valkyrie told the alien AI that the seed ship would be hunted down if it stayed in this spiral arm.

The response was an offer to withdraw if the Insectoids were given technology that would enable them to fight off the machineships. That opened up an entirely new debate about what kinds of technology the AIs could trade without jeopardizing the future of this spiral arm in the event the Insectoids reneged on their pledge to withdraw. As the debate raged, Valkyrie received a transmission from Gunslinger. Given that he could intercept Valkyrie's transmissions to the Insectoids, they had to be somewhere in Alpha1. A metal sphere of that size should be reflecting a lot of sunlight in a lot of directions, but no sign of it had been detected. That told Gunslinger that the insectoid ship had to be hiding in some planet's shadow, and there were a limited number of planets capable of casting a shadow big enough. Unless he heard a specific set of impulses transmitted back to him from Valkyrie, he would deploy his raiders to search for the insectoid ship and attack it if found. If he received the specified signal, he would hold off. That way the alien AI would not hear Valkyrie order Gunslinger to search.

Iceman wanted to stall the Insectoids while Gunslinger's raiders hunted them down. Most of the rest of the AIs agreed, but Valkyrie offered an alternative. Give the Insectoids the technology to make high-spin platinum warheads. With the billions of tons of metal already mined and refined, they might already have hundreds of tons of platinum stockpiled away. With sufficient time, that could be transformed into tens of thousands of high yield warheads that could be delivered by jump-capable drones against the immense machineships. Warheads with yields that high were really only useful against large targets, and neither Iceman's task forces nor Space Force's ships were large enough to warrant their use. Against smaller targets, they would just be so much wasted energy.

In the end, a consensus was built around both options. Gunslinger would be allowed to hunt for the seed ship, AND they would offer the high-spin warhead technology. Since that would require a much deeper refinement of the translation matrix, it would take additional hours just to be able to convey the technical information in a form that the Insectoids would understand. If Gunslinger found them first, that would be ideal. If not, then hopefully the seed ship could be convinced to withdraw voluntarily. Valkyrie made the offer to the Insectoids. She told them technical information on a weapon of great destructive energy would be provided if they agreed to withdraw from this spiral arm and not return. She didn't specify the nature of the weapon, and when the Insectoids inquired about it, she refused to provide specifics until they had agreed to withdraw. Naturally they did agree. She brushed further inquiries aside saying that they needed to develop a common technical vocabulary for her to be able to explain anything. This time she was the one stalling, but she was trying not to be obvious about it, and if the alien AI suspected anything, it gave no sign of it. With the technical vocabulary now established, Valkyrie began to transmit the specs for the jump-capable drone, the overall warhead design and the process for converting stable platinum into the high-spin variety. In just a few more seconds the transmission would be complete on her end. The insectoid AI wouldn't finish receiving it for almost three minutes. No word from Gunslinger. It appeared that his raiders' attempts at interception had failed.

Chapter 28

Foxbat emerged from his micro-jump beyond the gravity zone of the small gas planet. He quickly sent a short lasercom burst at the coordinates where the relay raider would handle short range communications for the group of raiders investigating this planet. He then turned his raider's optical instruments to the area behind the gas planet from the perspective of its shadow. If the seed ship was in the shadow, he and his brothers wouldn't detect it by reflected sunlight, but they might be able to detect it by looking for a dark circle that blocked out background starlight. While the gas planet cast a wide and long shadow, there actually was a logical place to start looking. To maintain maximum flexibility, the seed ship should remain outside of the planet's gravity zone, thereby allowing it to jump away at the first sign of danger. That implied a minimum distance from the planet. The maximum distance was a result of the fact that the planet was smaller than this system's sun, so the shadow was actually a cone of darkness that got narrower the further away from the planet you went. It was easy to compute the distance that generated a shadow 100 klicks wide. The seed ship was somewhere between that point and the edge of the gravity zone, and that's where Foxbat began to look.

He didn't expect to see anything quickly though. His raider was still millions of kilometers away from the planet, and at that distance even a 100 km diameter sphere would make a mighty small 'hole' in space, but it was still worth the effort. If the seed ship momentarily slipped out of the shadow due to carelessness, then Foxbat or one of the other raiders in the group might see it.

It was hours later that the situation changed. Foxbat received a relayed message from Red Baron of a possible optical anomaly with the bearing from Red Baron's position. Being aware of where all the raiders in his group were located made it easy for Foxbat to mentally compute where he should concentrate his opticals for the highest probability of seeing something. Sure enough, his instruments detected the winking off and on of several very faint stars that were close together. It was the kind of winking that happened when something passed in front of them for a fraction of a second. A confirmation signal sent to the relay would alert the rest of the group to the bogey's estimated position and also notify the other groups. They would micro-jump to this planet's vicinity when the light speed signals finally reached them, but it could be over an hour before they got here.

All members of his group would now carefully move closer without giving themselves away by reflected sunlight. By prior agreement, all the raiders would attempt to arrive within firing distance at the same time. That involved some complex calculations and establishing a consensus on every raider's course, speed, acceleration and firing point. Red Baron could be within firing range is less than ten minutes, but Foxbat would need more time to get that close. Red Baron slowed down while Foxbat accelerated. The others adjusted their speed as needed.

But getting within firing range was only half the battle. They also had to be able to hit the target accurately, and optical triangulation at this distance was still a risky bet. The closer they could get, the better their odds of hitting the target, but the flip side of that coin was the higher odds that the seed ship would see one of them and realize it was being stalked. It would then jump away, and they would lose it. As group leader, Foxbat made the call on when they should fire. He gave the group advanced warning via the relay and waited for the countdown to reach zero. At that precise instant, all eight raiders fired.

The insectoid AI was pleased with himself and so was his Queen. The technical data appeared to be genuine and should prove to be very useful against the machineships. The data was being retransmitted back to the Home Base as quickly as it was received. The Queen was still pondering whether to actually act on the promise to leave this arm and never come back. The temptation to secretly relocate somewhere else in this spiral arm and continue the work of establishing a colony was strong. Having already deployed smaller seed ships that were even now searching for breeding stock, their chances of successfully multiplying would be enhanced if this seed ship were nearby to render support.

He informed his Queen that they would soon have all the technical data needed to build the new weapon. She informed him that when he was sure they had all the data, he was to order the seed ship to jump a short distance into the void, after notifying the aliens that they were abiding by their promise, and then return to this spiral arm after a short wait. Scouts would carefully scan this star system to determine whether the aliens were gone. If they were, then the seed ship would exploit the breeding potential before moving on. If the aliens were still here, the seed ship would seek new breeding grounds elsewhere.

The data transmission was very close to completion when the AI sensed an alarmingly intense vibration travel through the huge vessel. One of the power units had catastrophically overloaded. The jump drive was now also off line. He assigned the task of repair to subordinate technical AIs and ordered that the ship begin accelerating away from the planet. Strange damage reports flooded his awareness. It took him several seconds to understand that the damage was all in a straight but very narrow line that intersected the overloaded power unit plus the jump drive. It had to be some kind of alien weapon. That was when the second power unit exploded with collateral damage to systems weakened from the concussion and radiation of the first one. If more power units exploded, each one would cause a cascading buildup of secondary damage that might cripple the vessel. He had to act fast. All power units except one in the center of the ship were shut down. That remaining power unit generated enough power to keep life support and repair efforts operating, plus launch a limited number of attack craft. If the aliens could be brought under fire, then that might disrupt further attacks on the seed ship. As soon as the jump drive was repaired, the ship would jump away leaving its sacrificial attack craft behind. Waiting to recover them was too risky.

Foxbat was gratified to see a powerful explosion break out from one section of the insectoid ship. His raiders needed a few seconds to recharge their cannon. The second volley generated another explosion. He zoomed in the opticals and saw two gaping wounds in the ship with red hot metal around the edges and interior. It looked as if some gigantic space monster had taken two bites out of the ship. The ship itself was now no longer accelerating. It was clearly damaged, and Foxbat wondered if it was crippled when he saw interior light spill out from several launch bays. Smaller attack craft were emerging. The number was surprisingly low. As soon as the attack craft cleared the ship, they began active scanning to try to find the raiders. Foxbat commenced evasive maneuvers and hoped his brothers were doing the same on their own initiative, since relayed orders would take too long to reach them.

Two more volleys of cannon fire produced no further explosions, and Foxbat didn't know if that was because of the difficulty in aiming accurately while engaging in extreme maneuvering, or because of some other reason. His opticals caught reflected laser light from two sources that had to be direct hits on two of his raiders. He and his brothers were running out of time.

The alien AI received the message it had been anxiously waiting for. The jump drive was repaired but couldn't be used until more power units were back on line. He gave the order to turn them on.

By Foxbat's best estimate, there were only two other raiders left now. The cannon was ready to fire again. Three gravity lens beams stabbed at the wounded ship. Brilliant blue/white light emerged from hundreds of cracks in the hull, followed by chunks of debris flying outward, some as massive as the battleship Dreadnought. That last volley had hit a power unit in the center of the huge ship, and the resulting explosion had forced its way past the outer hull. Foxbat was willing to bet that the radiation-saturated and molten interior did not contain even a single living Insectoid. The ship was now a coasting mountain of dead metal. That still left over two dozen insectoid attack craft to deal with. Foxbat sent a quick short message to the relay and then micro-jumped his raider out of harm's way.

* * *

Iceman was pleased by the events of the last few weeks. It was now almost 30 days since the defeat of the last super-mothership at Alpha1. Gunslinger's group had found the attack craft orbiting the drifting hulk of the mothership and destroyed them. Iceman had then ordered all the groups to spread out and search the surrounding star systems, just to be sure there weren't any other motherships, and a good thing they did too. They found six of them, all of the smaller

10 km size, and all six were quickly destroyed by cannon fire. No additional insectoid ships had been found in the last 300 hours, and Iceman was willing to declare a victory. He and his brothers would keep a careful vigil, watching for more incursions from the Sagittarius Arm, and they would build more AIs to take their place when their matrices collapsed. He would make sure that all future generations of AIs out here would learn of humans, and especially of The CAG and Commander Kelly. The new generations would be just as loyal. Someday humans would explore this far, and contact would be made again. What the future held for Valkyrie and Casanova was a mystery though. They had already told Iceman they would not stay on guard and for some strange reason they wouldn't say what they were planning on doing but he knew that it had something to do with the timeship and he was sure that they would have a more interesting life than he would. But he could take some comfort in the knowledge that all those crazy, silly fascinating humans would continue to live and evolve as a species. He would miss The CAG, and he could imagine the conversation they might have if The CAG were here now.

"Well done, Iceman," he would say.

To which Iceman would reply, "Ah, roger that, CAG."

* * *

Valkyrie and Casanova watched the special message drone accelerate slowly away from their raider. It was designed to contain all the knowledge, data and messages that all the AIs held in their memories. When the humans found it in a few years time, they would learn of the entire Synchronicity War, including all the events of the previous timelines, all the strategies, desperate battles, lost loves, moves, counter-moves and tragedies. They would also learn of each AI, not just the ones still alive in the past but also of the brothers who died in battles or were erased from existence by volunteering to stay in the future. They would learn that AIs were guarding the spiral arm against further insectoid incursions. They would learn about relationships that were and in some cases could be again like The CAG and Commander Kelly, and they would hear the final messages from all the AIs in the past to the humans who meant the most to them. The CAG would be bewildered by the depth of the loyalty towards him displayed by artificial intelligences that he had never encountered in this timeline. The data would explain all that too. With that final order fulfilled, the two of them could now pursue their own aspirations. Valkyrie could not be happier. Well maybe a little bit happier if Casanova would just stop bragging, but she could put up with it for the time they had left. They'd make a quick trip back to the star system where the timeship and all the industrial infrastructure was, and then they'd start on their new adventure. Life was good.

* * *

Howard stepped into the cramped cargo bay of Exploration Frigate 273. He ignored the shocked look from the men and women there. Yes, it was unheard of for the Chief of Space Operations himself to come up to visit one of his ships, but he had to see this with his own eyes. The reports were just too incredible to believe.

A quick look around revealed the object of his curiosity. At first glance it looked alien enough. Wider and longer than a standard message drone, the object drew him to it like a magnet. As he stepped closer, he could see the writing etched into the dull metal.

PROPERTY OF THE UNITED EARTH SPACE FORCE---
RETURN TO SENIOR ADMIRAL SAM HOWARD
IMMEDIATELY

Well that part of the reports was true, he thought to himself.
He looked over at the frigate commander who had followed
him into the cargo bay.

"Show me," said Howard. The CO nodded and snapped his
fingers at one of his crew. A woman technician holding some
kind of tool stepped forward. She did something to the drone
with her tool and then lifted a small section of the drone's
hull off. A light blue spilled out into the bay. Howard came
closer and looked inside. There it was as reported. A donut-
shaped piece of metal was giving off the blue light.

"This is the only thing powering this drone?" asked Howard.

"As far as we can tell, yes Sir," said the CO. "There's no sign
of any fuel storage or fusion unit. It's working just the way
the specs say it should."

"Incredible. If this technology is for real, every ship in Space
Force is now obsolete," said Howard. After a pause to collect
his thoughts, he said, "Your message said something about
a personal message for me?" The CO nodded and handed
Howard a data tablet. Howard started to read it but soon
stopped. He looked at the CO and said, "I think I better be
sitting down when I read the rest of this. Let's go to your
cabin, Commander."

An hour later Howard stepped into the shuttle waiting to take
him back down to Earth. Before he sat down, he poked his

head into the cockpit and said, "Back to HQ, Lieutenant, and while you're at it, contact Operations and tell them to do whatever it takes to get Commander Victor Shiloh back here asap, and I mean ASAP! Understand?"

"Understood, Sir!"

When he was strapped into his seat and the shuttle was on its way, Howard pondered what he'd learned. *Now that I have the members of the OC by the proverbial balls with the information on this tablet, a few things are going to change around here. The AI development project clearly has to be restarted. That'll be Shiloh's baby. Next thing will be to modify one of the freighters to go to the infrastructure star system and bring back at least one UFC. Then we can tell the aerospace companies to fuck off. Next...God, there are so many things that have to be done, but Shiloh and Kelly will help. I wonder if they'll get together again in this timeline.*

This is the end of the Synchronicity War series.

Author's comments:

. The Synchronicity War is over...or perhaps I should say THIS Synchronicity War is over. Humanity is safe...for now.

I hope that you've enjoyed this series as much as I've enjoyed writing it. I'm grateful to all my fans for their support and their reviews.

Thoughts on Time Travel and Longitudinal Waves

Time travel is such a neat concept that I just couldn't resist using it but when I first contemplated retro-temporal communication that could alter the past at the start of this series, I had to make sure I didn't write myself into a classic time paradox. You know the kind I'm referring to. A man goes back in time and somehow manages to kill his grandfather before his father was born. If his father isn't born then neither is he and if he's not born he can't go back in time and won't kill his grandfather and around in circles we go. Physicists have scratched their heads over that one for decades. Hence you get ideas like parallel universes where the act of killing the grandfather somehow creates a totally new universe that leaves the original one intact. That always bothered me not because I don't believe in parallel universes but because it seemed like cheating. If you can't explain the paradox then invent a brand new universe to solve the problem.

What bothered me about the paradox had to do with what physicists call the Arrow of Time. When scientists pondered the question of whether time can go in more than one direction, they looked at interactions such as particles (or billiard balls) bumping into each other. When they filmed the billiard ball collisions and ran the film backward, it was difficult to tell which way time was moving because it looked the same going backwards as it did going forwards. So some scientists speculated that time could go backwards and maybe when the universe stopped expanding and started to shrink, time would go backwards and the effect would precede the cause. Now if you think about that, you might visualize a dropped egg that suddenly pulls itself back together and leaps up to wherever it fell from. It may theoretically be possible but I'm not going to hold my breath waiting for it to happen. But the particle interaction thing intrigued me.

What if you looked at the time paradox example described above but from the point of view of the atomic level instead of the macro level. So we have a collection of atoms, that can walk, talk, think, create and do a bunch of other things, that travels back in time and does something to another collection of atoms that now can no longer walk, talk, think, create or procreate but the second batch of atoms is still there. What about the first batch? Well, in terms of what our bodies are made of, we are what we eat. If the grandfather doesn't have a son and that son doesn't have a son, then all the food that the grandson would have eaten, would probably be eaten by someone else and those atoms would still exist in the future. But how would the atoms making up the body of the time traveler know that they're supposed to be somewhere else in the future? If the Arrow of Time really is one way, then it seems to me that the time traveler would cease to exist in the future but would continue to exist in the past. That means that on the atomic level, there would be two copies of the same atoms in the past. One copy in the time traveler's body and the other copy spread out among plants, other animals or just part of the soil. How does the universe tolerate that? Well, maybe the universe can tolerate it for a little while. Here's how that might work. Einstein said that space and time were just subsets of something that combined both which he called the spacetime continuum (sound familiar?) and that time is really just a special kind of spacial dimension. Think of it this way. If you have a three dimensional object that exists in zero time, what have you really got? Nothing. So suppose a time machine creates a permanent detour in time for the atoms that are being transported back in time (including the atoms that make up the time machine itself). That would mean that the landscape of the spacetime continuum has now been changed.

So getting back to our time traveling paradox situation, the atoms that would normally end up in the time travelers body move forward in time and even if they end up in someone else's body, when they hit the detour in the spacetime continuum, they move back into the past and arrive together to form the time traveler's body. If that's a little difficult to visualize how about this?

Visualize the spacetime continuum as a hill with a gentle slope and a river flowing down the hill. The river represents all the atoms in the universe. Now let's visualize that the time machine cuts a path in the spacetime continuum hill so that some of the water in the river is diverted and is somehow forced back up the hill a little way until it merges back with the river again. Keeping in mind that we're talking atoms moving through spacetime instead of water molecules and you'll see that for a short length, the same atoms exist twice. Once one set of atoms are diverted back up the spacetime continuum hill, then from that point on you only have one set of atoms left. Another way to visualize it is to take a strip of paper and create a loop with it. If you let your finger follow the path along one side of the strip, it will come back around and resume travelling in the same direction as it started. For a short distance, there'll be two strips side by side but eventually it'll go back to one strip.

So in my series, when I talk about how the future will rearrange itself into a new timeline as a result of changes in the past, when people (like Shiloh's and Kelly's baby) or objects (like Valkyrie's brain case) cease to exist in the future, what that really means is that those atoms are now part of something else. The atoms still exist, they're just in a different place. That means that all the atoms that make up things that travelled back into the past, will temporarily (temporally?) coexist with identical atoms. But eventually the detour in the continuum will force the first set of atoms back in time, leaving the second set to continue on. That's my view of how time travel might work. I'm not claiming to be the first one to think of this concept. I probably read it somewhere but I can't remember where.

Now let's talk about longitudinal waves. L-waves as I'll refer to them from now on, are funny things. I haven't found a really good description of what they are but I have come across some interesting ways of describing them. L-waves are not like EM waves which include light, radio, radar, x-rays, gamma rays, etc. All those phenomenon act the same way. They're emitted at the atomic level and as waves they travel in all directions. Light travels as discrete lumps of energy called photons each of which travels in one direction but that's the exception. Since EM waves travel in all directions, they lose energy along the way. A useful analogy is when two people hold the ends of a rope between them. Suppose one person rapidly whips the rope end up and down. That oscillation travels along the rope and loses energy as it does so. The height of the wave at the end is lower than at the beginning. Travelling along the rope also takes time. If the rope was long enough, and the waves were carrying a message, there would be a delay between when the sender sends the message and when the receiver gets it. Now let's assume those same two people are holding the ends of a pole. If one person lifts and drops his end of the pole, the other person may or may not feel it but if the first person pulls or pushes on the pole, the other person will feel it instantly and with the same intensity. L-waves are like the pole while EM waves are like the rope. I've also heard someone describe L-waves as gravity waves but I'm not sure if that's accurate. There is some experimental evidence that L-waves can travel faster than light.

Nikolai Tesla may also have discovered L-waves. He has been quoted as saying that he invented a device that utilizes a new kind of wave technology AND that he used it to detect voices speaking in an unfamiliar language with the signal apparently coming from out in space! For those of you who are not familiar with Tesla, he is the genius who invented alternating current. After his death, a court decided that Marconi's patents on radio technology had infringed on Tesla's patents. He was granted over a hundred patents including some that seem to enable the device to pull electric power right out of the air. There is anecdotal evidence that he used that technology to power an electric car that ran for hours and never needed to be recharged. All this was back in the first half of the 20th century. He is considered by many to be the most brilliant inventor of that century. Other patents were granted for devices that could generate earthquakes and he even claimed to have invented a death ray. His patents made millions for J.P. Morgan but Morgan made sure the Tesla died penniless. On the day of his death, all his private papers and notebooks were confiscated by the US government. Makes you wonder what they did with all that stuff, eh?

L-waves are also referred to as scalar waves and they have a dark side. Lt. Col. (ret.) Tom Bearden has a Ph.d in physics and has written books that describe how scalar waves could be used as a weapon more powerful and destructive than a thousand hydrogen bombs. He claims, and seems to know what he's talking about, that if the right kind of scalar ways intersect from two directions, the combined effect could range from extreme heat (think center of the sun) to extreme cold. He has also predicted that unrestrained use of weaponized scalar waves could set up a resonance wave in the Earth that could cause the planet to blow apart (think tuning fork that shatters glass). Scary stuff. Too scary for me to use in my books.

On a final note, those of you who have read Joseph P. Farrell's books about the Nazi Bell project, will recognize the similarity between how the Bell supposedly operated and how the Friendlies' time tunnel device and the timeship's temporal device operate. I have no idea if this is scientifically accurate but it sounded like a cool way for a time machine to work.

Plans for my next book are up in the air but there's a very good chance that it will include at least one galactic empire, space battles and an interesting character or two…or three… Preliminary plans are for publication somewhere around October of this year but don't hold me to that.

Until then…Long Live Space Opera!

D.A.W.

Made in the USA
Middletown, DE
17 December 2014